CLAW

A NOVEL

Ken Eulo and Joe Mauck

SIMON & SCHUSTER
New York London Toronto Sydney Tokyo Singapore

SIMON & SCHUSTER
ROCKEFELLER CENTER
1230 AVENUE OF THE AMERICAS
NEW YORK, NEW YORK 10020

SIMON & SCHUSTER AND COLOPHON ARE REGISTERED TRADE-
MARKS OF SIMON & SCHUSTER INC.
DESIGNED BY EVE METZ
MANUFACTURED IN THE UNITED STATES OF AMERICA

1   3   5   7   9   10   8   6   4   2

LIBRARY OF CONGRESS CATALOGING IN PUBLICATION DATA

EULO, KEN.
CLAW : A NOVEL / KEN EULO AND JOE MAUCK.
P.   CM.
1. ZOO ANIMALS—CALIFORNIA—LOS ANGELES—FICTION.   2. TIGERS—
CALIFORNIA—LOS ANGELES—FICTION.   3. LOS ANGELES (CALIF.)—
FICTION.   I. MAUCK, JOE.   II. TITLE.
PS3555.U56C58   1994
813.'54—DC20   94-4321
CIP

ISBN: 0-671-79963-0

This book is dedicated with gratitude to Michael Korda and Chuck Adams, for the confidence shown and the wisdom shared.

PROLOGUE

THE GREAT CAT slunk low in the dark, limbs tensed in a stalking crouch. Its head, extended forward from a thick and powerful neck, was more than twice the size of that of an average human. The whitish face had a pointed, streamlined look: jaw clenched, whiskers and darkly tipped ears swept back against the head. The large round eyes, made sensitive to light by a transparent layer of guanine, penetrated the blackness with ease. It was this invisible membrane that caused the eyes to glow dimly, like two green crystals floating in the dark.

The cat raised his massive head; not to see beyond the bamboo cover around him, but to gather in more of the faint, familiar smells drifting over his territory. The steady stream of scent impulses was quickly received, processed, and identified by the highly developed brain. One huge paw lifted and froze, cocked at the wrist. The huge body was still, all its energies focused, much as a hunting hound points at concealed prey. There was no motion now, save for one imperceptible twitch of the black-tufted tail.

* * *

CLAW

"RAJAH, COME," called Carol Lewis, the young, red-headed zookeeper. She was standing at the viewing rail high above the tiger compound, and tonight she wasn't feeling well. She had just started her period, her muscles ached, and she was in a great hurry to finish her chores.

"Rajah, come!" she called again, peering into the darkened bamboo pit below.

In the wild, the large Siberians were night hunters, prowling the jungle brush for elk and wild boar. But here, now, Carol knew Rajah wasn't expecting a nine o'clock meal; all normal feedings were completed by 6:00 P.M.

Moreover, she had been instructed not to leave the food behind the safety gate at the rear of Rajah's compound. There he would drag it back into his cave and devour it in solitude. Nor was she permitted to simply toss the slimy contents of the feed bucket into the open pit and walk away. The whole purpose of her waiting at the rail was to observe Rajah's behavior at night, before, during, and after feeding.

"Dammit," Carol muttered, thinking that Dr. Brewster was being unfair. All one of the keepers had said was: "I think Rajah is acting strange." Then suddenly, without so much as a preliminary briefing, the workload of each keeper on staff doubled.

Carol frowned now and gave the railing a good kick. Then she moved to her left; partly to view the pit from a different angle, but mostly to get away from the stench wafting up from the feed bucket. The usual fare of ground horsemeat was bad enough—it always made her feel queasy. But for this feeding, she was told to include a half cup of liquid vitamins, which added a nauseating aroma to the raw meat.

Better move farther downwind, she thought, before I get sick and . . .

Downwind.

8

CLAW

The keeper stood still for a moment—an idea formulating. It was an idea that seemed too simple. Too easy.

She turned and stared at the feed bucket, wondering if Rajah had gotten a good whiff of its sticky, blood-soaked contents. She suddenly realized the breeze was carrying the odor in the wrong direction, away from the pit. If she could get the bucket upwind, there might be a chance of coaxing the big cat into the open.

Ignoring the smell, she picked up the bucket and moved to where the rail ended at the corner of the compound. Then she started to climb up one side of the pit, on the earthen embankment that buttressed its twenty-foot-high concrete walls.

Halfway up the embankment, Carol felt good about her scheme. The wind was stronger higher up, and it was blowing eastward, across the pit. But it was getting difficult for her see. The moonlight was pale, and the illumination of the walkway lights was blocked out by a thicket of trees. She gripped the high-powered flashlight fastened to her belt, then let go, remembering another part of her instructions: no sudden light. *Do nothing that might provoke him.*

Her cutoffs and bare legs were thwacked by waist-high twigs and thorns as she moved on. A scratch opened on her right knee and began to bleed. She knew it would be easier to walk closer to the top edge of the wall; the foliage there was less dense. But taking that way was dangerous. One false step in the dark and over she'd go.

High enough, Carol thought. She left her parallel course with the wall and turned toward the compound.

THE CAT SLOWLY TURNED, monitoring the keeper's movements, homing in, his senses peaking, synchronized. The massive jaws slacked open. White pointed teeth, specialized

9

for stabbing and anchoring large prey, shone faintly as his lips skinned back. His tongue, roughly textured for licking off flesh, lolled out of his mouth, its tip twitching to the pulse of an eager pant. Only once did he break the rhythm of the panting, just long enough to lick saliva away from his thick, taut jowls.

Suddenly the cat's nostrils twitched, sucking in the provocative odor carried on the wind: *fresh blood*. Again, briefly, his head rose, green eyes targeting the objective.

Only then did the cat move, advancing slowly, his stealthy tread perfectly adapted for concealment. Sharp claws flexed as he glided through substance and shadows, without effort, without sound.

As CAROL ADVANCED, the brush around her began to thin out. She knew the edge of the wall was only a few steps away, so she hunched low and stretched out her foot, holding her weight back, like a swimmer testing water before a plunge. The walkway lights glowed in the distance, but here it was very dark.

The tip of her sneaker touched something hard and flat. That's it, she thought. The roughly textured surface of the wall was unmistakable.

She dropped down and crawled through the dark on all fours, dragging the bucket after her. Her hand found the wall. She judged the top surface to be ten inches wide.

At last, sitting and facing the pit, Carol settled down to wait for the tiger to show himself. Shivering, she zipped up her jacket. Overhead she could see more clouds, swept in by a sea breeze, enveloping the tops of the trees, making the night darker.

There had been no mention of rain in the forecast, but Carol felt a few drops strike her face. Probably residue from the storm that had soaked Los Angeles earlier in the day, before moving rapidly eastward into the desert. January was always rainy in California, but this month had been worse than most.

Carol sighed, glanced up, and was surprised she could see the moon and a few stars.

For a moment, it was very quiet.

She lowered her gaze. From her new vantage point, she could see far more of the compound than she had before. To her left, beneath the viewing rail, the tiger's wading pool lay like flat, darkly polished jade. From the closest edge of the water, a small stream arched along the bottom of the wall and ran directly under where she sat, then snaked to her right at the mouth of the cave.

Her eyes had adjusted well to the dark, though she had to admit Rajah had the advantage in this peekaboo game. Her human night vision was pitifully inferior when compared to his. He could spot prey at two miles, even in half-light.

Then, suddenly, Carol thought she saw something, a momentary flash of motion.

There. Something *had* moved. Right on the edge of the small clearing in front of her. Yellowish. Faint.

Then it was gone.

She tipped the bucket slightly, letting a small portion of raw meat fall into the pit. That'll bring him out, she thought. What flesh eater could resist?

She leaned forward, watching, peering into the dark shadows.

THE TIGER DREW BACK, instinctively aware that his movement had been detected. A splatter of blood-soaked meat lay in the open not twenty feet in front of him. But he ignored it. The meal he hungered for was perched on the ledge.

A moment passed. The prey remained still. Unafraid. Unaware.

The cat crouched, hind quarters slightly spread. It was time. The muscles in his huge, sleek body tightened. Restrained force mounted. Time to strike. Tingling nerve endings set off small reflex spasms. Thick hide rippled, fur bristled. Time.

The cat released his fury in one explosive sprint to the wall. Muscles uncoiled, the beast sprang into the air, teeth bared, limbs surging, reaching out with his claws.

IN THAT FIRST, fleeting moment of awareness, when all other animals would have been instantly filled with terror, Carol was not. She did not comprehend. There was a sense of unreality. The vision coming up at her was like something out of a dream. Dark. Silent. A winged phantom rising to the moon. And when this horrible wraith rose no longer, hovering only inches away, it did not matter that she knew it was the tiger. To her, it was the green-eyed monster in every nightmare of every child that ever lived. This was the dreaded demon flying up from hell to get her—*to eat her alive*.

The tiger's roar struck her face like a hot deafening wind. A blow from its right paw sent her reeling. Stunned, yet starting to comprehend, she grabbed a bush with both hands and tried pulling herself to safety, but her body would not move.

At first, she thought her legs were hooked on the jagged edge of the wall. But when she glanced down, she saw the tiger's claws buried in her thighs. He was trying to keep himself from falling back into the pit by digging deeper, ripping away flesh to get at bone.

Carol flung her head back and screamed as claws dug deeper into the bone and cartilage of both her knees. Now the tiger's mouth surrounded one leg. His jaw slammed shut like a springed vise, splintering the bone in one bite.

"Oh God, help me!" the keeper cried. She was on fire, beyond pain. Nausea and heat rushed through her—also a fierce determination to stay alive.

Suddenly the tiger's shoulders jerked back, and he pulled. The trunk of the bush warped under the strain. Chunks of earth popped up from the snapping roots. A deep rumbling growl escaped from the cat's belly as the bush broke free, and the keeper slid over the side.

In an effort to save herself, Carol flung her hands out and gripped the wall. The cat slipped and lost leverage. His hind quarters and right front paw scratched furiously at the wall. Then his left front claw broke free.

Now only the cat's jaw held tight.

Hope surged as Carol felt her shinbone separating from her upper leg. The tiger was slipping down; her leg, gradually tearing away. She tightened her grip on the wall. She knew she had just enough strength to pull herself to safety. But only if the tiger was satisfied with that mangled portion of her leg and ripped it off cleanly as any normal tiger would.

But this tiger was *not* normal. He did not violently shake his head back and forth to capture the smaller prize. Sensing triumph, he abruptly altered his assault and let his tremendous weight dangle from the tattered limb and waited for his victim to fall.

For the first time, Carol felt the physical sensation of fear. Adrenaline shot through her arms and chest, generated a numbing chill, as she swayed helplessly above the pit. She could see a sliver of moon high to her right. Hear the shrieks of frightened animals responding to her screams, all sensing death. She tried to hang on, tried to muster the strength to resist the tiger's pull.

But she could hold on no longer.

A series of tremors shook her. Panic and pain erupted. Suddenly her hands slipped free, and she slid to the bottom of the pit, her descent on the wall marked by a crimson streak. Her body hit the cold concrete below with a muffled thud.

The tiger released her and took several swipes at her body; then his mouth slacked open.

Carol's pleading eyes closed. Christ of the crucifixion shone faintly in a mind preparing to die. But a prayer was never uttered. Illusion and reality had merged. Past and present were mingling in a final childhood memory.

You said it was just a dream, Daddy. You promised me the green-eyed monster couldn't hurt me . . . Daddy?

The screams lasted only a short while, the time it took for reality to end. Soon the only sound was the tiger's muffled growl, and the crunch of jaws grinding bone and sinew.

Overhead the moon was again obscured by clouds. Nearby a flock of geese erupted in a cacophony of squawks, then settled back into silence, while in the shallows of an adjoining pit, an alligator slipped soundlessly into the murky, pewter-colored water.

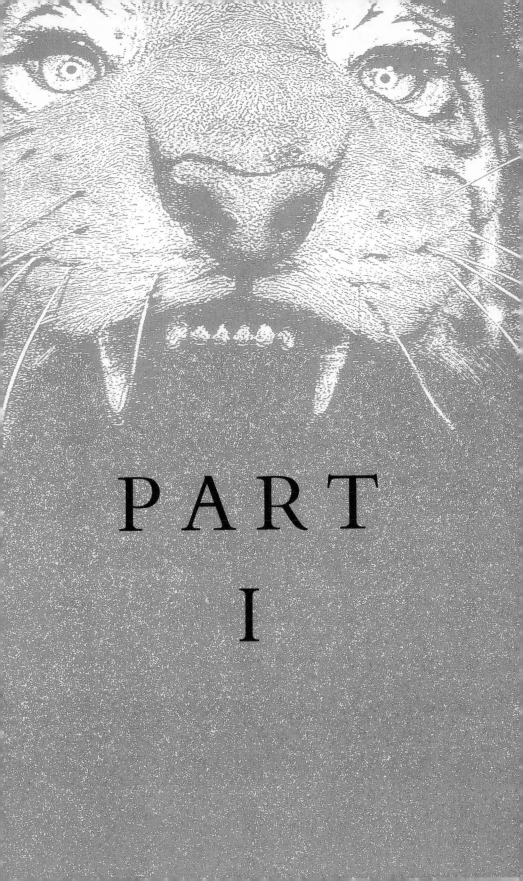

PART
I

1

T HE HISS OF the snake filled the classroom as its head shot upward, then flattened into a hood. Lifting the plastic lid, Dr. Meg Brewster used her right hand to quickly grip the snake behind its jaws. Then, in one sweep, she lifted the boa clear of the case so her Adult Ed students could get a closer look. The snake firmly in hand, she continued her lecture.

"Here is another favorite with people who enjoy snake pets," she said, carrying the coiling reptile past the front row of students. "*Constrictor constrictor*, better known as the boa constrictor. This particular specimen—her name is Suzie, by the way—is a hognose snake, and is about average size, although some have been known to reach six feet. If you're interested in viewing her larger relatives, you'll have an opportunity to do so next week at the zoo."

An elderly woman in the front row drew back and raised her hand. Meg nodded to her.

"What would one . . . I mean, as a pet, what would one feed it?"

"It feeds on toads and other amphibians and small reptiles. Yes, Mr. Richards?"

"And you wouldn't consider the boa dangerous?" The man leaned over to get a closer look.

"Heavens, no," Meg laughed, stroking the snake's body as it wound itself around her arm and up over her shoulder. "The hognose, sometimes called puff adder, spreading adder, or blowing viper, is entirely harmless. They are highly praised by snake fanciers as being interesting and friendly in captivity."

"That so?" The man's eyes narrowed. "Then how come it snapped at you like that?"

"Because the hognose is a mimic of exceptional talent, Mr. Richards. It can imitate the actions of venomous snakes so well it is often mistaken for one. Here, would you like to hold her?"

"No, ma'am," he said, sinking back into his chair. The class laughed nervously, and a young woman in the second row raised her hand.

Meg didn't know the girl by name. She was new, having entered the class only that evening, bringing the number of students to twenty-eight. Most of Meg's students were in their mid-forties. This young woman, however, couldn't have been more than eighteen, which pleased Meg, who at twenty-nine looked still younger and enjoyed teaching young people. Meg's hair was a brilliant strawberry blond and very wispy. When she worked, she wore it up. Her face was broad, with high cheekbones, her eyes deep set and pale blue with flecks of green, so that they changed color slightly in different light.

Meg had inherited her looks from her mother, who had died too young to be remembered save in treasured photographs. Her tough-minded survival instincts came of being the only daughter of natural scientist John Brewster, who had backpacked her on many a rugged location while she was little more than an infant, and had entrusted her, at an early age, with classifying and cataloguing their rock and mineral finds. John Brewster, Ph.D., had taught her things like the scientific names of trees and flowers and animals.

Perhaps, as a result, Meg had always enjoyed using her mind. She was dedicated to nature and wildlife. After graduating from Stanford, she had had no trouble getting into veterinary college.

"Yes?" Meg said to the young woman. "I'm afraid I don't know your name."

"Evelyn Gardner," the young woman said, her pen poised over her notepad. "I was wondering, Dr. Brewster, what—"

"Call me Meg, all right? Doctor sounds kind of formal."

The young woman hesitated, then went on. "Meg, I was wondering what made you become a veterinarian. I hope you don't mind my asking."

Meg glanced at the boa wrapped over her shoulder. Its body felt cool against her flesh. She was accustomed to the question. She had heard it a thousand times, especially from her friends, who never could understand why a beautiful young girl who "had everything" would choose such a career.

Looking at the young woman, Meg finally said, "I became a veterinarian because I love animals. When I was a little girl my father would let me bring half-starved animals into the house and care for them. My first was a baby raccoon. I called her Sarah. After that, my room was full of all sorts of animals on the mend. I enjoyed helping them. Especially when I would return them to the wild." Meg shrugged and smiled. She knew she could never give a complete explanation.

"Thank you," the young woman said. Then she added, "About the boa, can you tell me where it is most likely to be found?"

"Not in my backyard, I hope!" quipped Mr. Hadley in the back row. The class erupted again, a little less nervously this time.

Meg smiled. The snake, curled around her neck, peered

out at the class. "Well, they are mainly found in South America, Africa, and Asia. At least the larger ones. There are small boas too, some of them living in the United States, but only because, years ago, their ancestors were 'stow-aways' from South America, hidden in huge bunches of bananas."

"Jesus!" someone breathed. "In bananas?"

"Your fears are understandable," Meg said, uncoiling the snake from around her body, and placing it gently back into the container. "At some point, all animals must have been frightening to humans. Even today, any creature that proves a nuisance in our modern world is considered 'bad,' as well as 'frightening.' A gorilla's size and strength. A shark's knifelike teeth. The venom of some snakes and spiders. All potentially dangerous. But people are becoming more aware. Not all animals live up to their evil reputations. . . ."

At that moment, the back door of the classroom opened and Jason Hall popped his head in. "Dr. Brewster," he said, then broke off, staring at the class that was staring at him.

Jason Hall was the head of Beverly Hills Adult Ed Program, who had urged Meg to consider teaching a class or two as a kind of therapy following her divorce. Something to do outside and away from her job as veterinarian of the L.A. Zoo. Something to take her mind off her unhappiness.

She and David, her ex-husband, had said their last sorrys-about-that and goodbyes two years earlier. Or maybe it was three years ago. Meg had lost track of time. Never mind; their marriage hadn't set any records.

David had been "Christ, I'm restless" for almost the entire three years of the marriage. Or sometimes "No, not depressed, just antsy." He had drifted aimlessly during that time, lacking a definable group of friends to which he could attach himself. Worse was his absolute disdain for work. He did not mind the physical act of doing a job; what he couldn't stand was the straitjacket of regular hours.

"It's a bitch," he'd sigh, and Meg would lie there next to him, tears sliding away into her hair until he lost his temper, because what the hell was *she* crying about. It was he who had the problem, wasn't it?

Damn, Meg thought now, seeing Jason Hall waving at her from the half-open door, seeing the strained expression on his face, knowing that he and David, if only for a brief time, had called themselves friends.

"Meg, can I see you for a second?" he called out.

Meg turned and glanced at the wall clock, annoyed that the last fifteen minutes of her class were being interrupted. She was trying to think of something clever to say, when Jason's voice changed, suddenly sober, with a hint of fear.

"Meg, I think you should hurry. Uh, there's a call for you in the office. It sounds urgent."

"Right," Meg said. "Class, I'll be right back. In the meantime, feel free to take a closer look at the specimens." Once outside the classroom, she said, "Okay, Jason, what's up?"

But he was already ahead of her, holding open the next door, talking in a rush about a problem at the zoo. Something unspecified, but serious.

They crossed the small courtyard, hurried down the deserted hallway of Beverly Hills High, and ducked into Jason's private office. Meg would remember later that at that point she still felt no fear, only annoyance. The fear, when it came, would be unforgettable.

Jason nodded at the phone on his desk, pressed line two, and handed her the receiver. "Go ahead," he said, backing away.

"Hello?" Meg said, and held her breath. God, don't let it be Daisy, she suddenly thought, remembering the elephant whose skin wound she had been tending for weeks. Today, Daisy had stood around listlessly. Her appetite was gone. Some of her toenails were falling out.

"Hello?" Meg said again, hearing only the sound of muffled voices on the other end of the line.

Then: "Doc, that you? Hold on, it's her. No. Doc, Doc?"

It was Russell Biggs, night security at the zoo. He sounded agitated, confused, and barely able to get his words out.

"Yes, Russell, what can I do for you?"

"Oh, geez, Doc—there's . . . there's been an accident. Real bad. I don't know how it happened."

Meg struggled to stay calm. "What kind of accident?"

"The night keeper, Doc, she's . . ." His voice cracked. His clenched breath sucked in, held, then came whooshing through the receiver. "Carol Lewis," he finally managed. "She's dead, Doc. She fell into the pit, and Rajah got her!"

"Oh God," Meg said, watching Jason nibble his thumbnail. She was sure her face had turned as white as his. A chill gripped the back of her neck and quickly spread over her body. Her stomach tightened. She closed her eyes and tried to think. "When . . . when did it happen?"

"I heard her scream about twenty minutes ago. You know 'bout the strange sounds out here at night. But this wasn't like that, see? And the whole place starts up like the animals goin' crazy, squawkin' their heads off. Then I heard her scream again and I knew where it come from. So me and Herbert, we run up to the compound and there she was. Tore up. Dead. And Rajah, what he done . . ." Meg heard the man choke back a sob. "Doc, he—"

"It's all right. Never mind." Meg knew this was more than just a sudden mauling, a few quick strikes from the cat's powerful claws. Rajah had taken Carol as prey, and the last thing Meg needed was a full-blown description.

She sat on the desk, shoulders hunched, her free hand rubbing the gooseflesh on her skin. "Did you call Ray Menitti?" she asked.

"First thing. And Mr. Ellroy."

"What about the police?"

"I will. As soon as I hang up."

"All right. And tell Ray I'm on my way in."

"I will, Doc," Biggs said. "Right away."

A FEW MINUTES LATER, Meg jumped into her Jeep and sped out of the parking lot, the Jeep rattling as she ignored the speed bumps.

"Come on," Meg grumbled now, trying to make the old Jeep go faster than its maximum speed of fifty miles an hour. She crossed over Mulholland Drive, close to her house, and started down Beverly Glen to the Ventura Freeway.

A sudden cold enveloped her. She tried to shake it off, shivering, as she remembered snatches of her last conversation with Carol Lewis: *Observe Rajah's feeding habits closely. Maybe we can pick up something in his behavior we've missed.* Meg could see the young woman clearly in her mind. Tired. Annoyed. Carol had listened obediently to the instructions, but made no effort to conceal her displeasure. And when, after three grueling weeks of observation, she'd asked Meg to give the task to another keeper, the complaining tone of her voice was unmistakable. Meg's reply, she recalled, had been deliberately firm: *We work on rotation here. It's your turn, Carol. I'm sorry.*

Regret filled Meg now as she struggled with the double meaning of her final words.

I'm sorry.

"Dear God," Meg sighed, and realized too late that she

had missed the ramp. She doubled back, hit the gas pedal hard, and entered the fast lane of the Ventura Freeway. A light fog was spreading across the road, dampening the windshield.

Meg flicked on the wipers. Then, as if in sympathy with the mist, her eyes welled up with tears. Who was she crying for? she wondered. Herself? Save the pity for Carol Lewis, she thought. She's the only one who deserves it.

Meg pressed the gas pedal to the floor. The Jeep sputtered, coughed, then lurched forward.

2

MEG SLOWED DOWN only when she saw the familiar "Los Angeles Zoo" sign flash in her headlights. Her hands were slippery with sweat as they gripped the wheel. Her stomach tightened as she entered the parking lot and saw four squad cars angled up close to the front gate, lights flashing.

She drove past them to the smaller lot reserved for employees. Director Gordon Ellroy's Mercedes was in its slot. Philip Roueche, the curator, had also arrived ahead of her. Ray's station wagon was parked at an angle, its front bumper nosed against the cyclone gate.

Meg got out, zipped up her parka, and hurried up the deserted service road that snaked the eastern edge of the zoo. High on her left, the Santa Monica Mountains loomed like a sleeping giant. There were no street lamps or porch lights to be seen on this side of the mountain. Only thick woods—part of Los Angeles County's vast Griffith Park— separated the zoo from the Griffith Observatory.

Meg trudged over the first incline and stopped when she saw Russell Biggs leaning against the rail, eyes wide and staring. Herbert, one of Biggs's assistants, stood next to a tree with his head hung, vomiting.

"Russell, is he all right?" Meg called out.

"Just sick, Doc," Biggs sputtered. His face was milk white, and his hands trembled as the night air was torn by the howls and squawks of frightened baboons, timber wolves, and howler monkeys. Dominating the relentless din were the shrieks of exotic birds in the nearby aviary.

"What are those lights?" Meg pointed to a cluster of flashing lights above the tree line.

"Hell, Doc, they got half of L.A.'s police force up there."

Damn! Meg thought. If she'd been there when the police arrived, she would never have allowed the emergency lights. Herbert looked up at her, eyes rolling, cheeks red, then doubled over and retched again.

"Take care of him," Meg said.

She started upward again, angry now that Philip Roueche hadn't ordered the emergency lights turned off. His neglect meant the staff would be run ragged for days, trying to coax the more excitable animals to start eating again. Some of them would fall ill, which meant forced feeding, a task Meg loathed.

"You!" Meg shouted, reaching the tiger compound. "Turn off those lights!"

The surrounding area was clogged with police cars, their turret lights whirling and splashing red and white light on the faces of the men standing by. The morgue van and forensics station wagon were parked at different angles close to the viewing rail. The officer closest to Meg glanced up. "Beg your pardon?" he said.

Two lengths of cord had been hastily stretched from the rail to the handles of two radio cars. Meg straddled the cord barrier, pushed the rope down with her hand, and stepped over. "I want whoever's in charge here to get those lights turned off," she said.

"Lieutenant Dragleman," the officer said. "He's over there."

Meg glanced at the cluster of men standing behind a hot searchlight beam that was aimed into the pit. Abruptly the biggest of the men broke from the pack and shuffled into the brilliant light.

"Dr. Brewster, I presume?" he said in a deep baritone.

He had a good face and reflected a certain savvy that suggested he understood the trauma of chaos and death but had the strength to distance himself from it—probably an occupational necessity. His light brown hair was worn long and casual. Dressed in a dark sports jacket, open-neck shirt, and loafers, he was handsome enough to be an actor, but carried the unmistakable aura of cop. His blue eyes were at once keen and sympathetic. He smiled at Meg with one side of his mouth because the other side was again clamped down on a thin, sweet-smelling cigar.

Meg said, "Is that supposed to be funny?"

Dragleman removed the cigar from his mouth. "Right. Not funny," he said. "Not much to laugh about around here."

"Those lights—"

"My fault," he said. "I wasn't thinking." He lifted his large hand and pointed at the group of men. "Shut off the lights, boys. All but the floods."

As the lights started to go off, a vicious roar split the night air. Dragleman's gaze quickly shifted over his shoulder. "Makes your skin crawl," he said.

Meg, however, did not respond. The growls of big cats were all in a normal day's work. And when it came to Rajah, no one knew his sound better than she did.

"Hey!" Dragleman shouted as Meg turned and hurried away. "Where are you going?"

Meg never looked back and was halfway down the service path when Dragleman hollered: "Hey, Doc, wait up!" She didn't have to look into the pit to know what was happening. She had immediately recognized the character of Rajah's roar: *challenge*. Somebody was down in the tunnel leading to the back of Rajah's cave.

In the clearing below, on the edge of the light emanating from the tunnel entrance, was a green all-terrain vehicle with steel mesh cage built onto the back end.

County Animal Control, Meg thought. *Damn them!*

She had barely set foot in the tunnel when a stocky control officer in crumpled green uniform blocked her path. "Nobody allowed down here," he said.

"I'm the zoo veterinarian," Meg said sternly. "I'm responsible for these animals. Now let me through."

Further ahead in the tunnel, Meg could see her assistant, Raymond Menitti, arguing with a second control officer. When he saw Meg, he broke off and rushed toward her. His face was drawn and angry.

"Meg, tell these goons to get lost. They don't know what they're doing." He pointed to a third C.A.C. officer who was stooped over a tranquilizer rifle in front of Rajah's cave. "But that's not going to stop them from doing it!"

Meg turned, saw two men in white coats from the County Coroner's office standing with their backs against the wall. They were biding their time, waiting to see who was going to win the turf war.

"Asshole!" Ray shouted at one of the officers.

The man came rushing over, his jet-black mustache flaring as he said, "Watch your mouth, boy! Nobody tells me how to do my job. Got that?"

Meg's internal warning bell went off. If Ray couldn't budge them, there was no way they were going to listen to a woman.

KRA-BOOM! The sound of the tranquilizer gun was amplified by ten within the stone walls of the tunnel.

The son of a bitch with the rifle!

"No!" Meg yelled. As she rushed forward, Ray jerked

the man away from the heavily barred cave door. But too late. Rajah's paw shot through the bars and caught the officer's hand.

The man lurched back before Rajah could claw him again. "Goddammit, he clawed me!" he screamed, smashing one hand over the other to stop the bleeding.

Ray snatched the Cap-Chur rifle off the floor, then kicked the officer's darts and CO_2 cartridges across the floor.

Meg could see that the man's wound was deep; blood oozed then gushed from between his fingers. "That cat could have ripped your arm off!" she yelled.

She spun around and glared at the confused faces surrounding her. Her reaction was pure reflex. The muscles of her back and thighs contracted and she stiffened. "I'm only going to say this once," she said, pointing at the man with the mustache. "I don't care how bored you get taking potshots at coyotes and cleaning up roadkill. You're not going to get your kicks here. If you don't get out of here now, I'll have you arrested. And I *will* make the charges stick."

The man was livid. "Arrest us?" he boomed. "You and who else?"

"Me." Dragleman stepped forward into the tunnel. He was flanked by two uniforms. "Listen, boys," he said, "why don't you head down to Winchell's on Ventura." He flashed a companionable grin. "Joyce'll fix you up. Tell her it's my treat."

"What about my hand?" the control officer whined. His face had turned ghost white.

Dragleman said, "See the medics outside. They'll fix you up. Now whaddaya say, fellas, let's let the woman do her job."

As the three men reluctantly left the tunnel, Dragleman smiled at Meg. "Figured I'd lend you a diplomatic hand."

"Thanks," Meg said, and turned to Ray Menitti. "The dart, did—"

"He missed," Ray said.

"Of course," she replied.

Rajah's roar again filled the tunnel. Dragleman reflexively backed up against the wall. Meg, however, moved forward, and Ray followed. Both peered into the dimly lit cave. Eyes flashed in the dark, then disappeared behind a boulder.

"What are you going to use on him?" Ray asked. He was three inches taller than Meg, and his features were rugged and handsome. They were both the same age, had gone to school together at UC Davis, and had been having an on-again, off-again romance going since Meg had divorced David.

Meg looked at him now and was glad to have him at her side. Somehow, she considered him more friend than lover; she depended on him.

"Let's make it Zyzaline and Ketamine, 2 cc's each. And you'd better give me two setups."

"Right. You want the rifle?"

"No," Meg said. "Get me the Telinject and some extra darts. No telling how charged up he is. And tell Russell I'll need tarp and some rope. He can find everything I need in the locker behind the lab. And you'd better leave me your light."

Ray unhitched the flashlight from his belt and slapped it into her palm. "Are you going to place Rajah in the squeeze cage?"

Meg nodded and took hold of his arm. "And whatever you do, don't forget the shotgun."

Another growl rumbled through the cave.

Ray said, "Are you kidding?" Then he turned on his heel and hightailed it out of the tunnel.

"Shotgun?" Dragleman wondered aloud. "For what?"

Meg said, "Twelve-gauge, just in case Rajah wakes up while I'm examining him."

Dragleman's eyes grew wide. "Wait a minute. You mean you're actually goin' in there? With *him?*"

Meg flashed the detective a half smile, then got down on all fours and crept forward. Five feet from the steel bars that separated Rajah's cave from the service tunnel, she stopped. Close enough, she thought; if he charged again, she'd have enough space to avoid his claws.

Twenty feet ahead, where the interior of the cave widened, the shadows were too dense to see the tiger. Yet Meg knew exactly where he was: a pair of green spheres floated in the dark. She glanced at Dragleman. "Want to have a look?" The detective hesitated. "It's okay, Lieutenant. Get down on his level and move in behind me. But don't make any sudden movements."

Dragleman crouched, and carefully moved behind Meg's shoulder. Rajah uttered a low, rumbling growl and began to pace.

Meg took a deep breath and raised the flashlight. What was left of Carol's body was back there somewhere, guarded by the tiger. She flicked on the switch. Rajah spun around, eyes shining, lips curled back. He dipped his head, trying to avoid the bright glare. Dust particles swirled in the air. The sweeps of his tail quickened—erratic and sharp—signaling anger.

Suddenly his massive jaws slacked open. White pointed canines shone in the light. His tongue lolled out of his mouth. He flung his head back and roared.

"Jesus," Dragleman groaned. "How big is that thing?"

Meg felt the detective's fingers dig into her shoulder as the cat suddenly lunged at the light, then veered away. "He's the largest tiger ever held in captivity," she replied steadying the flashlight. "He weighs seven hundred pounds and has a shoulder height of four feet. He's eleven feet from nose to tailbone, and one of the rare few who can . . . oh my God!"

Dragleman tensed. "What is it?"

"There." The flashlight in Meg's hand began to shake. "Over there by the last boulder."

Half buried under a pile of leaves was the keeper's body, or what was left of it. Her right leg was nearly torn off, her eyes frozen open in stark horror. Most of her clothes had been ripped away; a few tatters of blouse still clung to her shoulder. She was sprawled on her back in a puddle of her own coagulated blood.

"Don't look at her," Dragleman said, lifting Meg to her feet.

Rajah roared again, and Dragleman turned. And as he turned, he thought—and the thought made him cringe— that he saw a small strand of human flesh dangling from the cat's mouth.

3

SEVERAL MINUTES PASSED before Meg felt well enough to help Ray with the equipment. Twenty minutes later Biggs and Herbert Tally arrived with another security guard. In the meantime, the level of tension had increased as nerves began to fray.

"I can't do it," Herbert said, glancing fitfully into the cave. "I can't, Doc. So please don't make me go in there."

Meg liked Herbert, despite his lack of enthusiasm in dealing with emergencies. She admired the fact that the old man had a great love of animals and even kept a pet monkey of his own in his small house in Van Nuys.

"Sorry, Herbert," Meg said, picking up a syringe dart. "I'll need you on the clock."

Herbert knew what that meant. Someone was needed to keep precise time from the moment the tranquilizer dart penetrated the cat's hide. Usually a stopwatch was used, but in emergencies a wristwatch was acceptable.

Herbert said, "I ain't got a watch."

Ray removed his watch. "Here," he said, "use mine." Then he picked up the shotgun and handed it to Biggs, who pressed the stock of the Remington 870 against his middle and pushed four shells into the chamber.

Dragleman said, "You know how to use that thing?"

Meg said, "Every zoo has to have two assistants who can handle a shotgun. Ray, Russell, and I are registered with the National Rifle Association."

"Yes," Dragleman snorted, "but does he know how to use that thing?"

A guttural roar split the air, and everyone glanced at the cave. A stench rose, filling the tunnel, an odor like the miasma at a particularly gruesome murder scene.

"What's that smell?" Dragleman asked.

"Rajah is marking his territory," Meg said. "Or, perhaps, he's marking his kill."

All eyes turned to Meg, and she stared back, assessing each man. Some looked frightened, some dazed, but all were tense, edgy. Meg didn't know the third security guard, but she could see panic in his boyish features.

"Here, hold this!" Meg pressed the flashlight into the young man's hand. Then she held a vial upside down, pricked the seal, and pulled back the plunger of the syringe dart, drawing the liquid into the hypo barrel. She repeated the procedure with the second vial. When the syringe was full, she held it up to the tunnel light and flicked her finger against the middle; the drugs blended into one solution. Then she gave the plunger a slight push, driving the last bubbles of air from the barrel in one tiny spurt. Ray handed her the Telinject blowgun, and Meg turned to Biggs. "Okay, hit the lights."

Biggs flicked a switch on the power box, and the tunnel lights went off, leaving only the glow of the flashlight in the young man's hand.

Meg leaned against the wall next to Rajah's cave and peered in. The cat was still agitated, but not as jumpy as before. She carefully slipped the blowgun barrel between the bars of the cave, then waited.

Getting a straight shot at the fleshy part of the upper torso was often difficult. If she fired too low, the cat would swipe the dart away before the full dosage could enter his bloodstream, too high, and she risked hitting the face.

"Hold the light directly on him," Meg whispered, and the young man steadied the flashlight.

The tiger made no motion now—there was no tail twitching, no ear movement; not even a whisker quivered. He appeared frozen, as stonelike as the large boulder to the left of the keeper's body. Meg steadied herself, took aim at his muscular left shoulder, sucked in a slow, deep breath and fired—a hit!

With a sudden roar, the cat charged, full weight slamming against the bars. Meg stumbled as she lurched back, barely avoiding the flexed claws that went for her throat. Ray dived forward and yanked her away as hard as he could.

Shrill voices overlapped in the dark. "Jesus!" "Now he's *really* pissed!"

"Are you all right?" Ray said, lifting her to her feet.

"Yes, I'm fine." Meg let out two slow breaths, then said, "Okay, Russell, turn on the lights."

Dragleman blinked, his eyes readjusting to the sudden glare. "How long do we wait?" he asked.

"About ten minutes," Meg said. "In the meantime, I can send up for coffee."

"You kidding?" Dragleman said. "After what I just saw, I'm about as wired and wide awake as I get."

"PHASE ONE OVER!" Herbert shouted when the cat's head fell limply to the floor.

Meg pulled out her key for the cave's padlock. "Time to move," she said. "And remember, we have fifteen minutes, tops."

As Herbert punched the reset button on Ray's watch, Biggs pumped one round into the twelve-gauge chamber. Moving in first, he stood behind the cat, nestling the twenty-inch barrel of the shotgun against the base of his massive skull. "Come ahead," he said.

Bodies moved into position.

Meg glanced quickly at the young guard, who kept looking over his shoulder at Carol's body. "What's your name?" she asked.

"Billy," the young man said.

"Okay, Billy, now I'll need you to hold the light steady, understand?"

The young man nodded, and Meg bent and ran her hands under the cat's torso, searching for surface injuries.

Ray knelt down beside her and slid the end of his stethoscope along the tiger's chest, listening. "Heartbeat, regular . . . respiration, good."

Meg hesitated. She had the sudden sensation that what was happening was a horrendous nightmare from which she rightfully should have awakened some time ago. She glanced at Carol's body, and then flinched when she felt the cat move. His breathing was heavy, on the surface, as if he were about to wake. She quickly slid her hands up the tiger's wide girth. "Lacerations and contusions on both rear pads," she said. "Middle claw chipped on both."

Ray dabbed the hind paws with disinfectant. Then, as quickly as he could, he slipped the rectal thermometer into the tiger's anus.

The tiger flinched. Everyone froze.

Biggs tightened his grip on the shotgun trigger.

Meg turned to Ray. "Well?"

"It's in," he said.

"Okay, let's keep moving. And hurry."

Meg picked up the cat's left front paw, fanning the thick

36

mitt with both hands. Then she checked the right paw. "Minor inflammation of both front pads, minor contusions—claws undamaged." She looked up at Biggs. "I'm going into the mouth."

Biggs nodded, sliding the shotgun barrel down the cat's spine to rest between the shoulder blades.

Wrapping her arms around the tiger's head, Meg heaved back, turning the face upward. Cat eyes gleamed up at her through narrow slits. His snout and tufted cheeks were blotched with dried blood. With both hands, Meg gripped the upper and lower jaws and pulled the tiger's mouth open. An acrid smell wafted up from the tiger's belly.

"Seven minutes to go," Herbert wheezed.

Meg sucked in a deep breath and held it as she put her hand into Rajah's mouth. She ran her fingers along the tiger's teeth, looking for recent damage. Then she repeated the action along the gums and deep into the wet jowl canals.

Suddenly she stopped, looking more closely at the rear of the tiger's raspy tongue. Resting on the back surface was something she could not identify. She reached in and pinched the object with her fingers. Then she pulled and pulled again, until the long, sinewy strand of flesh was dangling in the light. A wet pink shoelace was twirled around the strip of tissue like a string of macrame.

The young guard turned and started to gag.

"Easy," Meg said. "Take a few breaths, you'll be all right." She lowered the strand into a plastic bag and sealed it.

Ray said, "Turn the light a little this way."

The young man steadied himself as Ray removed the rectal thermometer and held it up to the light. "Temperature is two degrees above normal."

Suddenly the cat moved. All eyes went to Meg. She knew she had to find the saphenous vein quickly. Pressing down with her finger, she said to Ray, "Right there." Ray rubbed a small area on the cat's hind leg with a cotton ball dipped in disinfectant. Then he gripped the leg firmly with both hands.

Meg held the syringe needle directly above the target. "Drawing blood," she said, a warning for everyone to be on guard.

The needle pierced the hide. A deep, grunting protest rose from the cat's throat.

Herbert said, "Three minutes to go!"

Blood drawn, Meg picked up the pace. "We'll need a fecal culture."

Ray took the flashlight and redirected it to the far corner where Rajah had recently defecated. "Over there,"

"Fine, now let's get the tarp down."

As Meg and the young man spread the tarp on the floor, Ray sidestepped the keeper's body and knelt by the steaming pile of feces. With a plastic depressor, he scooped out a small lump and smeared it onto the chemically treated sampling tab. Then he dropped the tab into a plastic bag.

"One, two, three, heave!" Meg said, pulling on Rajah's hind quarters as hard as she could. The young man pushed from the other side, straining, barely getting the cat's rump into position.

"What's the time?" Meg asked.

Herbert hollered, "Under two minutes. We should be getting out of here!"

Biggs quickly stepped back as Ray moved to the front half of the cat's torso. Squatting, he encircled the massive head with both arms. They all knew this was a critical moment. With Biggs backing off, even a few feet, anything could happen.

"One, two, three, heave!"

They moved the cat, but not far.

Biggs hesitated, then crooked the shotgun over his arm and with both hands took hold of the tiger's leg. They heaved again, dragging the cat onto the tarp. Ray quickly folded the cat's legs under the white underbelly as Meg flung the corners of the tarp over Rajah and cinched the ropes.

"Thirty seconds . . ." Herbert said, backing out of the cave. Biggs followed, shotgun ready.

"Gangway!" Meg called.

Suddenly the cat moved, or maybe they did. No one knew for sure as they slid the tarp across the concrete floor toward the tunnel. Two uniforms at the door rushed forward, and together they yanked the cat into the holding pen.

"Five seconds . . ."

Meg moved frantically to untie the tarp. Hands groped, people drew back. Ray was about to roll Rajah onto the floor when Meg ordered him out. "Stand clear!" she shouted.

Ray rushed from the pen and Meg slammed the bars shut.

Suddenly Rajah kicked his powerful limbs and staggered up with a hissing growl. He swayed and stumbled, trying to shake off the grogginess. Then he slowly began to pace, moving in circles, his head slung low, eyes glaring. Then he raised his massive head and froze. There was no motion now, save for the involuntary twitch of a muscle in his left rear flank.

He was in position and ready, a beast looking for its next prey.

4

MEG BREWSTER MOVED silently into the compound and looked around. There was no color to be seen anywhere. The spotlight still shone, a particle-filled beam of light that cut the area in two.

Behind her, an awful smell wafted upward, filling the heavy, damp air. The odor came from the mouth of the cave, riding the murky breeze that would give way to warmer, gentler air when the sun came up. The smell could be compared to that of a moldy carpet or spoiled fish, but none of these comparisons did it justice. And once encountered, it was a stench that one could never mistake or forget.

Shivering, Meg zipped up her parka and glanced past the bright glare to where a group of reporters stood talking. She knew what was about to happen. Come morning, the story of Carol's death would be the lead item on news shows coast to coast. Broadcast services, utilizing the power of their shared satellite networks, were bound to pick it up. And, depending on how many things were exploding in the other parts of the world, the country would hear the story over breakfast, complete with grisly details.

Like a circus, Meg thought grimly. No usual fare of street violence and bombings today, folks, no sirree! Today we give you slaughter the old-fashioned way! Basic and primeval.

But no matter how the media presented their view of the incident, Meg knew they would lean hard on the difference between this tragedy and those that had occurred in the more remote areas of the world. This was Los Angeles, in the United States of America. The City of Angels. Here the beasts of nature were subdued for the sake of human curiosity and amusement. They were not supposed to cause harm. And they should never, *never* be allowed to kill.

But Rajah had killed, and suddenly Meg felt the weight of it all. Rajah was *her* responsibility. Under *her* care. And she wondered if an older, more experienced veterinarian might have prevented the accident from happening.

Ashamed, Meg turned now and watched Dragleman saunter from the cave, a light early-morning fog settling around his ankles. Voices rose from the railing above him. Some were hushed, others were full of laughter.

"Hey, Lieutenant! Have a look over here," a voice called from the bushes above the concrete wall.

Dragleman moved toward the south wall a few feet from the stream, Meg followed.

"What is it?" Dragleman hollered back, searching his pockets for a fresh cigar.

The voice came again. "Hey! Get that light on this so the lieutenant can have a look-see."

"Right," another voice barked.

The spotlight moved slowly up the side of the wall, tracing a wide streak of blood that ran from the bottom of the pit up to the bushes along the rim. An obese man was kneeling at the top, pointing to the crimson trail. Crumbs clung to his tie and a constellation of dandruff floated across the dark shoulders of his suit.

"She went over right here, Lieutenant," he said. "Not over the rail. We've got an uprooted bush, footprints, and this." He held up a metal bucket. "It's got some kind of stinky mush in it."

"That's Carol's feed bucket," Meg said.

Dragleman looked at Meg, his tan face crinkling some as he rubbed his forehead. "Was she supposed to be up there?" he asked.

"No . . . never." Meg eyed the wall, confused.

"Why do you think she went up there?"

"I don't know, Lieutenant."

"Hmmm," Dragleman said. Then he said, "A real tragedy, you know." He stuffed an unlit cigar in his mouth and began tracing a broken trail of blood—like skid marks— running the length of the compound to the mouth of the cavern. "He dragged her across these rocks and into the cave," he said.

Meg watched him amble through the brushy grounds, peer into crevices hidden from the light. "Just what is it you're looking for, Lieutenant? Maybe I can help you."

"I don't know," he said, scanning the wide pit. "Maybe nothing." He looked up. "Just habit, I guess. I like poking around. You understand."

Meg said, "Of course I do. Your line of work complicates things, I'm sure. Being involved with criminals all the time . . ."

"Yes, ma'am. You've got the picture." He paused to light his cigar. "I've been at this sort of thing for a while now," he said, shrouded in a fresh cloud of smoke. "And if I see questions without answers, I can't file a report. That's what I do, Doc. I write reports. Actually, my job is rather boring."

"What sort of questions?" Meg asked.

"Well, to be perfectly truthful, I don't really know." He paused again to consider the tip of his cigar. "We might start with: What do you know about Carol Lewis?"

Meg composed herself: a deep intake of breath and a stiffening of her shoulders. "She was an employee of the zoo. She'd been here a little over two years. We weren't friends, Lieutenant. We were friendly, in a professional way, but I don't know about her personal life."

"You were her boss. . . ."

"Not technically. She worked for the zoo staff."

"But she followed your orders."

"Ah, I see where you're going, Lieutenant. Tonight's feeding—this was an exception to the usual feeding schedule."

"An exception?" Dragleman looked at her with the intense gaze of a pro.

Meg hesitated, thinking of the zoo's director, Gordon Ellroy, who had a history of sensitivity over her obsession with Rajah. *What is it with you and that tiger?* he had finally demanded. *Cats aren't great in captivity—it's something we both know. So why won't you just admit Rajah hates being caged a little more than the next Siberian tiger and leave it at that?* Finally, Gordon had put it in the form of an order. Unless symptoms developed indicating some "real" danger, and by that he meant were the cat to suffer some life-threatening injury or disease, he didn't want to hear any more about Rajah.

And Meg was sure, standing here in the blood-streaked compound, spotlight moving slowly over every inch of walls and interior grounds, the detective very quiet beside her as if he sensed pertinent data in the air . . . that Gordon Ellroy wouldn't want her to mention a word about Rajah's erratic behavior.

43

"An exception, you were saying?" Dragleman looked at her curiously.

"Yes," Meg said finally. "I had ordered an around-the-clock watch on Rajah."

"No kidding."

"It was routine, Lieutenant. It wasn't the first time I've ordered observations on an animal that was restless, off his feed."

Dragleman gave her an unexpectedly winning smile. "Dr. Brewster, I have as little knowledge about what a zoo vet calls routine as *you* have of . . . well, what a police detective calls routine. But I'll tell you this. If you're talking about sending a young female keeper sneaking around up there in the dark with a pail of slop meant for that same beast I just saw with your fingers halfway down his throat, it doesn't sound all that routine. If it is, tell me how. I'm willing to learn, but my first impressions are, frankly, *come on, lady!*"

"Don't call me that," Meg said automatically. Her heart plummeted. Now she had done it. She had made the very mistake most likely to send Gordon through the roof. She had called attention to Rajah, and probably made the zoo legally culpable for Carol's death. "Look, Lieutenant, I have no idea what Carol was doing up there. I've already told you that. She wasn't supposed to take any chances. I hate to say this, but it was probably Carol's own *methods* that killed her. And it's Carol's methods that don't sound routine to you."

Meg saw him take in what she had said, doubt it, and then shrug.

Meg unzipped her jacket, feeling a nervous heat rush through her body, as if she were running a fever. She heard Dragleman ask what, exactly, the tiger's symptoms had been, and answered slowly, as though reading it from her own notes. "Constant pacing . . . occasionally broken by a

slow attack crawl . . . erratic twitching during sleep
. . . responding to ordinary sounds with aggressive mo-
tions like he was reacting to an invisible intruder."

"And you think he might be sick?" Dragleman looked at
her, engrossed.

Meg hesitated. "I'm not really sure."

"Well," the lieutenant said, "the way I see it, a zookeeper
makes a mistake. Then the biggest damned cat I *ever* saw
eats her alive—"

"Not alive, Lieutenant. A cat always kills its prey first."

Dragleman shrugged. "Small consolation. Anyway, it
seems cut-and-dried. She was on the wall observing a cat
that's been acting weird. The cat gets wind of her and, well,
he jumps up on the wall and pulls her into the pit."

For the first time, Meg got it. What had been bothering
her all along. With a jolt, she turned to the wall and stared.
"No," she said. "It couldn't have happened that way. It's
impossible. No cat could scale the smooth surface of a wall
at that height."

Dragleman sighed. "We've got those streak marks on the
wall, you know. And the uprooted bush. Some sort of
struggle took place at the top."

Meg continued to consider the height of the wall. No
way, she thought, but there was no point in saying so again,
since the visual evidence told both her and Dragleman that
she was wrong.

Dragleman turned to look at her, his gaze both sharp and
admiring. "You know, Doc, you handled yourself like a
pro in there. I was impressed. You tell me a cat can't jump
that high, I have to wonder. I have to wonder about adrenaline. People can do amazing things if their adrenaline goes
crazy. Maybe cats can, too, but you'd know better about
that than me. Anyhow, between the investigation and the
autopsy we'll figure things out."

"Autopsy? You're not sure how Carol died?" As tired as

Meg was, the idea of an autopsy struck her as a note of dark humor.

"It's standard procedure," Dragleman said. "When a person dies alone, no matter how obvious the cause of death may seem, I've got to ask the coroner for an autopsy. I wouldn't take it personal." He smiled blithely at her. "Well, good night, Doc."

As Dragleman ambled back to the cave, Meg turned and peered at the twenty-foot-high wall again, as though seeing it for the first time. Her eyes followed the streaks of blood upward, a chill sweeping over her. Above the ledge, the dark forms of two men hovered over the spot where Carol's feed bucket had been found. "Some sort of struggle," Lieutenant Dragleman had said. One of the men snapped a photograph of the spot; the brilliant flash briefly illuminated the other man's face.

Meg continued to stare at the bloodied ledge. That a tiger could leap to such a height and grasp a strong, full-grown human was incomprehensible to her. Studies of tiger behavior had shown that no matter how desperate or determined a tiger might be, it rarely attempted to scale a tree, let alone the smooth, perpendicular surface of a twenty-foot wall.

Meg remembered once being on the shore of a misty lowland marsh at sunrise, observing tigers for the World Wildlife Federation. A family of monkeys was thrown into a panic when a Bengal tiger sprang from a nearby thicket. When the dust settled, it appeared the monkeys had all escaped safely into the branches of a tree. It soon became apparent, however, that the monkeys were trapped; there was no way for them to climb to other trees, no way to spread out into the thick jungle canopy.

The tiger, sensing their predicament, began circling the tree, repeating a low, rumbling growl. The monkeys grew more frightened and climbed higher in the tree, onto smaller, less stable branches. When they were all at the top, the tiger stretched his long body up the tree trunk and let out a terrifying roar. The roaring then continued until one of the trembling monkeys lost his grip and fell into the waiting claws of the tiger.

Meg blinked as the camera flashed above her again, the memory of that morning, and of the cunning tiger at work, vanishing into the reality of the glistening red streaks on the wall in front of her. She could not explain how this tragedy had occurred. Everything she had thought she knew about tigers was suddenly being challenged.

All cats, given the opportunity, are people watchers. Meg knew that much. Cats know how to anticipate. But what would have caused Rajah to commit such a destructively hostile act?

Meg began to back away now as newsmen crowded around the front railing, their faces dead white and splotched under the spotlight, whistling and calling out to the detectives. One held a video camera.

Another made an indescribably evil cackle as he shouted: "Hey, hey, Ryan! Ryan, who the hell's in charge here?"

Turning her back on them, Meg started toward the tunnel. Ray suddenly emerged at the railing. "Meg, Ellroy's on the line." He dropped the portable phone down to her.

Meg caught it in one hand, raised the antenna, and hit the switch. "Yes, Gordon?"

The director said, "Are you finished up there?"

"Just about."

"I'll need to talk to you in my office before you leave." He paused. "Is that okay?"

"Fine with me," Meg said, thinking that now the real fireworks would begin.

* * *

GORDON ELLROY WAS a man of moods, and as a result, the art of conversation was sometimes difficult for him, and sometimes not. A large man, he was in his early fifties, drank too much, and lived his life with a certain amount of dash. He was also a notorious bully when he wanted to be. More times than not, obstinate was the word that came to mind when describing him. On the other hand, Meg had long ago concluded, Ellroy hadn't gotten where he was by being stupid.

When Meg arrived at the office, she found Ellroy and Philip Roueche alone. Roueche paced the room restlessly, a grave look on his face. Ellroy sat motionless behind his desk, watching the curator's every move. Despite the soundproofing, occasional snatches of excitedly raised voices, animal noise, and the high-pitched whine of sirens drifted into the room.

Finally, Ellroy looked up and noticed Meg. "Come in, come in," he said, waving to her. "Roueche was just saying—go on, Philip."

"I can't understand," Roueche said, "why our director here has never wanted to collect serious artists." He motioned dismissively at the paintings that were hung on the walls. "Why is that, Gordon?"

The director did not answer.

"I mean, even if you have no appreciation of art, paintings are an excellent investment. Am I right, Meg?"

He turned nimbly to face her, teeth sparkling through his sensuous lips, opened slightly in a flirtatious smile.

Roueche was a handsome man and fully aware of it. In his early forties, he had wavy black hair and a body kept trim by diet and exercise. He was also somewhat single-mindedly fascinated by women, and seemed to pursue them constantly. He had been born into money, ran with a politically chic crowd, and often spent his time in Washington dining with the newly elected. Meg had first met him three years ago while doing field work in India, an assignment she had accepted in an effort to flee the harsh reality of her crumbling marriage. Philip had zeroed in on her immediately, and when she made it known she wasn't interested, he took it as a challenge and offered her a job at the L.A. Zoo. He, of course, had continued to pursue her; she, to resist. It was a situation Meg found irritating, if occasionally comical.

Meg said, "Tell me, Gordon, was I asked here to discuss art appreciation, or is Philip's seeming disinterest in Carol's death a harbinger of things to come?" There was no humor in her voice tonight.

Ellroy looked up sharply. He sometimes moved with the temperamental energy of a squirrel, but not tonight. Tonight he seemed weighed down by the shock of events. "No, of course not," he said. "It's more complicated than that. I'm afraid it's quite disagreeable, actually." He rose slightly in his chair. "Please, sit down."

Meg hesitated a moment, making an effort to control herself. She knew that Ellroy held all the cards where Rajah was concerned, and that the next move was entirely up to him. She also knew Roueche often influenced his decision making. With a heavy sigh, she sat in the leather chair beside his desk.

"So, how'd things go up there?" Ellroy glanced nervously at Roueche, who hovered over Meg's shoulder.

Meg said, "Detective Dragleman is requesting the coroner perform an autopsy on Carol Lewis."

"Autopsy?" Roueche looked down at Meg. "What in God's name is the man hoping to find?"

"Nothing, really. He said it's standard procedure. Carol was alone when she died."

Ellroy and Roueche exchanged glances. As director, it

was Ellroy's job to oversee all aspects of the zoo's administration in addition to fund-raising, arranging donations,
and acting as a liaison between the zoo and the Greater Los
Angeles Zoo Association, GLAZA.

As curator, Roueche was responsible for orders, ship-
ments, and the transfer of animals, which included running
a data bank on the location of all animals in zoos across the
country. And, in Roueche's case, in zoos around the world
as well.

Neither, however, was directly responsible for the health
and safety of the animals in the zoo. Meg alone bore that
responsibility, and it was quickly becoming an exceedingly
heavy burden.

When she looked up, both men were staring pointedly in
her direction. "Autopsy—I don't like the sound of that,"
Ellroy said. "Perhaps, Meg, you should tell me exactly
what went on up there."

It took only a few minutes for Ellroy to learn everything
he felt he needed to know. Then, as much to seem efficient
as for any other reason, he asked Meg again for the detective's name.

"Draggleman." He scribbled the name haphazardly on a
pad, spelling it out loud as he wrote.

"Dragleman," said Meg. "One *g*."

Ellroy made the correction. Then he paused for a second.
He seemed to be choosing his words with care: "You know,
Meg, I don't mean to sound heartless. God knows, I liked
Carol like my own daughter. But her death may, in a cir-
cuitous way, prove . . . well, beneficial to us."

Meg said, "Beneficial?"

"An unfortunate choice of words, I suppose. Nevertheless, let me explain our situation." He rummaged his desk,
found the file he was looking for, and opened it. "I've been
going over our latest financial report. To put it bluntly,

Meg—our cash flow has dried up. I got a call from Gold-
man this morning and the gossip around town is that our
bond rating may be up for review. As you know, that
process can drag on for months. Meanwhile, we won't be
able to borrow a dime." Ellroy paused to catch his breath.

"What's more," he continued, "we're carrying large
debts from the previous two years. So in a very real sense,
we're heavily mortgaged."

"About our indebtedness," Meg said, "could you spell
that out roughly?"

"How about exactly?" Ellroy answered, pulling a sheet
from the file. "We're eight million in the hole, and this year
doesn't look good. At least . . ."

Meg said, "At least what, Gordon?"

Roueche said, "At least, not until now. Gordon and I
both feel that if Rajah were kept on display—"

"*Display?*" Meg nearly leapt from her chair. "I've ordered him into quarantine, Philip. Where he belongs. I'll
need to run tests. . . ."

Ellroy hastily said, "Meg, for heaven's sake, look at it
from our point of view. The city has slashed our budget
five years in a row. Attendance at the zoo is down. But with
the media and public fascination that's sure to follow this
terrible tragedy, we have a chance of climbing out of the
red. Carol's death was indeed a horrible accident, but we
cannot afford to pass up this opportunity."

"It's blood money," Meg said, staring the director down.
"Pure and simple. You can't do this. What if Rajah is sick?
If he's carrying a rare contagious disease? The health of the
other animals may be at risk."

Roueche had moved to the window and was peering
out between the blinds. He turned now, straightening the
lapels of his jacket, hands gracefully smoothing expensive
silk.

"You've spent—what is it now?—ah yes, three weeks, I believe, looking for this *mysterious* disease." He spoke as if he were talking to a four-year-old. "By your own admission, you've turned up nothing."

"Our laboratory doesn't have the equipment I need to make all the tests!"

He glanced at her tentatively, then sighed. "Yet you persist. Gordon and I both suggested you let it go, that Rajah was just going through an emotional phase. But you wouldn't listen. Surely you must realize that Carol might still be alive if not for your stubbornness?"

Meg got to her feet. She had expected a strong argument against her ordering a late night feeding vigil, but not so soon, and certainly not from Roueche. "That's unfair, and you know it. I do what I'm paid to do, Philip. I care for animals. I believe that's your job as well. Or have you forgotten that?"

Roueche smiled. "No, Doctor, I haven't forgotten. If you remember, it was I who suggested that we have Rajah declawed after acquiring him. For his own well-being."

"Oh, that's great. Remove an animal from his natural habitat, ship him ten thousand miles in a crate, then pull his claws out and stick him in a cage. His claws, Philip, are as important to him as your teeth are to you!"

Roueche nodded, eyes sparkling with challenge. He took a gold cigarette case from his pocket and opened it. He said, "As usual, Meg, you've overstated your premise." Then, lighting a cigarette, he said, "I've always felt that your attachment to Rajah was . . ." He paused.

"What?"

Roueche hesitated. "Too personal."

"My caring for Rajah was born of neglect, Philip, you know that. He was treated horribly in quarantine. You saw the deplorable conditions he was living under."

"Midway Quarantine was government run. And run quite well, I might add."

"Is that why it's been shut down?"

"Again, an overstatement," Roueche said, filtering his words through a mouthful of smoke. "Midway wasn't shut down, it was *closed* because of government cutbacks. Just as we will be closed, unless—"

"They held him captive for six months," Meg said. "He was only supposed to be there thirty days. He was underfed, in poor health—no, I won't allow him to be put on display. And that's final."

Meg looked at Ellroy, who was still seated at his desk. His eyes seemed unfocused, as though he were daydreaming, not even listening to all that had been said.

"Gordon?" Roueche said, wanting to bring him back to the present, over which he might have some control. "Perhaps you might say a word here."

Ellroy glanced up, then looked away sadly, his eyes drifting distractedly over the financial report. "I'm afraid neither one of us is dealing with this very well, Philip," he said. Then he said, "You know, Meg, I know you're not much interested in our financial dilemma. But things get pretty complicated around here. We're right on the edge. The whole state is. People are more cautious now about how they spend their money, where they'll vacation. There's something crazy in the air when things get this bad. Let me read you something." He searched through some papers on his desk, then adjusted his glasses. "Um—here it is: 'California's vast economy is slowly grinding to a halt. For the first time in recent memory, property values have plummeted, companies are leaving the state, and according to the latest U.S. Census, there was a decrease in Los Angeles County's population.' "

Ellroy looked up at Meg to reinforce his point. "So in the

strictest sense, Meg, we haven't any choice but to exploit our resources. And, in all honesty, I must tell you that unless our financial problems are solved, you might as well start looking for a new job."

Meg stiffened. "Is that a threat, Gordon?"

Ellroy said, "Not at all. I just want you to understand what's at risk here."

"I'm well aware of what's at risk here, Gordon," Meg said, making no effort to disguise her disgust. "That's why I'm stressing the quarantine. Or would you prefer I sweep the whole thing under the rug? That amounts to a cover-up." She glanced at Roueche, then eyed the director. "Tell me the truth, Gordon. Where's the pressure coming from?"

"There is no pressure. . . ."

"Don't kid me, Gordon. I may be junior here, but I've been around enough to know better than that. There's always a political pressure point somewhere. Is it the mayor? The City Council, maybe? Good grief, is the state of the economy that bad?"

"There is no pressure," Ellroy repeated woodenly, "unless I count the pressure from you. And I certainly am *not* suggesting we cover anything up. From what you've told me, Carol's own negligence may have caused her death. And despite all your tests, you really haven't found anything medically wrong with Rajah."

"Not yet, Gordon. But what if something *is* wrong with him? Tigers don't normally act the way he's been acting. Please, Gordon, at least give me the courtesy of time."

Roueche said, "Time isn't the issue, Meg. Money is."

"As simple as that?"

"Money is never simple, especially when one finds one hasn't any." Roueche smiled, a vague leer in his eyes as he glanced at Meg's breasts.

Overwhelmed by the absurdity of the man and the un-

reality of the moment, Meg needed all of her self-control
not to slap him. But then Roueche would be pleased finally
to have gotten a physical rise out of her. He doesn't belong
here, she thought. His money made ordinary concerns disappear. His was a life of grandeur, of sensual power and
domination. What was one measly tiger to him? Or a lowly
zookeeper, for that matter? And how could she have so
readily accepted his offer to come work for him?

Ellroy glanced at Roueche, then looked searchingly into
Meg's eyes. Finally, he nodded, his large chest rising and
then collapsing with resignation. "All right," he said, "out
of deference to your loyalty, and past service, which
you know I've always considered top-notch, I'll give
you three days to find the cause of Rajah's odd behavior.
Just three, Meg. Then I want him back on display. Is that
clear?"

"Fine," Meg said. "I've already taken a blood sample to
send to Dr. Shindler at UCLA. His equipment is far more
advanced than anything we have in our lab."

"Dr. Shindler?" The director raised an eyebrow. "Do
you know the man, Philip?"

"Not personally," Roueche said, "but I've read some of
his work. He appears to be a brilliant man, assuming he
isn't stealing his ideas from his students, of course. Perhaps,
Gordon, you've come across one or two of his articles in
Scientific American?"

"Yes, yes, I'm sure I have."

Meg said, "If you don't mind, I've still got plenty of
catching up to do."

Ellroy said, "By all means, go right ahead. But before
you go, I have a favor to ask. It's a nuisance, really. You
probably won't want to."

"Ask and find out."

"I'd like you to personally handle the press tomorrow.

I'll be out of the office most of the day. I don't trust PR, so just this once. I would count it," he added, setting his jaw in the way he did when he was giving an ultimatum, "a personal favor."

"I'll be glad to, Gordon."

Ellroy smiled as he glanced at Roueche, whose face remained impassive. Meg knew Ellroy's intent was to use her. Roueche, clearly, had something else in mind.

OUTSIDE, MEG STOOD for a moment and listened. It was something she instinctively did each day before leaving the zoo. If the sounds were normal, then she knew the animals were settling down for the evening.

But tonight, the sounds were anything but normal. The excited cries of the orangutans and the howling monkeys shattered the air. Somewhere in the distance a lion roared and kept on roaring, causing hundreds of birds to flutter and rush upward at the fearful sound.

Meg felt overwhelmed, and yet, at the same time, she was bursting with strength. Part of it was the strain of unanswered questions. The other part was the urgent need to restore the zoo to some semblance of order. Slowly at first, she began checking animals, calming the more restless ones as best she could. But there wasn't enough time to assess accurately the damage done to the zoo's entire population by tonight's disturbance.

The other keepers pitched in. Even Russell Biggs helped. Herbert, however, was too sick and grief-stricken to help, so Meg thought it best to send him home.

Everyone was obviously depressed. The same thought resonated in every mind. Carol Lewis was dead. The fatal error that all zookeepers feared but never spoke about had actually happened, and now they must all live with it.

Meg, however, was left with a more agonizing thought: Was Carol Lewis's death my fault?

It was almost four in the morning when Meg pulled the Jeep into her carport and killed the engine. Ray followed right behind her, pulling his station wagon into the driveway and quickly climbing out.

"The quiet up here seems odd after all the confusion at the zoo," he said, as Meg wearily lifted her satchel from the Jeep.

"Only the coyotes prowling," Meg said, and looked up into the still dark sky. She heard nothing but her own strong heartbeat, the slow quieting of her breath. She could smell the sweet scent of wild roses and the fragrances of her dampened garden. For a moment she thought about just lying down there, on the wet grass. The need for sleep had never seemed so urgent.

When Meg turned, she saw Ray smiling, shaking his head. "What?" she asked.

"You look exhausted," he said.

"I feel even worse. Carol's death . . . seeing Rajah locked in a squeeze cage . . ."

Taking her hand, Ray leaned casually against the Jeep. "You did the right thing, Meg. Rajah needed to be isolated. I'm sure there's something wrong with him."

"But what?" Meg persisted. "According to Dragleman, Rajah scaled a twenty-foot wall. You and I both know that he couldn't have jumped that high."

Ray shrugged. "Maybe he did."

"If he did, he accomplished the impossible." Meg paused. "But then nothing he's been doing lately is consistent with normal behavior. It's almost as if he's undergoing a transformation of personality. As if he doesn't know who he is, or who he used to be. As if he's lost control of the 'hunting factor.' "

"Hunting factor?"

"Yes, if Dragleman is right, then he stalked Carol, *hunted* her down and killed her as though he were still back in the wild. But why? What triggered his aggression? He had plenty to eat. His territory was clearly defined. Under normal circumstances, he would never have attacked Carol."

"Or any other keeper, for that matter."

"That's my point!" Meg turned away, eyes averted, burning with doubt. She felt exhausted, crushed by the night's singular catastrophe. In one motion, she picked up her satchel and slammed it down on the Jeep's hood. "There has to be a logical explanation! I want you to get that blood sample over to Shindler first thing in the morning."

Ray sighed. "It *is* the first thing in the morning, Meg. Or haven't you noticed?"

"Well, then, why are you standing here? Go on, go."

"Oh?" Ray said, an edge of disappointment in his voice. He paused a moment debating whether to protest. "Sure, okay," he said finally. "Are you going to be all right?"

"I guess."

Ray hesitated, and then slowly climbed back into his station wagon and let down the window. "Okay, you get some sleep," he said. "I'll handle things at the zoo till you get there." Before Meg could speak, he held up his hand to silence her. "I know, you don't know what you'd do without me."

"How'd you guess?"

"I've become very good at it, Meg."

Meg knew what Ray was referring to. Sometimes, on his way home to his small cabin in Beverly Glen Canyon, he would stop by. Meg had tried as best she could to be warm, even romantic. She really liked Ray. But somehow she couldn't quite pull it off. Not that she hadn't wanted to, but something always seemed to be standing in her way. Perhaps her divorce had made her lose confidence. Or perhaps she just wasn't ready to make another commitment.

She stared at Ray for a moment. Then she leaned in through the car window, draped an arm over his shoulder, and kissed him lightly on the cheek. "Hey—buddies, right? Anyway, you're my assistant. Work before pleasure."

Ray tensed. "Why can't it be—"

She placed her fingers to his lips. "Let's not discuss it now, Ray. In a few days, okay? I promise. We'll get take-out at Fab's, a bottle of wine. Just you and me . . ."

"And Rajah makes three."

"We might even get a bottle of your favorite. Dom Pérignon."

Ray started the engine. "Are you kidding—on my salary?"

"No, on mine," Meg joked, and kissed him again before he pulled out of the drive.

As he drove off, Meg took a step foward, waved, and then noticed for the first time a dark blue sedan parked fifty feet up the road. Its lights were off, but in the faint glow of the street lamp she thought she could make out someone sitting in the car.

Meg hesitated, noting that except for that car the street was deserted. And even from a distance she could tell the car was parked at an odd angle, beneath trees along a curve where parking wasn't permitted. She also didn't recognize the car; it didn't belong to any of the neighbors.

Abruptly, the car started up, its headlights went on, and whoever was in it drove off.

That's odd, Meg thought, then reasoned that it was probably someone who had had too much to drink. Boozers were always using Mulholland Drive as a rest area or a haven for heavy contemplation.

Ten minutes later, Meg straggled into her bedroom and

dropped into bed. "Only the coyotes prowling," she thought, and reached for the lamp.

A CLOUD-COVERED dawn crept across the zoo. Something moved just outside the tunnel. The cat edged closer to the front bars of the cage and peered out. Then he drew back, charged, his claws shooting through the narrow opening.

He growled; the hunger within him growled louder.

He backed up and repeated the charge, striking out at the invisible prey. Water dripping from the ceiling spun him around. He swiped at each drop.

Then he emitted a last cry—a moan, of hatred, of fury—louder and louder until it filled the tunnel. Then the huge beast sank to his belly, where he waited alone in the cold steel cage.

5

W HAT GOOD was aggression?

Meg flipped impatiently through pages of the *Animal Behavioral Science Manual,* expecting that any second it would shed light on her Darwinian question. In the background the voice of Dr. Lennox Hampton on the VCR tape could be heard, explaining the "killer instinct" in animals and man.

Meg sighed and flipped another page, trying to concentrate. From where she sat, she had a clear view of her garden, which contained a dozen varieties of rare and exotic roses. The entire area was enclosed by a wall of hibiscus and night-blooming jasmine.

Usually she found peace there. Usually, but not today. Not now, at 9:00 A.M. Not after so little sleep. The garden seemed to reflect her mood—weary, drooping.

A pity, Meg thought and returned to the manual, where she saw a picture of a dog caught in a moment of complete and utter rage. She knew that in nature, fighting was an ever-present process, its behavior mechanisms and weapons highly developed for preserving the species.

Laymen, however, imagined the relationship between the

various "wild beasts of the jungle" to be a bloodthirsty struggle, all against all. In a film she had seen recently, a Bengal tiger was shown fighting with a python, and immediately afterward the python with a crocodile. But Meg knew that such encounters rarely occur under natural conditions. There wasn't anything to be gained from any of these creatures exterminating the other. None of the three interfered with the other's vital interests.

However, Meg did know of ferocious contests between members of different species: at night an owl kills and eats even well-armed birds of prey, in spite of their fierce defense, while by day, these same birds come upon the owl and attack it viciously. Almost every animal capable of self-defense, from the smallest creature upward, fights when it is cornered and has no means of escape. This is known as *critical reaction*: a struggle in which the fighter stakes his all, because he cannot escape and can expect no mercy. This most violent form of aggressive behavior is motivated solely by fear.

But Rajah hadn't been cornered, had he? What did he have to fear?

Meg flung the manual aside. She felt exhausted, yet wide awake. She had spent the last hour in deep concentration going over journal articles, books on animal behavior, her own medical book, and her clinical text. Each dead end made her more determined than ever to find the cause of Rajah's aggressive behavior.

She glanced at the TV; Dr. Hampton was still rambling on about how lion tamers maneuver their beasts into positions in the arena by playing a dangerous game with the margin between "flight distance" and "critical distance." At flight distance the animal feels safe. At critical distance the animal attacks out of fear and self-preservation.

Meg sat back now and imagined herself in Carol's place.

CLAW

At minimum, a twenty-foot-high wall separated them. Flight distance. Yet Rajah did not retreat. He attacked. Perhaps Carol had slipped and fallen partially into the pit. But why would Rajah mistake her dangling presence as a threat?

No, none of it made any sense.

Meg glanced again at the TV screen, then, on sudden impulse, reached for the Los Angeles phone book. A few minutes later she had Dr. Hampton on the line.

"Now?" he said.

"Yes, you're right off Beverly. I could be there in twenty minutes."

The man was silent for a moment. "Well, I'm running short on time. But if you really believe I can be of some help . . ."

"I'm sure you can," Meg said. "And thanks."

DR. HAMPTON'S HOUSE was in Hollywood on a cross street between the boulevards. It was the kind of street people took pride in. Well-manicured lawns, sidewalks neatly swept; even the palms that lined the street looked as if they received special care.

Dr. Hampton opened the door only moments after Meg's knock. He was a tall man in his late fifties, with frighteningly big eyes behind glasses. His shock of white hair was freshly combed to one side and neatly parted.

"I'm Dr. Hampton. You're Dr. Brewster, of course. You got here in no time at all."

"There wasn't that much traffic coming over the hill. I got lucky."

"Come in, Doctor. Let me get you a cup of coffee. I was just having a cup myself. Perhaps you'd care for a bite to eat."

"No, just coffee will be fine. Black."

63

Meg stepped inside, and the door made a loud noise as it swung closed behind her. The hall was warm and smelled of wax.

"This is my office," he said, sliding open a large oak door. "Please, take a seat. I'll only be a moment."

Meg stepped inside and looked around. It was a small room, crowded with a large oak desk, chairs, a hassock, and bookcases. On one of the shelves was a stuffed squirrel. On the desk stood a stuffed bird. It wasn't until Meg sat down that she noticed the stuffed boar's head above the fireplace.

She was still staring at the gruesome-looking thing when the doctor came into the office carrying a tray on which sat two cups of coffee and biscuits.

"Are you a hunter, Doctor?" Meg asked.

He laughed shortly. "No, heavens no. My son, God love him, is a taxidermist." He sighed. "No matter how many times I tell him I don't like those things in the house, he keeps bringing them in, I'm afraid."

He put the tray down beside her on the desk. "Please, help yourself."

Meg reached for the coffee cup and sipped. Then she outlined for the doctor the events of the previous evening, and ended by explaining why she had sought him out.

Dr. Hampton sat quietly, listening attentively to her description of events. "Animal aggression," he said at last, "whether directed against members of the same species or against man is very complicated. Many things could have caused the tiger to attack the girl. Fear, for instance."

"How about jumping twenty feet into the air?" Meg said. "Could fear cause him to do that?"

Hampton thought for a moment. "No, I don't believe so. Twenty feet is—"

"Flight distance, I know. I've seen your tape dozens of times. Especially while in college."

He smiled. "I was only forty when I did that series. It's still popular." He sipped his coffee. "Tell me, was the girl using a flashlight when the incident occurred?"

"No, she was instructed not to. I knew any sudden glare might alarm him."

"A weapon, perhaps. Or something that might have produced a sudden, loud noise?"

"Nothing like that. She was armed only with a feed bucket filled with ground up horseflesh."

"Yes, so you've said. And thus far you haven't found anything in the way of sickness, a virus, perhaps? Or perhaps a chemical imbalance?"

"That's correct. Other than showing aggressive behavior patterns, he appears to be perfectly normal."

"Aggression," the doctor said, "is frequently equated with the death wish. Perhaps—"

"Death wish?"

"Yes, it's a destructive principle which exists as an opposite pole to all instincts of self-preservation. Yet I believe them to be one and the same."

"Are you suggesting *thought* alone might have caused him to attack Carol?"

He smiled. "A bit Freudian, I know. But, nevertheless, his thought process must be considered. Let me give you an example. It was actually a case study of mine. Very unusual. A few years back, in Reno, a man kept his dog chained in the yard and beat the animal regularly. This went on for over a year. One day the man decided to take a week's vacation. He left the dog chained to the post. While the man was away, the dog somehow managed to break free.

"Now here is the interesting part. The dog did not run away. He merely crept under the back porch and waited five miserably hot days for the man to return. When the man came home and entered the backyard, the dog sprang from his place of concealment and viciously tore the man's body apart, killing him. After that, the dog simply returned to his post and lay back down. All those who examined the dog afterward, physically as well as psychologically, declared him a healthy and contented dog." He paused. "Interesting, is it not?"

Meg shook her head. "And you think that thought, rather than instinct, caused the dog to act the way he did?"

"Absolutely. Flight distance was clearly in effect, yet the dog chose to stay. Not to fight, mind you, but to actually launch an attack. In my opinion, the dog was seeking revenge."

"Revenge?"

"Yes, one of the age-old emotions. Remember, the dog's actions were carefully thought out. He knew exactly where to hide to gain the tactical advantage. He attacked the man from the rear. He never let up on his attack until he was certain the man was dead. And once he was certain, he did not flee. His thoughts, his emotions, you see, had been satisfied. You could hardly classify his behavior as merely animal instinct."

"But in Carol's case?"

"An authority figure, perhaps. Her presence in the dark may have triggered a thought process derived from some horrible incident in his past. Surely he took her by surprise. Such an attack takes planning, even cunning. After all, it's not part of his normal instinct to scale a twenty-foot-high wall and take a human as prey. He surely must have given it thought. Thought, of course, driven by emotional need." The doctor hesitated, and then glanced at his watch.

"In any case," he said, "I'm afraid I have to get along."

"Yes, yes, of course," Meg said.

"If you like, I'd be glad to observe him. Perhaps I could

set aside some time on Monday. I'm afraid I'm terribly busy over the weekend."

Meg hadn't heard him.

Revenge, she thought. She glanced at the boar's head mounted on the wall and shuddered.

6

At LAPD's Northeast Division, Lieutenant Dragleman leaned against the computer-room door with a bag of fresh doughnuts in his hand. He was watching Marty Walsh, a thin, scrappy captain pull at what little was left of his graying hair.

"Damn!" the captain muttered. He quickly crossed the room to where a young officer was punching commands into a high-powered computer. He was a kid, actually, fresh out of the academy.

Without warning, the division switchboard had suddenly been flooded with phone calls. All were from angry merchants doing business along the eighty-seven-hundred block of Sunset Boulevard; all were complaining about the demonstration taking place in front of a three-story gray building that engulfed the entire north side of the street. None of the callers knew who owned the building; there was no sign on the marble-scrolled edifice, merely an address plate mounted discreetly above the door. And no one seemed to know for sure what the building was used for.

"Well, Lenny," the captain said to the rookie, "I don't wanta throw you off stride, but it's ten minutes since the first call and you still haven't given me what I need to know."

Dragleman inched further into the room.

"Sorry, sir." The rookie kept his eyes pinned to the monitor. "Getting closer now."

Dragleman watched as rectangular images flashed across the screen behind a constantly expanding luminescent grid. The most numerous shapes were outlined in blue, indicating residential structures. Those, as well as the rare white-edged government buildings, were ignored. The rookie was concentrating on all shapes in red: buildings zoned for commercial use only.

Without looking up from the screen, the captain called to the dispatch officer, "Five twenty-five, Janet. We'd better do it now."

The dispatch officer hesitated. "But what do I tell them?"

The captain turned. "The address, Janet. That's all we know, right?"

"Yes, sir," she said. Then she sent out the code for crowd control.

"Still searching, sir," the rookie said nervously.

"I can see that, Lenny." The captain turned to face Dragleman. "Look at my face, Dan! Am I a happy man? No!"

Dragleman knew Marty was wondering if the new Rapid Location Identification Network was all that it was cracked up to be. On line less than three months, the system's effectiveness had been, at best, marginal. It had shut down seven times. And now, when quick action was needed, it seemed that R-LIN was crawling its way to another dismal performance.

"Want a doughnut?" Dragleman asked, searching for neutral territory.

"Can't. Damned things give me gas."

Dragleman nodded. He liked Walsh. They were both

loners, and both had been high school football stars back when schoolboys received as much fame as professional athletes. Both had lost their wives early on to cancer, a topic of conversation that would crop up now and again, always unexpectedly, and always leaving both men deeply depressed.

But most of their late-night bull sessions were given over to talk about their work, how they planned to handle certain aspects of a case. As time passed on a particular case, they would grow more and more filled with the mystique of the crime and how they identified with the victim.

Dragleman sighed, suddenly remembering last night and the sight of the young girl's body. And that tiger! Like nothing he'd ever seen. Or heard, for that matter. The uncanny roar as it separated itself from all other sounds, breath chuffing across the hanging tongue, growls of murderous excitement. If he hadn't seen it, he certainly had dreamed it a hundred times as a boy.

Walsh looked at him now, curiously.

"Heard you got called in on an interesting one last night."

"Sort of."

"Hell of a way to go, being eaten by a tiger. Reminds me of the old Wong case, remember? Had that pit bull—"

Suddenly, R-LIN's chaotic flashing stopped. In the middle of the screen was a large red rectangle. "Got it!" Lenny hollered. The captain moved to look over the kid's shoulder, Dragleman followed. The rookie leaned in slightly, concentrating. "Here we go now." He tapped a key on the top row of the key panel, and the rectangle began to rotate as a three-dimensional image. Flashing yellow dots appeared, unevenly spaced along the perimeter of the structure.

"It's 8742 Sunset," said the rookie. "One of the side streets, Wilton Avenue, comes to a dead end. Prospect

Place, here, leads to a Catholic school two blocks away."
He pointed to the yellow dots. "The building has six street
exits. Four more inside, leading to the garage below."

"That's more like it." The captain glanced at Dragleman.
"Now the question is, who the hell owns it?"

Dragleman watched the rookie tap in another command.
The rectangle blinked in and out for a split second, and
white lettering spread across the bottom of the screen.

The captain leaned in. "Albert Richter Institute
. . . medical research facility . . . eighteen to twenty employees, and—"

"Captain," the switchboard officer yelled. "I've got them
on the line now." Her finger pressed the mute button on
her panel. "Transferred from 911, a Dr. Auston. Says she's
the head of research inside the Richter Institute."

The captain said, "Put her on the box."

"Right." She tapped her key panel twice and nodded for
him to go ahead.

"Dr. Auston? This is Captain Walsh. Has anyone attempted to enter the building?"

The woman's voice came rushing through the speaker.
"Got to stop them," she shrilled. "You can't let them in
here!"

Everyone in the communications room looked up. Even
Dragleman, after years of experience, was surprised by the
tone of the woman's voice. She had let loose one of those
ungodly shrieks. A sound from deep down, from under so
many twisted layers of fear.

"It's all right," the captain said. "Units are at the scene.
Our crowd control unit is on the way. But we need to
know some facts before we can—"

The woman said, "You don't know what these people
are capable of!"

"Yes, Doctor. Now please . . . one moment." He

snapped his fingers at the switchboard officer, who immediately took her cue and punched the mute button. Following procedure, the captain was about to press Dragleman for information he deemed critical. The book was clear on that point: don't let the caller pull you away from first-priority inquiries. And the first priority was assessing danger to human life. But his gut instinct told him that standard questions should be put off for the moment, that he should let the caller lead the way.

The captain nodded, and the mute button was released.

Dr. Auston was beyond panic. "Are you there? HELLO!"

"I'm here, Doctor. Now slowly, tell me who these demonstrators are."

There was a long, disgusted sigh before Dr. Auston spoke again. "They're radicals, Captain. They call themselves Humanity Against Animal Torture and Exploitation. If you know anything about them, you know they're not going to stop at a few sound bites on the evening news."

The captain was perplexed: animal rights activists? There were lots of them in L.A., although he had never heard of this particular group. "One moment, Doctor." He signaled and the mute button was clicked on. He had seen the hard, apprehensive look on Dragleman's face.

"What is it, Dan?" he asked.

Dragleman leaned against the console. "They call themselves HAATE for short. They're mean sonsabitches, Marty. I had a run-in with them a few years back. They jumped all over this small college for kicks, demonstrating against their animal research program. Burned down two science buildings. Two people were killed."

The captain's face went ashen. "You think this has got anything to do with the mauling at the zoo last night?"

"I doubt it," Dragleman said.

The captain said, "Okay. Janet, send a three-twenty-one to the Fire Department. Then pass the word to crowd control—full riot gear. Lenny, get me Kaulman at the mayor's office." He nodded, and the mute button was released.

"Doctor, we know who they are. Our units at the scene have been informed." He paused, made an effort to sound relaxed. "Are all your doors and windows secured?"

"Absolutely." The woman's voice was softer now, but trembling. "*Everything* is locked. My staff and I are in the upstairs lab, on the north side of the building. I don't care what you have to do, Captain, just don't let these people in here!"

"Okay, stay calm. An officer will stay on the line."

The switchboard officer shut off the conference box.

Dragleman sighed. "You know, Marty, I think it's time you consider retiring. This damn place is becoming a zoo."

As Dragleman moved into the hallway, a plainclothes cop took hold of his arm. "Hey, Dan, heard about that gal getting torn up last night. You were there, right?"

"Yeah, so?"

The cop glanced conspiratorially around the deserted hallway. Then he leaned in, face wildly animated as he said, "Tell me, Dan, what'd she look like?"

"She looked dead, stupid!" Dragleman said, pulling back. "Now let go of my arm."

As THE MORNING progressed, the mood of Dragleman's co-workers changed from mild curiosity to a frenzy of speculation and myth-making. Already stories were starting to circulate about how Beauty had finally met the *real* Beast. Suddenly, everyone had a tiger story to tell, some dredged up from childhood, some complete fabrications from over-active imaginations.

Dragleman himself was unapproachable. After grabbing a cup of coffee, he had locked himself away in his private cubicle. At intervals, a couple of narcs had jokingly tried to draw the gory details out of him. But he proved to be as impenetrable as a stone wall.

Finally, around noon, Detective Reese stuck his head into Dragleman's cubicle. "I picked up the Lewis photos from the lab, Lieutenant." He waved the manila envelope enthusiastically in the air as if he'd just purchased the latest, hottest issue of *Playboy*.

"So, okay, put them on the desk." Dragleman lit his cigar and sat back, eyeing his half-eaten corned beef on rye. His stomach felt tight; his head ached.

Reese dropped the packet on Dragleman's desk. "Christ, what a story. It's like one of those massacres you see in a B-movie. Monster and all."

"Only this isn't a goddamn movie, Billy. Am I right? A girl's dead, for chrissakes."

Reese absently scratched his earlobe. It suddenly dawned on him how deeply affected Dragleman was by last night's events. "Sorry, Lieutenant. It's just—"

"Just what?" Dragleman started pulling at the envelope's seal. "Homicide isn't gruesome enough for you? The Valdez mutilation last week, Christ—what's this compared to what he did to his wife?"

Reese shrugged. "This is different, that's all. Are you all right, Lieutenant?"

"Yeah, yeah, I'm fine."

The clenched muscles of Dragleman's face went slack as he glanced at the first eight-by-ten glossy. Carol Lewis wasn't a pretty sight.

He scrutinized the photograph carefully: same gore as last night but from a different angle. Then he glanced at the report still in his typewriter. He hated paperwork. Especially the unfinished kind. The next two photos of Carol Lewis were even worse than the first. Beauty had certainly confronted the Beast. And lost.

"Jesus," Dragleman muttered and got to his feet. As he stood, the phone rang; he picked it up on the first ring. "Lieutenant Dragleman."

"Cusack, Lieutenant," said the voice from the morgue.

"What is it, Cusack?"

"I think you'd better get over here."

"Why's that?"

"Well, it's like this, Lieutenant . . ." Cusack obviously didn't want to go into details. Dragleman heard him say something to someone else, then return to the phone. "Listen, Kirkwood says he wants to speak to you personally. He's got something to show you."

"To do with the Lewis autopsy?"

"Yeah, some unusual physical evidence that complicates things. I'll tell ya, Lieutenant, it's really bizarre."

"What kind of evidence?"

"It's . . ." Cusack faltered, then said quickly. "I'm not supposed to talk over the phone. But it's weird."

A slight chill shivered Dragleman's spine to hear Cusack, a tough detective, nonplussed by the Chief Medical Examiner's findings. "I'll be right over," he said, and put down the phone.

"A problem, Lieutenant?" Reese asked.

Dragleman felt the blood rise to his neck. He said simply, "Sort of." Then he tore the report from his typewriter and headed for the door.

"Where are you going?" Reese wondered aloud.

"To the morgue, Billy-boy. To the morgue."

7

DARK SHADOWS suddenly crept over the tunnel wall. The cat spun around, steamy breath shooting from his nostrils. He looked intently in several directions, then drew back, his striped head and tawny fur becoming invisible in the dark cage.

Again the partial-streaked light outside his cage changed. He could hear soft padded steps, as if he were being stalked. He crouched, ready to attack. He bared his teeth, laid back his ears, and growled as the steps came closer.

Quickly he lowered his head, switched his tail angrily. A cough-roar erupted from his throat.

"EASY, RAJAH," Meg said, stopping within view of his cage. She had heard the cough-roar, and knew exactly what it meant. Many a hunter had heard just such a sound as the hunted tiger sprang from cover to attack.

"It's only me," Meg whispered, letting Rajah take in her scent, letting him scrutinize her. Still, he kept his ears back, exposed his teeth, and growled deeply. The meaning of his gestures was unmistakable. He meant, "Leave me alone, go away."

"Easy," Meg whispered, "easy." She had enough sense not to move. Even to raise her hand or to turn her head would send Rajah charging.

Meg stood motionless, facing him. Her wildlife studies in India had served her well. There she had learned how tigers mated, slept, and fed. She had also learned how they communicated.

The most noticeable method of communication, and the one Meg understood best, was through the sound the tiger made. When tigers approached each other in a friendly way, they made a puffing sound through their nostrils; it sounded harsh but was friendly. They also meowed when pleased to see one another. A sharp *woof* meant they were startled. A *pok* call simply meant, "I am here." The cough-roar, well . . .

Meg shivered now and drew her coat tightly around her. Rajah had settled down. She dropped to a crouch position and rested her back against the brick wall.

Outside, the day was bleak and overcast, so typical of January in Southern California, not unlike the day she had first laid eyes on Rajah: an awesome vision in fiery orange and black stripes, gliding effortlessly through the small compound at Midway. Meg had followed his progress outside the chain-link fence.

She remembered the day well. Sunlight had briefly lit up the meadow of tall grass. Suddenly two eyes glinted in the light, and he rose above the high grasses. Then, carefully placing one foot in front of the other so as not to make a sound in the litter of dry leaves, he insinuated himself from bush to bush, his eyes fixed on a flock of scavenging birds skipping about on the ground in search of food. In a single movement Rajah crouched. One of the birds shrilled an alarm. Before the others could look up, Rajah burst from cover. In one unbelievable lurch, he attacked. The birds scattered.

Missing his prey, Rajah lifted his head and uttered a loud moan like a baby denied its bottle of milk. Then he rested, lying in a pool of sunlight.

Meg had drawn closer to the chain-link fence and was greeted with a low, rumbling growl. Then silence as Rajah's eyes settled on her face.

"Friends," Meg had whispered. "You and I are friends."

Rajah had seemed to understand her that day; his eyes slowly rolled back and he lowered his head to the ground. It was then that Meg had noticed a festering sore on his right ear, the open wound on his jaw, and felt her nursing instinct come alive. Before the day was done, she had carefully tended each wound. She wanted only for him to be well. To live as best he could in confinement. And until recently, everything had seemed fine.

Meg straightened now and got to her feet. She had already made her rounds of the zoo. Most of the animals had survived last night's ordeal unharmed. One of the zebras had picked up a limp, but nothing serious. A few of the primates were refusing to eat, but Meg knew they'd be chowing down before nightfall. The elephant, Daisy, wasn't any better, but she wasn't any worse either. Meg made a mental note to look in on her again before the press conference.

Rajah's head rolled to one side, and he groaned. A meow would have been better, but Meg understood. It pained her to see so magnificent an animal held in a squeeze cage, and once again she felt a rush of guilt.

"It's okay, Rajah," she said, voice choked. "I'm going to help you. Help us both."

Rajah stared at her for a long moment, then stretched and closed his eyes.

"I promise," Meg said.

She hesitated. She wished now that she had never spoken to Dr. Hampton. Revenge, indeed. She turned—Rajah's eyes remained closed—and left the tunnel.

CLAW

*   *   *

A FEW MINUTES later Meg entered her narrow, L-shaped office. Her desk was sleek, black, opaque Plexiglas, dwarfed by miniature palm trees and birds-of-paradise plants.

As usual, the *Los Angeles Times* stared from her desk, where the secretary left it each day. Removing her coat, Meg stared back at it with something approaching real dislike. She was of the unwavering opinion that newspapers deliberately set their own agenda, getting people all worked up over the wrong things. She always put off reading the paper as long as she could, and sometimes refused to read it at all. Today, with Carol's death front page news, she had no excuse. She had to read it.

ZOOKEEPER MAULED BY TIGER

LOS ANGELES, Calif., Jan 8, Carol Lewis, a twenty-year-old zookeeper with the Los Angeles Zoo was mauled last night by a tiger and died from her injuries a short while later.

The Chief Medical Examiner, Dr. Larry Kirkwood, speculated that the upper torso wounds suffered by the young zookeeper would, in most cases, have proven fatal. When the doctor was asked if he could be more specific, he refused further comment. In China, India, Tibet and along the peninsula of Southeast Asia, tiger attacks occur every few months. But none has ever been recorded in the United States.

What caused the tiger to attack is not known.

Meg pushed the paper aside. She knew this sketchy account of Carol's death was merely the first installment. Already the office phones were ringing nonstop with reporters interested in Meg's press conference scheduled for this afternoon.

Meg glanced at her own telephone now, wondering if Harry Shindler had gotten around to analyzing Rajah's blood sample. When she hit the intercom button, the secretary said he hadn't called yet. But then Meg knew Harry Shindler was a busy man. His wife, Joyce, had often joked about his intense work habits. "If he could do ten jobs at once, instead of five, he'd get no sleep at all."

Meg had first met the Shindlers at a party in Westwood. She and David, newly married, were still living in his two-bedroom apartment in Malibu, and the gathering was one typical of young intellectuals: subdued music on the stereo and joints being passed around. There were two biochemists in attendance, along with a few painters, one sculptor, a host of musicians, and one physical anthropologist. Meg was twenty-four at the time and eager to meet interesting people. Harry Shindler fit the bill.

Meg had found him at once charming and outrageous, and never, never dull. He had piercing green eyes, which seemed to increase the earnestness of anything he said, and he affected a resigned incredulity when he listened. The dark-rimmed glasses he sometimes wore gave him the look of a friendly owl, and she never thought of him as the oldest man in the room.

Thereafter, Meg and David had run into the Shindlers often, mostly at parties back when things were still fun, back when they still enjoyed being together. David had seemed so happy then, so much in love.

. . . If only, Meg thought.

Stupid, too late; David was gone. Yet she couldn't help wondering what her life would be like if she were still married and if David hadn't changed.

Useless, self-indulgent thinking, she reminded herself. As though she could spiral back through time to safety. She was never safe. If David and she had stayed together they might have worked things out for a while, but that wouldn't have changed his nature. Nor would she have avoided the horrible situation she now faced.

The thought froze Meg for a moment. Suddenly everything seemed just beyond her reach. Her knowledge, all of her experience seemed useless. Miserable at the thought, she shook her head, then sat and began combing through Rajah's daily log report, which detailed three weeks of meticulous observation. Reference books covering aggression in both man and beast literally covered the entire surface of her desk. She had combed through the books earlier that morning before making her rounds, but had discovered little of help in solving her problem.

One subject, however, had caught her attention. The subject was *dehumanization*. The author, in covering aggression, theorized that if the terrified figure trembling before the hunter was no longer considered a person but an animal, his or her death would be of little consequence. Just as foxes routinely slaughter rabbits, an accepted rule of nature, likewise a person dehumanized by the hunter becomes nothing more than an animal of prey. Like the rabbit, his death is of little concern.

Meg paused, wondering: Had Rajah mistaken Carol for an animal? Had he, in some way, dehumanized her, thinking of her only as quarry? As wildlife?

The thought sent a chill through her body. She knew aggression worked the same way in the human race, and that once dehumanization occurred, man achieved the dubious distinction of being the most murderous species alive.

Has Rajah's aggressive instinct become so dominant that it is the only force that drives him? she wondered. Has Rajah lost all sense of cohabitive life? Is his only instinct to kill?

As Meg nervously searched through the books on aggression, Russell Biggs bustled into the office and dropped heavily into the chair beside her desk. Meg looked up, hands trembling, and asked him about the reporters. Biggs made a face and said they were swarming all over the place. Then Biggs asked, "What are you gonna tell them, Doc?"

"I don't know," Meg said, and for the first time felt a genuine sense of fear.

CORPSE RACKS and corpse vaults and the heavy smell of disinfectant greeted Dragleman as he entered the autopsy room. He squinted into the blue-white fluorescent glare as the attendant slid the girl's body, stretched out beneath its sheet, from the corpse vault onto the examination table. Dr. Kirkwood slipped on a pair of rubber gloves, then came to stand between Cusack and Dragleman, both of whom looked like apprehensive students at a forensic convention. Cusack had already been briefed, so he watched Dragleman's reaction from the corner of his eye as the attendant left the room.

"Well, Dan, let's have a look," Kirkwood said, pulling the sheet off of the corpse. He hesitated a moment, his heavy eyelids concealing the medical curiosity in his eyes.

Kirkwood was the kind of doctor who refused to be shaken by life's complexities. He was first and foremost a professional. Dragleman knew him to be the best forensic analyst the department had ever had. Yet conversations with him were typically breezy and light. Today, however, Dragleman could detect a slight edge to the man's voice.

"Like I was telling Cusack, Dan," said Kirkwood, snapping one green glove, "I'm not quite ready to draw up my preliminary report because I can't say for sure what caused the girl's death."

Dragleman froze, staring at Kirkwood in open curiosity. "Not certain?"

Cusack said, "I told you it was weird, Lieutenant."

Kirkwood edged closer to the examination table and pointed to the corpse's neck. "Usually cats go for the throat when bringing down their prey. So, naturally, I assumed cause of death to be asphyxiation. That, however, was not the case.

"In the wilderness," continued the doctor, "it's usually cut-and-dried: a cat seizes its victim by the throat and strangles it. But the deep puncture marks of the cat's canines are clearly visible on the girl's right shoulder." Rubbery fingers touched corpse flesh, indicating the wounds. "Apparently, that's how he dragged her into the cave. By the shoulder. Deep wounds, plenty of blood loss. But also not the cause of death."

Dragleman shook his head. "If there was that much blood lost, why rule out the possibility she bled to death?"

"Because quantity is not the issue, Dan. She definitely lost a lot of blood, but not enough to cause her death. Yet the *quality* of her blood proves more interesting. And more perplexing."

Dragleman could feel his temples throb as the doctor flashed him a smile. "Jesus, Larry, I sure hope you can tell me what you're driving at. I mean, did the cat kill her or not?"

"I wish wholeheartedly I could say yes. But then—"

Kirkwood broke off as the attendant reentered the room. "The slides are ready, Doctor."

"Thanks, Jimmy. See to it that we're not disturbed, all right?"

The attendant glanced worriedly at the doctor. "The reporters are back," he said. "Saperstein's talking to them now."

Kirkwood sighed. "Tell them I'll be tied up for a long time."

"Reporters been dogging you?" Dragleman asked.

"A few yellow-rag types. Most of the legit papers feel they've already gotten their story. Now, if you'll follow me."

Kirkwood led the way down the deserted hallway, the detectives following. Dragleman loosened his tie. Cusack popped a mint into his mouth.

"Want one, Lieutenant?" He held out the roll.

"I want answers for God's sake, not fresh breath. I got a report to get out."

"Patience, Dan," Kirkwood said, flashing a boyish smile. The room they entered was small and airless. Hot spots of light shone on stainless-steel cabinets, reflected off glass screens. Most of the west wall was given over to electronic equipment: transmitters, terminals, monitors, computers, high-speed printers . . . it all looked jumbled together. But it was one of the best systems in the county.

Kirkwood sat down in front of a console, and his hand stroked buttons, keys, switches. Small lights glowed and gleaming sine waves undulated across the screen. "Data should be up in a second," he said. "In the meantime, I want you to look at something."

He sat Dragleman down before a microscope, made a few adjustments. "Comfortable?"

"Yeah, yeah, so what am I about to see?" Dragleman huffed.

"Perhaps your future," Kirkwood quipped, but Dragleman could tell there was little humor in the remark.

He pressed one eye to the sight, squinted, and saw a swarm of little somethings racing around below. It was like watching a circus performed by unidentified objects.

"Any idea what they are?" Kirkwood asked.

"Haven't the foggiest."

"Would it surprise you, Dan, if I told you I haven't the foggiest either?"

Dragleman looked up. "I assume those squiggly things got something to do with Carol Lewis, right?"

"Unfortunately, yes." Kirkwood reached for a cigarette and then thought better of it. He carefully pushed the cigarette back into the pack. "It goes something like this, Dan. Those *squiggly things,* as you put it, were found in the girl's blood, also in her saliva. Millions of them."

Before Dragleman could speak, Kirkwood said, "Hold on, Dan. There's more." He stepped to the table and removed the slide from the microscope. "This blood sample is twelve hours old. And whatever those things are, they're still alive."

Dragleman's eyelids dropped with chagrin. "Be straight with me, Larry. What's happening here?"

Kirkwood smiled sardonically. "If I could answer that question, Dan, I'd have submitted my report."

"How about a guess, Larry?"

Kirkwood stared at him for a second, then went to the console. "No guess, Dan. Not enough data. All I know for sure is the girl underwent an invasion of some sort, and one of massive, if not overwhelming proportions."

"Maybe she caught something from the cat. You know, bacteria or something."

"I don't think so."

"Why not?"

"Because those 'squiggly things,' at least as far as I can tell, are completely unheard of in the animal kingdom. I've already called a friend of mine, a zoologist with the National Zoological Park in D.C. He ran the info through his data bank. Zero. I've been running it through ours as well. Again, zero.

"And I'll tell you another thing," Kirkwood went on. "Whatever invaded the girl's body isn't part of the human chain, either. I've had a pathologist confirm this."

Dragleman stared dumbfounded at the doctor, who returned his gaze calmly. "What the hell is going on here?" Dragleman barked. "A girl is killed by a cat the size of a house and yet she isn't. She's got something in her blood, but nobody knows what it is! Not animal, not human . . . Jesus, Larry, what about all those rules of scientific evidence I'm always hearing about?"

Kirkwood's eyes drifted distractedly to the computer screen, which was continuing its search for data. "You know, Dan," he said, "it's like when you die of a heart attack, only the heart attack is caused by a long bout with cancer, so who's to say if you died of the heart attack or cancer? If it's AIDS, some families want to pay the doc extra to say it was the heart—"

"Wait a minute," Dragleman said. "What are you saying? You're speaking in some sort of hieroglyphics. Can I put mauling as cause of death on my report or not?"

"If you like. But I'm afraid I'll have to qualify mine."

Dragleman threw up his hands in disgust. "Jeez, Larry— you know the department. They want answers. Not more mysteries. They'll have me on the carpet before the day is out."

Kirkwood nodded sympathetically. "Seems we have a dilemma on our hands, doesn't it?" He tried to sound casual. "Look at it this way, Dan. The girl could have suffered an attack of some sort and was dead when she fell into the pit."

Dragleman tried to affect the same casual tone, but it was no go. "I've been all through that, Larry," he boomed. "The damned cat dragged her in. From the top! And then he ate her!"

Kirkwood said, "I'm sure that occurred posthumously, so we're right back where we started. What killed her in the first place? He wouldn't have eaten her if she wasn't dead. And none of her wounds were fatal."

"Then what do I do, Larry? You tell me."

"I'm afraid this is out of my league, Dan," said the doctor, softly, sullenly. "I recommend you find yourself a good microbiologist. Or a sorcerer. Yes, I'm sure that's what you're going to need."

8

"Yo, Doc, do tigers acquire a taste for human blood? I've heard that. Is it true?"

"No, *that's*—"

From the rear: "Can't hear you. Can you speak up?"

"I said—"

"Louder!"

The press conference was crowded, and loud, and Meg found herself stepping back from the podium.

"Yo, Doc, did you hear my question?"

The reporter was standing right in front, a wiry, hard-looking man of middle height—Hector Cataro, he said his name was, from the *L.A. Weekly*—and he kept interrupting Meg. The heat and glare of the television lights were intense. Meg squinted as she reached for a glass of water, the room a blinking haze. She could barely make out Cataro's face. She saw a silhouette and the bony angle his shoulder made when he jotted something down in his pad.

Other reporters were crammed into the small room behind him, jockeying for position close to the rostrum. There were photographers and television cameramen. There were microphones and tape recorders and lights. One of the reporters, a woman, stood on a chair. She kept waving her notepad in the air, demanding Meg's attention.

The freak show was on again.

Meg had asked PR to schedule the conference for 4:00 P.M., hoping for little or no attendance. But the reporters showed up early at the administration office and began shouting for the conference to begin. Meg thought fleetingly about running from the press. She had her coat on and her keys in her hand. She had done it before. It was no use this time. She knew she'd never get away from them. Besides, she had given Ellroy her word.

Roueche, of course, was conveniently absent, so the PR staff gladly handed Meg the spotlight. Ray stood by, helping out as best he could. Early on, one of the reporters had been particularly abrasive, arguing with Ray in the parking lot, yelling, "*I don't mean to bother her. I just want to talk!*" But he didn't care about Meg, just as he didn't care about Carol Lewis. This wasn't about solving problems. This wasn't about righting wrongs. All this man wanted was another installment in the ongoing freak show, more gory details to sell papers, sensationalism to boost circulation.

"Doc, my question," Hector Cataro repeated. "Do tigers acquire a taste for human blood?"

Meg leaned into the microphone and said, "Definitely not. That's a holdover of superstition and primitive thinking." She glanced at Ray, who stood off to the side, nodding grimly.

Before she could speak again, a reporter elbowed his way front and held up a newspaper carrying the banner headline: RAJAH THE LADY KILLER.

"It says here," he said, "that tigers are literally brutes, that they have no self-awareness, no recognition of their existence in nature. In light of this, do you feel Rajah should be put to sleep?"

Another eruption in the crowd, louder this time. The man's question stunned Meg. But only for a second. She knew the next instant meant everything. The woman reporter was on the chair again, shouting, "Dr. Brewster, Dr. Brewster!" The crowd swelled up. The ceiling pressed down.

"All right!" Meg shouted into the microphone. "You've asked your dumb questions and now you're going to shut up for a minute!"

Her remark startled the reporters. En masse, they all quieted down. Lights flashed. Voices grew hushed. A solitary coughing sound rose above the rest.

"Now it's important that you understand the tiger as a species," she said, catching her breath. "Almost everything you *think* you know about the cat family is false, pussycats included. We've worshiped them, burned them, and hanged them as witches and worse. Some of us love them, some of us hate them, and not just a few of us are terrified of them. But that's because we don't understand them. Our egos tell us that they are different from us and therefore they must be bad."

"Say, Doc?" The reporter with the newspaper had drawn back, but was still waving the damn thing in the air.

"Okay," Meg said. "Now I'd like to give you a few statistics—"

"Say, Doc?" He held the newspaper up higher, taunting her with it. "People aren't interested in statistics."

A low rumble again from the crowd.

Meg said, "Background, then." She picked up her prepared notes and began to read, a light sweat covering her forehead. " 'Widespread in Asia until the late nineteenth century, the tiger appears in the fossil record of the early Pleistocene, more than a million years ago. The carnivore adapted to diverse habitats. . . .' "

"Janet Lewis," a voice interrupted.

Meg looked up and saw Hector Cataro standing below her. He had moved forward and leaned one elbow on the rostrum. "Beg your pardon?"

Cataro turned to the other reporters, like a gang leader on a street corner, then turned back to Meg. "Janet Lewis," he said. "Carol Lewis's mother. I spoke to her this morning. She's quite upset. Said she was forced by the county to have her daughter's body autopsied. Was there a reason for performing an autopsy?"

Meg lowered her notes. She felt flushed, almost feverish. Guilt and anger blended into a solid knot of pain. She felt at once betrayed and betrayer. She had wanted to quarantine Rajah three weeks ago, hadn't she? But Roueche had made her feel ridiculous about the notion. Merely an "emotional phase," he had said. And she had acquiesced.

Perhaps, she thought, Carol would still be alive if I had had the nerve and the professional integrity to stand up to Roueche. But she hadn't, and that made all the difference. Meg suddenly hated herself. And just as suddenly, she felt a deep, gut-wrenching self-pity.

She turned and looked Cataro in the eye. "You'll have to ask the LAPD about the autopsy," she said.

"But you spoke to them last night. Spoke to a Lieutenant Dragleman, right?"

"No comment."

"He must have questioned you."

The room had fallen into a deep hush. Meg could hear pens scratching across paper, see lights flashing, and she drew back. "I'm sorry," she said. "But . . . ."

Ray stepped to the microphone. "Dr. Brewster has a busy schedule. She's prepared a press release. Copies will be given out at the PR office."

The woman on the chair shouted, "Dr. Brewster, is Rajah sick? Dr. Brewster?" Her notepad fluttered in the air as she repeated the question. "Is the tiger sick, Doctor?"

In the next moment Meg had a horrible realization. The press was three steps ahead of her. No matter how she answered the question, she'd be courting disaster.

Meg spoke into the microphone. "Rajah is in quarantine at this time. We're as stunned by this as you are. We are checking out all possibilities. That's all I have to say."

The crowd erupted again. People shouted, moved closer to the rostrum. Biggs, who was standing behind Ray, came forward to block the steps. A cameraman pushed him aside and climbed on the stage. The whole room appeared to be jumping up and down in agitation.

"Press releases in the administration office!" Ray snapped, taking hold of Meg's arm. Biggs raced to the side door and opened it. Questions were hurled at Meg's retreating back. "How long will he be in quarantine?" "What about the autopsy?"

For Meg, the conference was adjourned.

THERE WERE no other lights on in the science building; only Dr. Shindler's lab was awash with a soft glow as he paced in a circle, perplexed by the specimens taken from Rajah's blood sample.

His preliminary examination had uncovered nothing out of the ordinary. Under standard binocular microscopy, he did not see the undulations and quiverings typical of mammalian cell activity. Everything was dead—precisely what he would have expected from a blood sample fourteen hours old. He had made a rough count of the various microorganisms at three hundred nanometer magnification. This revealed the same problem Meg had encountered at the zoo laboratory: the number of antibodies, which would have been high if the cat were suffering from any of the common feline diseases, was at a normal level. He then ordered a full range of chemical analysis tests, performed by his highly skilled and respected lab technicians. Again, everything in the cat's blood appeared perfectly normal.

With night falling, Shindler had decided to send his team home and tackle the problem alone, without distraction. He combed through research data hoping to uncover examples of similarly rare feline disorders.

When he found himself at a dead end, he backed off and allowed his mind to open up to whatever thoughts might enter. He read the newspaper, had a bite to eat at the staff cafeteria, and then returned to his lab to reflect quietly on the mystery confronting him. For a man like Harry Shindler, such problems were no more than a healthy challenge, a way of breaking up the normal lab routine. And not much different, he thought, from many of the challenges he had faced in his youth.

He had once been a good lightweight boxer in the Navy, and even now his body looked capable of going three or four rounds against a man twenty years younger. He ran four miles each day, did fifty pushups and fifty situps, jumped rope for five minutes on his back porch. "Narcissism," he explained to his wife. "I don't like being sixty-three."

He did not, however, expect his wife to appreciate his obsession with staying fit. A microbiologist had especially keen insights into the slow disintegration of living tissue; the way muscles grow weaker with . . .

Wait a minute, he had thought. *Disintegration.*

That was the moment Shindler had hit upon a strange revelation, an oddity so conspicuous that he was amazed he hadn't thought of it before.

According to information received from Raymond

Menitti, the two vials of blood were drawn from the tiger at about 11:30 P.M.—eight hours before the sample arrived by special messenger packed in dry ice and fourteen hours before Shindler had broken away from his demanding schedule to examine the first specimen. In that time, no nutrients or growth hormones had been introduced to the sample. No culture solution had been prepared. No tampering of any kind. And yet, those dead cells, which should have been flat and opaque, were still firm, full, and round. Every visible microbe was distinct. Ridges and membranes of each organism were perfectly discernible. There wasn't the slightest hint of the nubilous film that usually envelops all microorganisms in the process of slow disintegration.

The evidence had pointed to only one conclusion—the blood was *fresh*, as though it had been drawn within the hour.

Now, nearly an hour after his startling detection, a strange foreboding crept over him; a fear connected with his past.

How many times had he tried to believe the horror was dead forever? How many times had he prayed to forget?

The eerie silence of Shindler's contemplation was broken by a soft *ping* emanating from the critical-point drier, a boxy metal unit mounted on the lab counter. He stopped pacing and slipped on a pair of surgical gloves. He opened the CDP chamber and removed a copper disk that held his last specimen, a wisp of warm air wafting over his strained features.

He turned the disk in the light, searching for visible imperfections.

Very good, he thought. The CDP process had performed flawlessly, precisely raising the temperature and pressure to the point where all liquids in the specimen passed from an aqueous phase directly to a gaseous phase.

He mounted the specimen onto a thin carbon stub by applying a tiny amount of silver paste as an adhesive. Then he applied a fifteen-nanometer-thin coating of palladium to the surface, just enough to give the specimen electron conductivity.

Sucking in a nervous breath, he sat down at the scanning electron microscope. To his left stood two heavy units comprising the X-ray microanalyzer, an accessory component used to augment the image-analyzing capability of the SEM process. The large unit to his right, packed with switches, button, and monitors, integrated computerized control of the imaging system with the advanced image recording section. Directly in front of him stood the ten-foot-high lens column, a powerful yet highly sensitive device that looked like the periscope of a nuclear submarine.

He flicked on a long row of switches. The hum of internal vacuum pumps rose quickly to a high, whirling pitch as air was sucked from the lens column chamber.

Sweat covered his brow as he pulled out the specimen carriage, a hinged disk that fit midway between the electron gun mounted inside the dome of the lens column and a fluorescent screen at the base. Carefully, he placed the specimen in the carriage and locked it back into the column chamber.

His hand trembled as he hit the switch activating the generators that powered the electron gun. He flipped up the safety cap on the firing button.

One more glance at the controls: the focus meters for both condenser and objective lenses indicated perfect alignment. The compression regulator light was green; all residual particles had now been evacuated from the column chamber.

He pressed the firing button.

A rasping buzz rose from the monolithic steel column as

the gun shot an electron beam down through the center of the chamber void. The accelerating beam trajectory criss-crossed off powerful magnetic lenses mounted on the internal walls.

Shindler's face grew expressionless as he peered closely into the lead-shielded window at the column's base. The image on the fluorescent capture screen was fuzzy, and appeared to be wobbling. Without looking away, he reached up to adjust the magnetic flow on the condenser lens control.

Now the image was crystal clear. Only . . .

Shindler suddenly lurched from his stool and stumbled back. The metal stool crashed to the floor. He sucked air deeply into his lungs, desperately trying to calm his frayed nerves. After a moment, he fumbled for his glasses in the pocket of his lab coat and approached the image recording monitor.

"Dear God," he whispered, staring at a screen filled with a million quaking creatures. Pulsating, quivering—*alive!*

He steadied himself, tapping in a command on the computer keyboard. The image grew larger in segmented jumps. He tapped another command and the image held steady.

Now the screen was filled with the flexing body of a single cell, a primitive kind of neuron, a spiderlike microbe that should never be able to survive outside of a living brain. He reduced the image. Yet there they were, by the millions, alive, feeding on the soup of a tiger's blood. Long, sinewy tendrils flexed outward, continually reaching for more nutrients.

And the presence of an axon, the longest and most supple of neuron fibers, was an indication of higher development. Its primary function in the brain was to stimulate the synapse of neighboring cells by electrochemical impulse, thereby releasing thousands of neurotransmitters—the messengers of the brain—to penetrate brain receptors with fantastic speed and precision. But what were these highly developed axons doing in this freakish environment? What good were neurotransmitters without receptors?

Shindler stood back, his complexion white with fear. The implications of mutated neurons capable of surviving in feline blood were terrifying.

What a fool he had been. He had walked away from the experiment on ethical grounds. But also because he had never believed they would be able to get these creatures to survive.

"Oh God," he whispered. Whatever he *thought* he was prepared for, nothing had prepared him for this. He reached for the phone. He knew that once the phone call was made, the madness would begin.

The question was: Where would it end?

9

GADDIS "DOUBLE D" checked his watch again. It was exactly 10:15 P.M.—time to move. The rain had momentarily stopped, and the street was so quiet he could hear the plaintive cry of a cat the next street over. He picked up his brown leather bag and stepped quickly from his place of concealment in the shrubs. He glanced around; lights were on in two of the houses at the end of the street. But those few TV watchers would present him no problem.

In darkness there is death.

This knowledge had been part of his earlier training and he never forgot it. He could also move unobserved in daylight. But the night was his special friend.

He moved softly around the perimeter of the house and entered the garage through the side door. Joyce Shindler's Buick was parked crookedly beside the west wall. Gaddis smiled at the sight, imagining the doctor complaining to himself as he tried to maneuver his BMW into the slot beside his wife's car.

The Shindlers were creatures of habit, Gaddis knew. And old habits could be a man's worst enemy. Both lived quiet lives, uncomplicated by children. Joyce Shindler was asleep in the upstairs bedroom. She had gone to bed at her usual time: ten o'clock. Dr. Shindler would be along shortly. Though he often worked after regular hours, he rarely worked later than eleven.

Gaddis surveyed the garage, then quickly unscrewed the overhead light bulb so that when the garage door opened the interior light wouldn't go on. Next he locked the side door. Then he went to the door leading into the house. It opened into the kitchen. Beyond the kitchen was the dining room and the stairs that led to the three bedrooms on the top floor. He leaned in, listened.

Satisfied that the house was quiet, he dropped down behind the Buick and waited. There was no need to check his watch again. He could feel the moment drawing near; could sense, almost, Dr. Shindler winding his way up the canyon road toward home.

As Gaddis expected, only a few minutes had passed when the automatic garage door opener clicked; a buzzing sound followed. Gears rattled and the big sectional door opened. Shindler's tan BMW idled at the edge of the drive for a second, then rolled slowly into the garage.

As Shindler inched the car forward, Gaddis removed a silencer-equipped automatic pistol from his bag. Then he removed a plastic pouch and took out a cloth. It was cold in his hand, dripping with chloroform.

Shindler killed the motor, then snapped off the headlights. The garage dipped into darkness as the door came down again, cutting off any outside light. As the doctor stepped from the car, Gaddis said, "Stop right there."

Shindler blinked at him, surprised. "Who the hell—"

Gaddis rammed the barrel of the pistol into Shindler's left cheekbone. "Get back into the car," he said. The doctor hesitated, his eyes darting to the interior door. "Don't do anything stupid, Doctor."

"My wife," Shindler stammered.

"Cooperate, and she won't get hurt. But try something foolish, and I'll blow her face off." Gaddis smiled. "Now get back into the car."

Shindler frowned and looked again at the interior door. Gaddis knew he was thinking things over; that he cherished his wife, and would do anything possible to protect her.

"Goddammit, do as I say," Gaddis hissed. "You and I are going for a ride. Cooperate, and your wife'll never know I was here. Now *move*."

Shindler took a hesitant step backward, eyes glued to the pistol.

In the distance Gaddis again heard the cat's cry and the low roll of thunder. Rain began falling on the garage roof, mixed with the sound of a car whizzing by outside. Gaddis's heart began to pound. Accident . . . it must look like an *accident*.

"Okay," Shindler finally said. "But don't hurt my wife."

Gaddis waited for him to turn, then lunged and smashed the chloroform-soaked cloth over his face. The doctor was a little man but somehow found the strength to resist. Hysteria came next and he spun away and was halfway to the door when Gaddis grabbed him but he was a powerhouse by then and Gaddis couldn't keep hold, and he couldn't get the cloth over his face so he used the butt of his gun and smashed it into the doctor's skull. The man staggered forward, fell limp against the Buick, then fell face down onto the garage floor.

Gaddis knelt down. Time was working against him now. He quickly lifted the doctor and put him, unconscious, behind the steering wheel of the car. Taking Shindler's keys, he turned on the ignition and lowered the front window. Before closing the door, he doused Shindler's body with chemicals and removed all the papers from his attaché case.

Tossing the papers into his own bag, Gaddis took out a

pack of Camels; Shindler was a secret smoker, and Camels was his brand.

Gaddis hesitated before striking the match. No effort was needed to concentrate now. He lit the cigarette and took several drags. Shindler looked peaceful slumped over the wheel, as if he knew that his long life of excruciating and complex work was coming to an end.

Gaddis took one last drag on the cigarette, and flicked it into Shindler's lap. Flames erupted with a sudden roar and the interior of the car was engulfed in a cloud of sooty black smoke. By the time Gaddis had reached the side door, Shindler was nothing more than a blazing corpse.

JOYCE SHINDLER turned in her bed. In that gray, shadowy place between sleep and waking she was vaguely aware of a noise. It seemed to her that it had started to rain and that it was the sharp, sudden impact of an incipient downpour pelting the windows that had roused her. As her mind swam lazily up from sleep, she reached for her husband.

"Harry?" She stretched languidly, and rolled over to snuggle against her husband. Instantly she was seized by a fit of coughing as smoke filled her lungs. She sat bolt upright, gasping, and fumbled to turn on the lamp.

Nothing happened.

"Harry!" she called out. Wearing nothing but her thin lace nightgown, she got up and raced to the bedroom door and threw it open. Stumbling to the head of the stairs, she looked down. Smoke was pouring from the kitchen. Beyond that she saw flames, and heard the crackling and hissing of wood and the shattering of her good china and crystal in the dining room. Her mind froze, rejecting what she saw and heard; denying, too, the searing heat that rushed toward her.

"Harry?" she cried out, and started down the stairs.

Flames shot into the hallway, spread rapidly upward, cutting off access to the front door.

She drew back and quickly retraced her steps to the darkened bedroom and closed the door. Smoke swirled, stung her eyes. She groped for the window and flung it open. The concrete driveway twenty feet below stretched out beneath her. There was no ledge she could climb out on, no tree, not even a rain gutter to hang on to.

Panicked, she ran back to the door. Even before she opened it, she realized the flames had reached the top floor. Heat stung her face and scorched the soles of her feet as flames shot beneath the door. Instantly, all of them doubled and tripled in size.

Now the entire bedroom was on fire. Windows exploded and a long orange arm reached in and torched the curtains. Then her hair. Screaming, she climbed out onto the window ledge, slipped and fell forward, her arms flailing the air until her body crashed against the pavement below.

She felt nothing; no pain at all.

There was only a brief moment of shock, and then Joyce Shindler's eyes closed.

10

Heavy rain beat on the roof of Meg's Jeep as she made a right turn and headed up Beverly Glen. The Jeep skidded around the next bend and she slowed down. She was exhausted, tired beyond feeling much of anything.

A sudden glare in her rearview mirror made her squint and cock her head to one side. A damned car was riding her rear bumper; as she accelerated, so did the car behind her. She knew she was driving too fast given the weather conditions, but the car behind her wouldn't let up. It kept inching closer.

She pulled to the right side of the road, hoping the car would pass. But it didn't, it stayed right with her. More glare from a car's headlights coming down from the mountain momentarily blinded her. She blinked, drew her head back, and as the car sped by, the Jeep started to spin out of control. She flung the steering wheel in the opposite direction of the skid. The Jeep slid across the road. The canyon five hundred feet below flashed before her eyes.

It fell away with the finality of a guillotine.

Meg spun the wheel again and jammed on her brakes. The Jeep swerved right, slid off the road sideways and slammed into a chain-link fence. She heard the impact, then herself scream.

"You bastard!" Meg shouted as the car behind her sped by. She sat for a moment, trembling. "You bastard," she mumbled again into the sudden stillness. There were only the distant sounds of traffic on the Ventura Freeway, the Jeep's idling motor, and a tinkle of glass from its broken taillight.

Meg started to get out to check the damage; the hell with it. She stamped her foot a few times and placed it on the gas pedal, and eased the Jeep inch by inch back onto the road. She drove carefully now, as though maneuvering the tires through a mine field.

At the top of Beverly Glen, she halted and waited for the light to change. There were few cars on the road; the rain had suddenly stopped. If only her troubles would go away that easily, she thought, and turned off the wipers. *If only*.

The light changed, and she made a left onto Mulholland Drive. She glanced at the dashboard clock: it was 11:15 P.M. A minute later she pulled into the carport, shut off the engine, and got out. The carport roof had a large leak, and she stepped into a puddle of water.

Will this day never end? she wondered.

After closing the front door of the bungalow-style house, Meg flicked on the light and looked around the living room—at her white cabinets, her books, the flare of lamplight hitting the shag rug near the window—as though surprised it was still intact. As usual, the room was untidy. Near the office door was a pile of books and papers she'd used while preparing for the news conference. A black evening shoe with a broken strap sat on the coffee table. By the closet door was a shopping bag labeled The Broadway, filled with unread magazines.

Meg stood there as though in a trance, then dropped her

satchel and jacket on the couch, punched the playback-call button on her answering machine before dragging herself into the open kitchen area where she turned the heat on under the kettle and spooned instant coffee into a cup.

A beep: "Dr. Brewster, this is Hector Cataro, *L.A. Weekly*. I'd like to get your opinion on what happened to one of your keepers, ah . . . Carol—"

Meg pressed the fast-forward button, sending Cataro's words into a high-pitched, garbled squeal.

A beep: "Meg? It's me. I just heard about the mauling at the zoo last night. Jesus Christ!"

Meg sighed. It was her ex-husband's sister, Denise, a high-strung but lovable young woman who had been Meg's best friend until the divorce. They had drifted apart afterward. Meg supposed the divorce had been as painful for Denise as it was for her. Talking about her broken marriage seemed inevitable whenever they got together. As a result, they seldom got together.

"Call me," Denise said on the recording. "You must be climbing the fuckin' walls."

If you only knew, Meg thought.

Another beep: "Meg, this is Dr. Shindler . . ."

Meg drew closer to the machine, listening intently. "I . . . I don't know how to say this. The blood sample you gave me . . ." She could hear the tension in his voice. The strain and fatigue.

"We . . . we have to talk, Meg. It's ten o'clock, Friday night. I'm leaving for home now. Call me, and we'll set up a meeting. I'd prefer we don't discuss matters over the phone." The recorder clicked off.

Meg rewound the message and listened again. It sounded less urgent this time but more ominous. She played it a third time and then called Shindler. Outside, a low rumble echoed across the canyon, but at first Meg thought nothing of it. Static shot from the telephone. She hung up and dialed again.

The rumbling outside grew louder. This time Meg recognized it as thunder. Lightning flashed. The weird noises coming over the telephone were harsh and loud. Meg called the operator and was told there was trouble on Shindler's line.

"What kind of trouble?" asked Meg.

"Not sure," the operator said. "Could be the storm has knocked out one of our lines."

"Thanks," Meg said, and turned abruptly to face the hallway. She had heard the bedroom door open. Or had she? She put the receiver down and listened.

The house was quiet.

Still, Meg had the odd feeling that she wasn't alone. She inched forward a little to get a better view of the hallway. Outside the hoot of a wood pigeon mixed with the sound of rainwater beating tattoos on the tiled porch.

Meg suddenly felt profoundly tired. She stood there, not wanting to hear, not wanting to deal with anything but the need to rest. Her exhaustion was absolute; the tension of the past eighteen hours had dissolved in the physical effort of deciphering Shindler's call.

"*Meg . . .*"

"What?" She turned. Not a door opening this time, but a voice. Who was calling her?

"Meg?"

"Who's there?" Meg called out. She could feel her heart falter; she was more frightened than she wished to admit. Then her mind swiftly changed gears. Suddenly she felt anger. It steadied her. She clung to it. Let it build, she thought. The anger burst forth, pushed her forward. She quickly moved into the hallway and flicked on the light.

"Good grief!" Meg shrieked when she saw David standing there. "Damn you, you scared the living hell out of me! What are you doing here? How did you get in?"

"You left the garden door open," David said.

"And you think you have the right to barge in here like this? I hate when you do things like this. Just hate it. This is my house, David. You have no right to be here."

"Relax, Meg."

"I won't relax!"

David came forward and draped an arm over her shoulder. "Come on, take it easy. We're no longer married, but we're still friends, right?"

"Oh God." Meg shivered and tried to draw back, but David held her close.

Tall, rugged, his hair sandy brown, David Sorel had an animal grace about him that drew women to him almost against their will. At thirty-three, he retained a seductive youthfulness: blue-eyed, bearded, his smile was often that of a boy. He was dressed casually, as always: a pair of Levi's, leather jacket open to a white cotton shirt and brown boots. A pair of aviator sunglasses stuck out of his jacket pocket.

Before Meg could calm herself, another young man stepped from the bedroom; a brown satchel was slung over his shoulder. There was nothing particularly remarkable in his looks. He wore an expression that was thoughtful and possibly a bit amused.

"And who the hell is he, David?" Lightning flashed outside the hall window, bright enough to sting Meg's eyes. She drew back.

The stranger said, "Name's Farris. Stan Farris." His words were almost lost in the loud roll of thunder.

Meg looked him up and down but never directly in the eyes. "And what were you doing in my bedroom?"

David laughed quietly. "Meg, relax," he said, his blue

eyes flashing. "We've been waiting for you since six. Stan got tired—"

"So he decided to grab a little snooze, right?" Meg could feel her anger building again. She resented the intrusion. Worse, she resented the way they had broken into her house. "Listen, David, the first time you pulled something like this, I thought it was charming. But the second time I thought I made it clear that I never wanted it to happen again." She went to the front door and opened it. "Now I want you both out of here. Now!"

David came to her and pushed the door closed. "It's not that easy, Meg. Stan's gone to a great deal of trouble to be here tonight. He's one of the organizers of HAATE."

"Figures," Meg said. She knew HAATE was an extremist group of animal rights activists, intent on stopping all animal research. Some people admired them. Meg, however, loathed their methods and their stubborn, combative, sharp-tongued, headline-grabbing organization.

She turned sharply to face Farris. "I suppose you took part in the bedlam at the Richter Institute today."

"I helped organize it," Farris said. "But that's not why I'm here. I've come to share information with you concerning Rajah."

"Ah yes—Rajah," Meg began. Her tongue was thick, her heart beating fast. "And what do you know about Rajah, other than what you've read in today's newspaper?"

"I know more than you think," he replied.

"Like what?"

Farris's cold brown eyes regarded her for a moment. Then he dug into his satchel and took out a videotape and slipped it into Meg's VCR.

Meg turned to David. "For God's sake, David, what is going on here?"

David held up his hand. "Stan has something to show

you, Meg. Something that should interest you." He motioned to Farris, who clicked on the TV.

"This tape was shot in a lab at Midway Quarantine in San
Francisco," Farris said. "Watch."

Meg turned to face the television set. A grainy image
came onto the screen. As the camera pulled back she saw a
baby tiger with electrodes attached to its skull writhing and
twisting against restraints that held its limbs down.

Off camera, a female voice said, "Forty cc's ought to do
it." Hands draped with lab cuffs entered the frame. A needle
was pierced into the cub's shoulder. The cub cried out.

Meg looked away. "How do I know this tape was filmed
at Midway?"

"It was," Farris said. "You'll just have to take my word
for it."

"Turn it off," Meg said, sickened. Farris did not move.
"I said, turn the *damn* thing off!"

Reluctantly, Farris retrieved the tape and shoved it back
into his satchel. "It goes something like this," he said, his
gaze focused on Meg. "I know Rajah came through Midway after your zoo acquired him from the Chinese Zoology
Ministry. It's my guess they used him in an experiment
while he was there."

Meg said, "Guess? What about proof?"

The evasion in Farris's eyes was instantaneous and brief,
though his answer was casual. "We're working on it
. . . but we know *all* tigers going through Midway during
that time were used in experiments. Midway was heavy
into DNA hybridization techniques and embryonic im-
plants. . . ."

"And I'm supposed to believe all this without proof!"
Meg exploded. "You come in here with an undocumented
tape and expect me to jump on your bandwagon? Rajah's
not a cause, Mr. Farris, something you can exploit. I've

already gotten enough of that from Ellroy." She picked up Farris's satchel and shoved it into his arms. "Now I want you out of my house. Before I call the police!"

David stepped between them. "Take it easy, Meg. Stan only came here to help you."

"Help *himself*, you mean. And how about you? Is that why you're here? To help me? You should have done that three years ago, but you were too busy then to care."

David's face grew pale. "That's not true. We separated because we were living different lives. I asked you to come to San Francisco with me."

"Yes, well, San Francisco wasn't exactly the answer to our marital problems, David."

"And I suppose Montego Bay was?"

"I thought so. But then I forgot who I was there with."

Suddenly the kettle in the kitchen was whistling. "I forgot. I put some water on for coffee," Meg said.

Farris moved to the front door. "I'll wait in the car, David. Don't be long. We still have a full night's work ahead of us."

As the door closed, Meg went into the kitchen and shut off the burner under the kettle. David came in and stood behind her, slipping his arm around her waist.

"You look exhausted, Meg."

"I am, David." She stood there, her thoughts wrapped in a crazy quilt of feelings. For a brief moment it felt good to her to be with David, as it had been in the early days of their marriage. But even then those moments had come only occasionally, and then only because Meg strove to make them happen.

David turned her around slowly to face him. Meg stared down at the floor. At last she broke the silence: "Why is it we always end up fighting? Can you tell me that? You come waltzing back into my life with the Prince of Darkness . . ."

"Stan's all right."

"All right? David, he's part of HAATE. Everywhere they go, there's trouble. They don't care who gets hurt, as long as they're part of the action. They aren't naturalists, Dave. They're terrorists."

David hesitated, then leaned forward slowly and kissed her; a light kiss, with his lips parted.

Meg stiffened and drew back. "Was that meant to change my mind, David? Do you really think so little of me?"

"You used to like it, Meg."

"I used to be twenty-four, too." Meg turned deliberately and poured hot water into her cup. She reached for the instant coffee. Her hands were trembling, which annoyed her.

"Why don't you let me fix you a real pot?" David said. "Like I used to do in the old days."

Meg sat down heavily with a sigh. "No, this is fine. I don't even want this. Help yourself, if you like."

David fixed himself a cup and sat across from her at the table. They sipped their coffee in silence, then he said, "Stan usually knows what he's talking about, Meg. He's pretty sharp. You should share information with him. Show him Rajah's records."

"There is nothing to show him, David. Up until three weeks ago, Rajah was a perfectly normal cat."

"Maybe Stan can spot something you've overlooked."

"So you're asking me to hand my records over to him? A complete stranger? David, I wouldn't trust him with my library card, let alone confidential records."

David thought for a second. "If Stan is right, Meg, then other people are involved. People that might try and use you as a scapegoat."

"People? Like who? Roueche? Ellroy?"

David shrugged. "They might be involved."

"This is insane, David. Stan is just trying to start trouble. He's an opportunist, feeding on everyone else's misery—" Meg broke off, realizing there was nothing more to say. She was too tired to argue. She had once thought that David could convince her of anything, that he could heal any wound. But tonight he made her feel hopelessly depressed, inadequate to deal with all that was going on. "Please, David, I'm tired. I just want you to leave, okay?"

David seemed perplexed. "Is that really what you want? For me to leave?"

"Yes, David, that is what I want."

"Listen, Meg, I know we've been angry with each other for a long time. But most of it is frustration over a situation that we couldn't handle. But this is different." He reached his hand out to hers and she pulled away.

He waited a moment and then made a vague gesture to show he bore no grudge. "All right," he said. "But I can assure you this whole affair will get worse before it gets better. I only hope . . . that you don't get hurt in the process." He paused. "I mean that, Meg. More than anything else, I just don't want to see you get hurt." He got to his feet slowly. "Anyway, thanks for the coffee."

After he had left the house, Meg swept into the bedroom and pulled her shirt over her head without unbuttoning it, kicked off her boots, and got out of her slacks. Then, scooping up her nightgown, she stared at herself in the dresser mirror. The face she stared at had black smudges under the eyes. The lips were tentative.

David Sorel had been there. Now he was gone.

Slowly the white silk nightgown slid to the floor.

11

THE NEXT MORNING, the sudden, shrill command of the telephone hurtled Meg into startled wakefulness. While her confused mind sought to right itself, her hand instinctively groped for the receiver. Her heart hammered painfully in her chest, more from a disquieting dream than from the rude awakening.

She had lain awake most of the night, sometimes in darkness, sometimes—jumping at every sound—with the lamp burning by her bed. She glanced at the clock now; it was ten-thirty. Oh, God . . . she'd overslept! She flung the covers aside, inadvertently knocking books to the floor as she groped for the receiver. "Hello?"

"Meg, it's Ray. Have . . ." He hesitated. "Have you heard about Shindler?"

"Dr. Shindler?" Meg said, dazed, her tongue as thick as a tree trunk. "Rajah's blood sample, you mean?"

"Meg, uh—I don't know how to say this. There was a fire last night. At Shindler's home in Bel Air. I'm afraid—"

"Oh no," Meg said, sinking back onto the bed.

"It's been all over the news, Meg. Shindler was in his car in the garage smoking or something. No one knows for sure how the fire got started, but Shindler and his wife both died. Jesus, from the sound of things, it was awful.''

Tears came to Meg's eyes. ''That's why I couldn't reach him last night. I tried, Ray—but I couldn't reach him.'' A sudden grief washed over her. The receiver wobbled in her hand. She steadied herself. ''Where are you?'' she asked.

''At the zoo,'' Ray said, and all at once Meg could detect the faint murmur of a crowd, and a surge of laughter and shouting in the background. ''More bad news, I'm afraid. Roueche called me early this morning. He told me to get my ass down here and put Rajah back on display.''

''Display?'' Meg got to her feet. ''Oh God, Ray—you didn't?''

''I tried talking him out of it,'' Ray said. ''But he insisted. He said this was the first Saturday in weeks that it hasn't rained. And, Meg—the attendance, the parking lot is full. The phones haven't stopped. Anyway,'' he said, remembering to breathe, ''Roueche is in charge of animal display. I couldn't override him. And Ellroy agreed with him.''

''But I placed him in quarantine, Ray. Ellroy promised me three days. We're in the middle of running tests!''

''I told Roueche that, and he asked me about the fecal analysis.''

''And?''

''It was negative, Meg. No blood in the stool, no parasites. According to that test, Rajah's fine.''

Once again the raucous sound of merriment came swooshing over the line. Meg hesitated, heard Ray shout to someone before he spoke again into the phone. ''Meg? Meg, are you still there?''

''Yes.''

''Meg, I don't know what else to say. Things have gotten crazy around here. You're the only one—''

''I'll be right there,'' Meg said. ''In the meantime, I want you to keep a close eye on Rajah. Don't leave the compound. Not for any reason."

"Okay," Ray said. "And, Meg, about the Shindlers. I'm really sorry."

Meg answered, "So am I."

12

EVERYTHING IS HAPPENING too fast, Meg thought as she passed the Hollywood Freeway intersect. Everything is out of control. The day was unseasonably warm, but she couldn't stop shaking. She shivered and rolled up the window.

Harry Shindler dominated her thoughts. And his wife, Joyce. Kind, unassuming people, always willing to sacrifice themselves for the good of others . . .

"No," Meg commanded, putting the thought aside. Her grief was bound to eat away at her in the days and weeks to come. But she knew she would have to control it as best she could. Just bury it, she thought. Hysterical outbursts would accomplish nothing.

Meg glanced at her watch; noon exactly. She looked up at the sky. A black dot appeared out of nowhere and grew larger. The helicopter passed directly over the Jeep, its propellers spinning in the heavy air.

Meg looked through the windshield at the traffic ahead. It was backed up, stretching into the pass for at least three miles. The helicopter banked and flew over the line of traffic. Meg had the creepy feeling that this midday jam wasn't the result of an accident. She was certain that the cars around her were heading for the zoo.

Damn Ellroy and Roueche, she thought. Damn them both.

She slowed, inching the Jeep forward. A row of hitchhikers dressed in khaki parkas stood at the roadside. Two were waving signs: L.A. Zoo. One of them lowered his head, peered into the Jeep, and waved. But Meg changed lanes and drove on. As she glanced back she saw one of the hitchhikers flip her the finger.

"Up yours, too," Meg barked.

She was absolutely furious when, an hour later, she pulled into her parking space at the zoo. The stream of visitors that had packed the mile-square parking lot moved steadily up the main walkway. Families, couples, tourists, even school groups moved like lemmings to the river, hellbent on drowning themselves in sensationalism. Some were somber, others talkative; but all were anxious to see Rajah the Lady Killer.

Meg pushed her way through the crowd, cursing the reporter who had given Rajah that loathsome title. A newspaper fluttered at her feet, and she kicked it aside. She noticed now that the surrounding area looked like a garbage dump.

"Herbert!" Meg yelled through the open security station window. "Put that phone down and get out here!"

Herbert nearly jumped out of his skin, eyes darting between Meg and the row of blinking lights on the telephone. "But what do I do?" he asked frantically. "The incoming lines—they just stay backed up. What do I do?"

Meg took a deep breath. No use taking Herbert's head off. He was doing the best he could. "Stay put," she said. She moved through the side door, locked it, and pulled down the shades.

"Russell said I . . . I should stay here and, and handle the phones," Herbert wheezed.

"Is he at the compound?"

"Been there since we opened."

"Okay. Please listen to me." Meg sat Herbert behind Russell's desk. "First, don't answer any more phones. Call the librarian at research and tell her *she's* answering the phones. If she refuses, tell her Mr. Ellroy said she works the phones or she's fired."

"But—"

"Don't worry," Meg said, "I'll clear it with Gordon later."

"Okay," Herbert replied. "But the government workers' guidelines—"

"I don't care what the policy book says. Get her down here. Then call the main gate and tell them to crack down on people bringing in food. They're coming in with picnic baskets. There'll be cupcakes and potato chips in every cage. I don't want the animals sick and vomiting for the next three days. All right?"

"Ye-yes, Doc," Herbert said. He gave Meg an exaggerated nod. "I can take care of that."

"Good. Please get Russell on the speaker and tell him I don't want to see a circus when I get up there."

Herbert jumped to his feet. "Right. You got it, Doc," he blurted, apparently relieved to finally have someone in charge. "I'll do it right now."

"That's fine, Herbert." Meg reached for the door. "And if you see Mr. Roueche, tell him I've gone to Ellroy's office."

Meg elbowed her way through the crowd again, did a quick sidestep, and stopped before a door marked Administration. The door was open and there were lights on, but the office was deserted. Meg paused, giving herself a moment to figure out how best to handle the situation. Come on too strong, and Ellroy would rebel. Come on too weak, and he'd brush her off. Middle ground, she reminded herself, and padded silently down the hallway to the director's vast mahogany-paneled office.

Knocking on the half-open door, Meg entered the office and saw Ellroy bent over a woman, offering her a handkerchief. The woman was seated in one of Gordon's overly stuffed chairs, crying.

"I'm sorry, Gordon," Meg said. "I—"

"No, come in, Doctor," Ellroy said with a sigh of relief. "Dr. Brewster, this is Mrs. Lewis. Carol's mother."

The woman turned to face Meg, the flesh below her eyes red and swollen. Her hair was pulled into a knot in back, and she wore no makeup. She held a crushed newspaper in her lap.

"Mrs. Lewis, I'm sorry."

The woman held up the crumpled newspaper. "I came about this," she said. "Doctor, tell me if it's true."

Meg inched closer, took the newspaper, and glanced at Ellroy, who shrank back behind his desk. Eyes downcast, face white, he shook his head.

Meg looked at the morning edition of the *L.A. Times*. In the lower left-hand corner on page one, she saw the caption:

SICK CAT KILLS
KEEPER AT L.A. ZOO

Meg shook her head and began to read.

> Carol Lewis, a 20-year-old L.A. zookeeper was killed the night of January 7 when she was dragged into the tiger compound by Rajah, the zoo's prize, 700-pound Siberian tiger.
> According to Lieutenant Dragleman of the Los Angeles Police Department, no one witnessed the violent

death. Apparently, Carol Lewis was alone, observing Rajah's feeding habits, when the cat attacked her.

"I heard her call out for help, but it was too late," said zoo's security guard Russell Biggs. "By the time I got there, Rajah had dragged the girl into his cave."

According to one of the zookeepers, Head Veterinarian Dr. Megan Brewster ordered the unorthodox vigil, hoping to determine the cause of the cat's erratic behavior for the past three weeks. One source stated off the record: "Rajah isn't right. He's been acting damn weird for three weeks now."

When Dr. Brewster was asked during a recent news conference whether or not Rajah was sick, she stated—"

"Is it true?" Mrs. Lewis said.

Meg looked up and saw the woman had gotten to her feet. She stood there, hands kneading her pocketbook.

"It says you knew the cat was sick three weeks ago. Is it true? Because if it is . . ." She broke off, wiping tears away with the back of her hand.

Meg didn't know what to say. It was true, and yet it wasn't. Not exactly. She said, "Mrs. Lewis, let me explain. Animals often display odd behavior, but that doesn't necessarily mean they are sick. In Rajah's case—"

"Odd? Dangerous, you mean?"

Meg sighed. "All zookeepers know the danger their jobs entail. Carol was—"

"Twenty years old. And now she's dead! Someone is responsible; is it you?" The woman's voice grew shrill as her agitation increased.

"It's . . ." Meg fumbled for words. "Carol worked for the zoo, Mrs. Lewis. Not me directly."

"But she was carrying out your orders. You weren't standing there alone in the dark—she was. Where were *you* when that thing killed her? You should have been there, not her! You! And now you've put the cat back on display, so he can harm someone else."

"Mrs. Lewis, I give you my word that right after Carol's death I placed Rajah in quarantine."

"But he's out there!" the woman shouted.

"Our curator is responsible for displaying the animals. Not me. All I can do is advise."

The woman wheeled on Ellroy. "You're the director! Why isn't that cat locked up where he belongs?"

Ellroy sank into his chair, mouth agape. "Mrs. Lewis, please, your daughter's death was an accident. The zoo's policy—"

"No more lies!" she shrieked. "I'm going to get to the bottom of this. All of you, damn liars!"

Before Meg could speak, Mrs. Lewis brushed past her and bolted from the room. As the door slammed closed, Meg turned to Ellroy.

"Well, Gordon?" she said.

The director shook his head, then buried his face in his hands.

"HEY, YOU, back in line!" Russell Biggs shouted, and the skinhead teen in leather stepped back with his girlfriend, a fourteen-year-old with gold-studded jacket and a rhinestone in her pierced ear.

"How's it going, Russell?" asked Meg, coming to stand beside him. "You look half dead."

Biggs rolled his eyes. "Thank God you're here, Doc. Are we shutting this compound down or what?"

Meg glanced distractedly at the newspaper in her hand. It was still folded back, revealing the headline: SICK CAT KILLS KEEPER AT L.A. ZOO.

"Can't," Meg said. "Roueche won't budge. Neither will Ellroy."

"Uh, hell, Doc, I don't have enough men," Biggs complained. "They didn't even call GLAZA for volunteers."

Meg scanned the crowd jammed along the viewing rail. Four security guards were doing their best to keep bodies moving through the maze of rope dividers. Gawkers still tried to cheat, craning their necks through breaks in the line, trying to see Rajah. Two gawkers, both teenagers, pushed one of the security guards as he attempted to move them along.

"Hey, knock it off!" Biggs shouted. He turned to Meg. "Listen, Doc, we gotta shut this place down before things get out of hand. You need someone to back you up, I'm your man. I've been lookin' to tell Roueche what I think of him, and the way things are goin', I'm damned good and ready!"

Meg shook her head. "You don't have to stick your neck out."

"Listen," Biggs said. "There's at least fifteen city code violations I can hit him with. Sanitation, crowd control, capacity . . . hell, I can't go checking every paper bag for beer cans!" He glanced at the crowd, then shook his head with a warning. "You wait and see. Come four-thirty, this crowd'll refuse to leave."

"Where's Ray?" Meg asked.

Biggs pointed over the crowd. "Somewhere near the rocks. He's been watching things from the other side."

Meg said, "I'll see what I can do."

As she worked her way through the crowd she caught the sickly-sweet odor of marijuana. Three boys and two girls, all very young, were passing around a joint. Meg bent and slipped under the rope barrier separating the crowd from the rising boulders.

"Welcome to Rajah mania," Ray said cynically. He was sitting on a ledge ten feet above the left side of the viewing rail, arms folded, wearing sunglasses and a wry grin. A bullhorn rested in his lap.

"This is crazy," Meg said, climbing up to meet him.

Ray reached his hand out and pulled her up to sit beside him. "Look at it this way," he said. "When we get through this, *if* we get through this, we'll have a new one-day attendance record. Twenty thousand, I bet."

"At least," she answered, and was amazed at the view from her new vantage point. Three or four hundred people were packed into the small pavilion, with more heading up the main walkway. The single line of bodies snaked back and forth between the rope dividers, edging closer to the pit.

Ray softened his tone and said, "I was sorry to hear about the Shindlers."

Meg said, "Things like that happen, I guess. I only wish it wouldn't happen to such nice people."

"Yeah," Ray said. "Anyway, I'm sorry."

"Me too." Meg handed him the newspaper, hoping to change the subject. "Have you read this?"

Ray nodded. "Whole staff has. That reporter gave you a bum rap, Meg."

"Any idea who the talkative keeper was?"

Ray shrugged and tossed the paper aside. "Gomez, maybe. Or Peterson. Both have been antsy lately."

"Yes, well, when this day's over I'd like to find out." Meg leaned across Ray's middle to get a better look at the pit. "How's Rajah?"

"So far, so good. I don't think he likes the extra attention, but he's cool."

"For the moment," Meg said. She studied the big cat closely. He was pacing between two rocks in the middle of the compound, eyes glaring up at the humans lining the rim of the pit.

Ray suddenly turned toward the front row of visitors and raised the bullhorn. "Please *do not* lean over the rail," he warned. A little girl in pigtails was stretched perilously over the railing. Ray was about to call again when the girl's father yanked her back.

"Whatever happened to common sense?" Ray said, shaking his head. "Don't these people know anything?"

Meg didn't answer. Her eyes had been drawn to the sound of a crying child. The mother, standing center of the long line, cooed and rocked the boy, but he would not be consoled.

Suddenly, a threatening roar careened through the pavilion. The crowd gasped. Meg scurried higher up the rocks for a better look at the pit.

"What is it?" Ray asked.

"I don't know," Meg said. Rajah's behavior had turned erratic, his massive head twitching and shaking back and forth. Yet his eyes never left the human ring staring down at him.

The crowd drew back, then surged forward with excitement. Titters and shrieks of laughter filled the air. Bodies pressed against the rail; fingers pointed, eyes glared with perverse joy.

"Move away from the railing," Ray shouted through the bullhorn. "If you don't move back *immediately,* you will be escorted from the zoo."

No one listened.

Biggs's men tried to disperse the front line, but it was hopeless. For each body they peeled away, there were thirty more pressing forward, leaning, shoving, all anxious to get a glimpse of the angry tiger.

Rajah snarled and hissed at the crowd surrounding his domain, all the while feverishly darting between the rocks.

Meg felt utterly helpless. Something was wrong. This was not the way he was supposed to react. She knew Rajah should have retreated to his cave by now, but he refused to give ground. Nothing Rajah did was indicative of normal behavior. He was primed to fight, as if sensing the crowd was closing in, preparing to attack.

The huge cat snarled angrily at his watchers; teeth gleaming in the sun.

In a chorus of harsh provocation, taunts and jeers and imitative growls were flung at the furious cat. Popcorn boxes and paper cups sailed over the railing. A child's teddy bear flew into the pit but never hit the ground.

Rajah exploded upward, tearing the bear to shreds in a flurry of swiping claws. Plumes of white stuffing filled the air like fluttering snow.

The crowd roared.

Meg turned, saw that three boys—none over twenty— had sneaked past the viewer's barrier to the bushes directly over the pit. They were getting their kicks by shooting spitballs at the tiger through straws. Rajah swiped the air and growled as a spitball hit his face. Then, somehow sensing that one of the boys had leaned in too far, he sprinted and leapt up at the boy, who, in his panic, slipped; the boy's legs dangled into the pit.

There was a horrified hush as Rajah missed and fell back. Before Meg could call out, the crowd merged into a single mass with the unpredictable spontaneity of a mob. Shrieking, they pressed closer to the rail as the cat lunged at the boy's legs again.

"Get Herbert on the two-way," Meg yelled to Ray. "Tell him to get the police and medics—now!"

As Ray quickly relayed the command, Meg was gripped by a new fear. Ray must have felt it, too. "What's happening?" he yelled, eyes frantically searching the crowd.

"Oh my God!" Meg cried. "The railing!"

The curved metal barrier had snapped free of the steel posts at either end. Only six thin bars, spaced evenly along the frame of the rail, remained anchored to the ground.

It all happened so quickly that no one had a chance to react. The middle of the railing bowed and twisted, warping under the tremendous weight.

"Get back!" Ray yelled over the bullhorn. "*Away from the rail!*"

Meg yelled, "Get the rifle!"

Ray scrambled down from the rocks but too late. The bars of the railing broke free.

Meg gasped as men, women, and children fell into the pit.

THE CAT SUDDENLY drew back.

Humans swarmed and shrieked around him. Visions of wild boar darting through the jungle unfolded in his brain, and his whole body jerked spasmodically.

As he lunged at the first man, memory erupted—images collided. The feeling of burning alive. The massive shock inside his skull. The loss of eyesight.

The cat tore at the man's flesh.

Sharp memory . . . cage . . . somewhere . . . long ago. He could feel the rubber pads beneath his feet forcing him to run . . . faster, faster—he lunged at a second human, sank his teeth into the soft flesh. Into the belly then into the buttocks.

New image . . . dense foliage . . . pale sun burning away the morning chill. Enormous trees. Spots of color: red blossoms, like blood. The cat roared, lunged again, hearing another roar, an echo of a roar, light-years away in the ultimate blackness, not quite a roar, rather a moan, like the pain of an animal.

He leapt onto the broken piece of steel dangling over the pit and climbed it like a ladder, trying to get away from the horrible shrieking. Trying to get away from his own pain.

He brought the security guard down with one lunge, then with long strides dashed up the walkway, veered off through bushes onto the service road, where he rammed his head under the fence and heaved upward. The fence lifted and then snapped.

Seconds later, the cat ran into the wooded hills of Griffith Park, away from the howling, shrieking sounds of the zoo, to freedom.

PART

II

13

THE COUNTY OF LOS ANGELES is enormous—larger, in fact, than a number of European countries. Aside from the City of Los Angeles, there are any number of other civic entities in the county: unincorporated areas, villages, smaller cities; and to make the situation worse, each of these civic entities has its own police force or is the private domain of the county sheriff. No one had planned this crazy quilt of authority; it just happened. And when word began to travel throughout the county that a tiger was on the loose, chaos ensued, fed by panic whipped to a fever pitch by the always excitable media.

Nobody knew who was in charge, whose area was being violated by whom. Helicopters took to the air, only to be driven down again by a sudden heavy downpouring of rain. Switchboards were jammed, and people ran to the safety of their homes. Gun sales skyrocketed. Hunters became self-styled vigilantes, adding to the danger. Reported sightings made tigers out of everything from a neighbor's dog to a man strolling through the park in a dark trenchcoat.

Well after dark, Meg steered her Jeep to the top of Griffith Park. The storm clouds that had swept through Southern California had passed into the eastern desert, leaving behind a hazy carpet of fog. The mountainside, swollen from days of rain, had begun crumbling into mud slides. Twice Meg had to swerve sharply to avoid rocks and debris that were tumbling onto the roadway.

The second time Ray stirred beside her. He was slumped in his seat, half asleep, curled against the window. Poor guy, Meg thought, he looks terribly uncomfortable, and he's probably had even less rest than I these last two days.

The road began to straighten, then leveled down to a mild incline. The Griffith Observatory parking lot was dead ahead. Meg reduced speed as she approached one of the five checkpoints, clear in the night under the harsh glare of the arc lamps.

As Meg slowed to a stop at the gate, the LAPD officer stationed there barely noticed her. He stood perfectly still, eyes scanning the shrouded woods. Meg wondered if he was listening to a roar or perhaps an approaching growl.

The officer turned suddenly, and Meg pressed her zoo ID against the window. He came closer, studied her photo for a second, then waved her on.

"Hey, sleepyhead," Meg said to Ray as she inched forward. "Time to look sharp."

Ray blinked, momentarily confused by the surrounding fog. "Right, I'm here," he said, and sat up.

Images appeared in the area ahead, everyday objects made unreal by the glow of powerful floodlights: CHP Chevys, patrol cars, and a paramedic's van. In the distance, barely visible, the observatory dome appeared through the grayish clouds.

As Meg slowed to a stop, she saw something rising up from a copse of trees. "Look there," she said, pointing to the edge of the visible area. Flashlight beams bobbed against the fog, drawing closer, until six men emerged into the clearing. Animal Control, Meg thought. Their uniforms were sopping wet, weapons dangling at their sides as they dragged themselves wearily to the top of the ridge.

"Who in their right mind would send trackers out in this fog?" Ray wondered aloud. "They won't be able to find Rajah until this stuff clears."

Meg said, "No, but Rajah could sure find *them*."

At that moment, a gloved hand rapped on the window.

Startled, Meg turned and saw the peering eyes of a high-way patrol officer, his leather jacket slick and glistening from the heavy mist.

"Dr. Brewster?" he called loudly.

Meg rolled down her window. "Yes, I'm Dr. Brewster."

Shivering, the patrolman leaned closer to the window, arms scrunched against his sides. He gave a slight nod over his shoulder. "Over there. Mr. Ellroy from the zoo wants to see you."

"Thanks," Meg said, and started to climb out of the Jeep.

"Maybe Gordon has some news," Ray said. He picked up Meg's thermos.

"Perhaps." Meg glanced past the CHP officers who stood before an open trash barrel, warming their hands over the fire. They were all wearing long raincoats, rifles slung over their shoulders. Beyond, in a patch of light, stood Roueche's chauffeur-driven limousine.

"While you talk to Gordon," Ray said, "I'll mosey over and share some of this coffee with the troopers. See what I can find out."

"Right," Meg said.

She glanced at her watch. Eleven o'clock, exactly.

As she approached the limo the darkly tinted rear window slid down. Roueche's smiling face appeared, perfectly backlit to set off his sculpted hair. His jaw line was pronounced, raised slightly, but not too far. His expression was that of complete self-confidence.

"Hello, Meg," he said smoothly. "Won't you get in?"

Interesting, Meg thought as she climbed into the limo and sat in a swivel chair across from the two men. Even in a situation such as this, a disaster of significant proportion and threatening to get even larger, this vain, egotistical man continued to play at seduction. Or was it guile he was exuding? Meg wasn't sure.

"Would you care for something to drink?" Roueche asked. He held up his own large snifter.

"No, thanks," Meg said, regarding him closely.

Gordon Ellroy didn't look at Meg right away. He sat wedged against the window, arms folded, peering out at the misted landscape. With his shock of untidy gray hair, tie askew, crumpled raincoat, he looked as out of place in this fancy car as Meg felt.

"Gordon?"

Ellroy turned and looked at Meg vaguely. He passed his hand over his forehead. It trembled and he took it down quickly. "We just got word," he said. "Another person, a man, died less than an hour ago. Internal injuries. Jesus. That makes four people dead so far. Who knows how many others there'll be."

"What about Rajah?" Meg asked. "Have there been any sightings?"

"Nothing," Roueche said. "Unless, of course, you count the roar someone *thought* they heard around nine o'clock."

"Any confirmation on that?"

"None. But it does reinforce your theory that Rajah headed straight into the park after his escape. And there isn't any evidence to suggest that he isn't still here, so—"

Ellroy abruptly raised his hand. "Look, they're calling them in." He pointed out the window to a dimly lit area at the road edge.

Meg peered into the gloom and saw two LAPD officers. They swung open the rear doors of a Chevy Blazer with K-9 Unit markings. A German shepherd, held close to his handler's side by a taut leash, pranced forward and leapt into the rear compartment.

"The dogs can't pick up the scent," Roueche said. "No surprise there. Everything is wet."

"Dammit!" growled Ellroy. He took a surprisingly large cambric handkerchief out of his pocket and wiped his face. "Have you seen the latest television reports? Those bastards. CNN called my office six times."

"And what did you tell them?" Meg asked.

"What *could* I tell them?" Ellroy said. He gulped. "Everything that goes on in the zoo, that's me. I'm to blame. I told them I was unavailable for comment, naturally."

"In any case," Roueche said, "there's over a hundred men stationed along the perimeter of the park. Rajah won't escape."

Meg said, "What about the mayor, Philip? You were at City Hall for two hours. What did you and the mayor talk about?"

Roueche was back to swirling his snifter of Armagnac in slow circles. "I've decided the mayor is a complete ass," he said. "He would like us to believe he must consider every detail, every minuscule point before he acts, strictly for the sake of administrative propriety. 'I have to consult with the County Sheriff's Office,' he says. 'I'm waiting to hear from the Park Service and the highway patrol,' he says. And then he has the gall to say, 'So you see, I can't give you an answer right now. *My hands are tied.*' God, what a cliché."

"So what's the bottom line?" Meg demanded. "Do we have official control over this search or not?"

Roueche glanced at Ellroy, and then placed his snifter on the bar. "No, for now it is strictly law enforcement. The mayor calls it 'first level emergency response.' But in truth, *he's* in charge, not us. Let's face it—City Hall isn't very happy with us right now."

Meg suddenly felt strong apprehension. If Roueche's

swagger had made her suspicious before, the fact that the mayor, as well as the Park Service, were declining her help in capturing Rajah made her even more suspicious.

"But why?" Meg said. "Ray and I are the only ones schooled in safe-capture techniques. At least, where a tiger is concerned. The Park Service can't handle that. Neither can any of the other units. So why exclude us?"

Roueche calmly folded his hands in his lap. "I don't know. But only those of specified administrative rank will be advised of any further proceedings. And frankly, that doesn't include us."

"*Me,* you mean. That doesn't include *me!*" Meg could feel her anger getting the better of her. "Well, I'm not going to stand for it. Not you, the mayor—the governor himself is going to push me aside. Do you understand me, Philip?"

"Of course," Roueche said. "But in the meantime, you have a responsibility to the other animals in the zoo. Frightened animals are animals at jeopardy. It would be costly to replace dead exotic animals because of your neglect."

"My neglect? It was you who ordered Rajah put back on display. I warned you, practically begged you." She turned to the director. "Gordon, you promised me three days to run tests on Rajah. Didn't you?"

Ellroy turned slowly to face her. His hands were trembling. "Philip and I listened very carefully to what you had to say Thursday evening. You stated that Carol's own negligence caused her death. You also stated that Rajah's tests, thus far, had proven negative. But I certainly don't remember discussing a three-day quarantine."

"What?" Meg watched him glance at Roueche, then turn away, directing his attention again to the scene beyond the window.

"Gordon, let me get this straight. Are you actually saying we *never* discussed a quarantine? That I wasn't in the process of running tests? Gordon?"

CLAW

Ellroy refused to look at her. Even Roueche looked away.

Clearly a reversal, Meg thought. From boldfaced lying to utter silence.

AS MEG RETURNED to her Jeep, filled with anger, she indulged in a truly hostile fantasy. If only I could lure them both into the woods, she thought, then Rajah would do the rest!

Suddenly Ray approached from the opposite direction, the empty thermos swinging at his side. They stared at each other for a second. Meg frowned, and they climbed into the Jeep without saying a word.

She started the engine, flung the gear-stick into reverse, and backed up until she found room to turn around. Ray blinked, held on.

"You're angry," he said.

She said, "You're very observant."

Meg's fury glimmered like ice as she cleared the checkpoint, adding to the chill inside the Jeep. She switched on the heater. Warm air blew through the vents onto their hands and feet. Behind them the glare of the arc lights grew dimmer.

"I'm sorry, Ray," Meg said, slowing the Jeep to a crawl. "Ellroy and Roueche really steam me, that's all. Ellroy's now claiming that I never asked him for a three-day quarantine. And I'm sure Roueche is prepared to support his claim."

"I'm not surprised," Ray muttered. "Kinda what I expected, only I guess I allowed myself to hope. They've always got to find someone, something to hang the blame on."

"How long do you figure it'll be before they actually get around to me?"

Ray shrugged. "Ordinarily, they'd want a week or two.

Really tool up for it. But they haven't got time for that now. Not with Rajah on the loose. They'll want to get this bandaged up fast."

"I suppose you're right," Meg said. "I suppose that's why the mayor doesn't want me heading the search."

"Oh? Did Roueche tell you that?"

Meg nodded. "Put simply, you and I are out, Ray. It seems we are not of 'specified administrative rank.'"

Ray was unperturbed. He bent and stuffed the thermos back into the satchel. "It's okay," he said. "I know how irritating the city bureaucracy can be. But you can't dwell on what you can't control. Just keep your mind on Rajah."

Baboons, worms, hyenas, Meg thought as she rounded the next turn. Night creatures. Another storm was approaching; she could almost see the turbulence in the air—trees bent and swaying, fog swirling in the headlights. She pulled over to the side of the road and stopped.

The vastness of Griffith Park had suddenly overwhelmed her. It was large, more than four thousand acres of hills, rocks, and wild land. With over fifty-five miles of trails to explore, Rajah would not be easy to find, and, once located, not easy to trap.

"About Shindler's phone call," Ray said, reaching for her hand. "You mentioned that he sounded . . . what was it?"

"I don't know, strained, I guess."

"Can you recall exactly what he said?"

Meg thought for a second. "It was a short message, I remember that. He wanted to set up a meeting to discuss Rajah's blood test. He said he didn't want to discuss matters over the phone."

Ray shook his head. "I don't like any of this."

"What do you mean?"

"There's a lot of stuff happening but no context. Shindler

didn't want to discuss matters over the phone. Ellroy and Roueche are both scrambling for cover. . . ."

Ray broke off and glanced around the deserted woods. The weather was clearing, even if only momentarily. The moon was up now, hazy, its ghostly light haunting the woods.

"Listen," he said, "I've got one more vial of Rajah's blood. I figured it wouldn't be safe at the lab, so I stuck it in the potato salad in my refrigerator. A friend of mine, Eddie Crowell, lives in Loma Linda. Nice guy, great microbiologist. I think it's important he test the blood right away."

"It's a little late for that, don't you think?"

"Hell, at least it might help clear your name. Let's face it, Meg—that story in today's *Times* really did a number on you. They came damn close to saying Carol's death was your fault. Who knows what they'll be saying next? So I get Eddie to check things out, right? Only this time we don't tell anyone, okay?"

"Yes, all right," Meg said softly.

Suddenly Ray turned away. He stared at the bleak landscape, eyes unfocused. Headlight beams washed over his face as another K-9 Unit van wheeled toward them, then passed.

In that brief moment Meg saw confusion; a mind shifting through a flurry of troubling thoughts. He seemed oddly vulnerable. Almost pained.

"Where are you?" Meg asked.

Ray hesitated, his gaze far off. "I did a little male bonding over your coffee back there."

"And?" Meg asked hesitantly.

Ray looked at her. "All that time we spent in school together, and later, working on safe-capture techniques, remember?"

Meg nodded.

"I loved it. I still do. I like to think we're both good at it." He sighed. "Those officers back there made no bones about it, Meg. Mayor's orders: Rajah is to be shot on sight. No exceptions."

For a moment Meg sat there, sagging under the weight of the news. A chill passed through her, far deeper than anything the weather could produce.

"Why, Ray?" she said finally. "Why do we use things up, places, people, animals, and then destroy them? I know Rajah has hurt people. That the public needs to be protected. But it isn't his fault."

Ray put his arms around her. "We'll just have to find him, that's all. Before they do. We can do that, can't we?"

Suddenly, unexpectedly, tears welled up in Meg's eyes. She was clinging to Ray, and kept on clinging, hoping to hold on to the last ounce of her courage.

She had no doubt she was going to need it.

14

THE CAT CAUGHT them when they least expected it. Linda and Tom Adams had just entered the cabin, and it was exactly as Linda remembered it. Heavy beams overhead. Comfortable furniture. Country kitchen and a marvelously old staircase leading to the twin bedrooms on the second floor.

"You get the firewood," Linda told her husband. "I'll put the food away."

"Are you sure your father's not going to mind us sneaking up here like this? This is his personal retreat, isn't it?"

"He hasn't been here in months. By the time he gets around to using it again, I will have told him about our little adventure."

"Okay, you're the boss." He smiled, drew her close, and kissed her. She clung to him for a moment, her breasts pressed against his chest.

"Promise me something?" she said, staring up into his pale green eyes.

"What?"

"That you'll never leave me. Or stop loving me."

He smiled. "I promise. But if we're ever going to get this place warm, I'll need to leave you to get the wood." He laughed, kissing her again. Then he ducked outside, heading for the woodshed.

Linda picked up the bag of groceries and popped into the kitchen. Through the dutch windows, she could see the Santa Monica Mountains dwarfing the rear of the cabin. Her father had bought the cabin when she was a little girl, and the only change from then until now was how large the trees had grown up around the property.

"There's no wood in the shed," Tom called through the back door, his voice nearly obscured by the wind.

Linda glanced over her shoulder. "Father always keeps spare wood in the downstairs bin. The cellar door is beside the stairs, to your right. The light switch is at the bottom, so watch your step."

"Right," Tom said.

She listened. The outside basement door creaked open. She heard footsteps on the basement staircase, some rustling below. She put the bag of groceries on the counter and turned on the radio. Loud music erupted.

"Linda!" Tom called out.

"What?" Linda fumbled with the knobs on the radio, accidentally turning up the volume.

Music blared; Tom's voice blared even louder. But guttural, more animal than human. As she grabbed for the on-off knob, she knocked the groceries to the floor. "Dammit!" she muttered, shutting off the radio. She turned. "Tom?"

The cabin was quiet now. Only the wind could be heard, and the rustle of tree branches brushing the house. A peculiar sense of numbness spread through her as she bent and started putting the groceries back into the bag. "Tom, what are you doing down there?"

When he didn't answer, she went to the cellar door and yanked it open. She glanced down. Below, everything was dark. Stepping onto the landing, she flicked on the stairwell light. Nothing. Something was wrong; she could feel it. Her stomach doubled into a knot as cold perspiration dampened her skin. Taking a flashlight off the ledge, she turned it on. Then she started down the stairs, the wood creaking noisily beneath her feet. She called Tom's name as she descended. No answer.

She paused at the bottom to look around. Toward the back of the room were several old chairs, a love seat, and a dozen cardboard boxes filled with dishes and glassware. Her father liked using the basement for storage. The woodbin was under the steps, next to the south wall.

As she focused the light on the bin, she felt a cold draft blow across her legs. She realized now that the outside door was still open. Abruptly a strange odor, a kind of acrid stench, assaulted her nostrils. She sniffed and drew back. She had never smelled anything like it before.

"Tom, are you down here?" she called out again, shivering.

The smell came again, swirling through the basement. She swung the flashlight toward where she thought the smell was coming from—the boiler. As she stepped closer she noticed a trail of slime streaked across the floor. And blood.

Fresh blood.

Oh my God. She opened her mouth, but no sound escaped. She kept going, following the trail of slime and blood around to the other side of the boiler, and yet the resistance to continue seemed almost physical.

When at last she had managed to reach the other side, she froze. She simply could not move. Like a statue, a tableau, she was frozen in time—staring down at her husband's body. He lay propped against the concrete wall, arms dangling at his side, legs spread, his eyes still open in shock. A tearing laceration ran from his forehead down to his throat. At the edge of the wound, the flesh was shredded.

CLAW

For one split second, Linda hesitated. Then she screamed. Over and over, she screamed, shrill, loud, mad—as though her voice belonged to someone else, as though her body were a recording device that had suddenly gone berserk.

And in that instant a shadow appeared.

A shadow that moved. That breathed.

Linda stopped screaming. Reached out and took hold of the boiler for support. Listened to the breathing of someone or something not ten feet away from her, hidden behind the pile of boxes. She could barely make out the form now. Huge, monstrous.

Dear God, was it even human?

As she stumbled back, the room exploded. Dishes and glassware crashed to the floor as whatever it was lunged. She felt glass spray across her shoulders and neck, then her face. At that same instant she stumbled and fell, dropping the flashlight. Then she smelled an animal stench in her nostrils and felt a hard object brush against her chin, before plunging like a dagger into her right eye.

Screaming, beating her arms and fists wildly in the air, blinded by her own blood, she stumbled to her feet and ran toward the cellar door that led into the yard. She ran out of the cabin, her feet slipping through the mud and wet grass, ran from the horrible roar that wasn't far behind her, ran until her lungs felt ready to burst.

Finally, unable to run any farther, she sank to her knees, there in the damp grass and mud. She felt—she didn't even know what she felt really. She wanted to feel some sense of closeness to her husband—some of the love she'd felt only moments ago. But all that remained were memories.

Before losing consciousness, she instinctively rolled herself into a ball in a final, futile gesture of defense. Then the cat was upon her, claws tearing into her flesh.

15

SEVERAL MILES AWAY in the Hollywood Hills, Dan Dragleman parked his Chrysler convertible in the narrow driveway in front of his apartment complex. He killed the motor, snapped off the headlights, and got out.

The street was dark and empty. Most of L.A.'s eight million plus were obeying the mayor's curfew. Only the homeless were out and the criminals.

After closing the front door of the flamingo-pink building, he climbed the two flights of stairs to his apartment. He found the wall switch just inside and to the right of the door. It turned on a small lamp beside the couch.

The apartment was damp and cold. Dragleman put his small deli bag on the dining room table. In the kitchen he found a glass. He got out of his jacket and unsnapped his shoulder holster. The gun made a thudding sound as he dropped it on the kitchen counter. He pulled a hard, straight-backed chair up to the table and sat down. He broke open a beer, poured, then unwrapped a tuna sandwich on rye and flicked on the TV.

As he ate, the screen flickered and warmed; all the local channels were covering the story of Rajah's attack and escape.

CLAW

As Dragleman watched, he was amazed at the security measures taken within the city. Road closures included the Hollywood Freeway from Universal to the Sunset Boulevard exit, the Ventura Freeway from Burbank Studios to San Fernando Road, and the Golden State Freeway from Western Avenue in Glendale all the way down to Los Feliz Boulevard in Silverlake. As predicted, traffic at the barricades to those freeway closures was backed up for miles. The highway patrol urged all commuters who normally used those freeways to find alternative routes to the downtown business district until further notice.

Absolutely incredible, Dragleman thought, chewing. Dr. Brewster's "cat" had become a big story. All over the city, perhaps all over the country, people sat glued to their TV sets.

Reporters and camera crews were flocking to L.A. from everywhere. The more Dragleman thought about it, the more remarkable it seemed. Movies and stories about Africa and its beautiful wildlife had fascinated him since childhood, but watching Meg Brewster go into that cat's mouth, seeing it rise up afterward and prowl the cage was something else. It was breathtaking to witness, but in a way that had more to do with horror than with nature's beauty.

Halfway through the sandwich Dragleman got up and turned on the heat. He set the thermostat at seventy-five, and was just sitting down to finish his sandwich when the phone rang.

He groaned and pushed himself stiffly to his feet. The hands on the small clock above the refrigerator pointed toward twelve-thirty. He groaned again as he lifted the receiver.

"Dragleman?" the voice said. It was a voice he did not recognize, muffled and low.

"Yes?"

"Lieutenant Dragleman," the voice said. "I have news for you. Information that I'm sure you'll find interesting."

"What?" Dragleman said, eyes glued to the TV. "Who is this? What news?"

"Now, now, we mustn't rush things, Lieutenant," the voice said. "I read the *Times* today like everyone else. How you're handling the Carol Lewis case. A pity, really. The way that cat . . ."

"Listen, it's twelve-thirty at night. Just what do you think you're doing?"

"It's Sunday morning, Lieutenant. Time for prayer, wouldn't you say? Especially with that cat loose . . ."

"Listen, wiseguy," Dragleman said, "why don't you quit it and let me get to bed!"

"Shindler," the man said. "Dr. Harry Shindler, from UCLA. Does the name mean anything to you?"

"Not a thing." Dragleman allowed his anger to sharpen his voice. "And where do you come off calling me at this hour? I'm hanging up now, and if you—"

"My advice is not to hang up, Lieutenant," the man said. "Not if you're really interested in what happened to Carol Lewis. In a way, it was murder, Lieutenant. Same with Shindler. Now if I were you I'd look carefully into Dr. Shindler's death."

Dragleman had been leaning across the kitchen counter, but now he stretched the telephone cord and sat on one of the stools. It suddenly occurred to him that perhaps the caller was one of his friends, drunk at an all-night party, having fun with a few buddies. "You know," he said, more calmly, "I think you've been seeing too many cop movies. Either that, or you've had too much to drink."

The man laughed, a sharp, brief bark. "Okay, Lieutenant, I won't call you again. But one last warning. Dr. Shindler was murdered. Check it out. He used to live in Bel Air.

He doesn't anymore. His house was deliberately torched. So why don't you climb out of your jammies and go see for yourself. Oh, and don't forget to brush your teeth and comb your hair first, Lieutenant, because it's a real high-class neighborhood."

"Screw you," Dragleman said, and banged the phone down.

He ran his hand through his hair, then shivered. Heat or no heat, he was still cold. He walked stiffly into the bedroom and put on his robe. The wounds he'd received in Nam, especially in his right leg, always acted up once the California weather turned nasty.

Finishing his sandwich, Dragleman sat back and sipped his beer. As he watched the news on CNN, he glanced at the telephone. He had expected his caller to call back. Prank callers usually did. But then, the man had stated that he wouldn't call back, and the fact that he didn't somehow added more weight to the call.

Dr. Shindler was murdered. Check it out. Who was Shindler anyway? Or was there even a Dr. Shindler to honestly consider?

Dragleman got to his feet. The Pacific Bell White Pages that he kept buried under his couch had six Shindlers listed. But only one with M.D. after his name.

What the hell, Dragleman thought glancing at the clock, and dialed the number in Bel Air. After the third ring a recording came on and stated that the number dialed was temporarily not in service.

"Interesting," Dragleman said aloud as he went back to the table and carefully swept the crumbs into his cupped hand. Nobody ever had to pick up after him; cleanliness was simply part of taking care of business. It was like exercise, a steady job, or emptying the garbage can. Take care of business, or they mop the floor with you.

He carried the crumbs to the garbage disposal, then took a fresh beer to the bedside table. He stretched out on the bed and rotated his neck on the pillow to relieve the tension. The bed felt soft and warm, and he settled in, realizing suddenly just how tired he was.

Shindler, he thought, eyes closing.

Shindler.

Microscopic images swarmed and rose up. Kirkwood's face: "Not human, not animal, Dan." The body of Carol Lewis. Jesus, what the hell was going on? Dragleman wondered, but there was no answer to his question as he drifted off to sleep.

16

MEG BREWSTER FLINCHED as the steel gate clanged shut behind her and the bolt shot home. The keeper walked slightly ahead, down the cement corridor that smelled of disinfectant and that reverberated with animal shrieks.

"You think she's gonna be all right, Doc?" the keeper said.

Meg nodded. "Place her near a heat lamp right away. Then inject milk from its mother. Use a small tube down its esophagus. Wait a while, then put warm mother's milk into a bottle with a special lamb's nipple."

"How about massage?" the keeper asked.

"After the injection of milk. But be gentle."

"I will," the keeper said, his eyes seeking more reassurance.

Meg couldn't give it. For the moment, there was nothing more she could do for the baby tapir except prescribe warmth, massage, and periodic injections of milk.

Outside again, Meg glanced at her watch. It was 2 A.M. Tense, exhausted, running entirely on nervous energy, she started down the walkway toward her office.

She had just completed her tour of the zoo, which was

still in utter chaos. One of her favorite orangutans, Tina, had miscarried. Another had broken his mate's arm. Because of all the disturbances earlier, fear among the animals had become life-threatening. Oryx, antelope, and kangaroos raced around the edge of their barns at dangerous speeds. Rabbits, hedgehogs, and other burrowing animals cowered in their holes, refusing to appear for food and water.

The larger mammals displayed their fear in a subtler fashion. The acrid smell of rhinoceros urine wafted through the African Plaza hour after hour, while the symphony of anxious cries persisted, echoing.

Meg stopped in front of the administration building, wondering if the harsh cries weren't a sign that Rajah was still close by, stalking. But where? She and Ray had already combed the Mount Hollywood Loop Trail.

Later, Meg alone combed Mineral Wells to Mount Bell Trail. Then the Bronson Cave Trail that snaked through Brush Canyon to an abandoned rock quarry and the Bronson Caves, a perfect hiding place for a cat. But she did not find Rajah. Nor did she see any signs that he had been there.

Meg entered the administration building. Most of the lights were on, but the place was deserted. The secretaries had all gone home; Ray was on his way to Eddie Crowell's house in Loma Linda. As much as Meg hated to admit it, Roueche was right. She was responsible for the zoo's *entire* population, and right now she needed help.

As soon as she was in her office, Meg began flipping through her Rolodex. She found a seldomly used phone number, and dialed.

"Hello?" came a raspy, sleepy voice.

"Hank, it's Meg Brewster. Up in L.A. Don't bother looking at your clock. It's two A.M."

Hank Marley made a grumbling noise, followed by a

clumsy rattling sound. Meg visualized the big man fumbling with the receiver as he struggled higher on his pillow.

"What's the problem, Meg?"

"Everything. Don't you guys in San Diego watch the news?"

The senior keeper let loose a gruff laugh. "Yeah, but I don't dream about it. And that's what I was doing when you called. Dreaming."

"Sorry, Hank," Meg said. "But things are getting out of hand."

"I can imagine. You've certainly got one mean Siberian on the loose. I suppose you could use some help."

"Desperately. I just had an orangutan miscarry, and I'm afraid one of our mandrills, Pattie, might be next." Meg listened to the long, pained groan. Hank was an expert on primate captive breeding, and she had known he would be sympathetic.

After a slight pause, Hank said, "Okay, I'll clear it with my front office later, but there shouldn't be a problem. We won't be drawing big crowds tomorrow. I'll be there before breakfast."

Meg breathed a sigh of relief. Hank was the best. He had a master's degree in zoology and twenty years of keeper experience in one of the finest zoos in the world. She said, "You're saving my life. You know that, don't you?"

"Forget it. When this blows over, you can fix me a spaghetti dinner."

"It's a deal," she said. "And thanks again."

MEG FELT a sense of relief when she hung up. A few minutes later, she was tense again. Glenn Foster, assistant chief of the Department of Natural Resources, showed up and began to grill her about the state of Rajah's health.

"Was there a bacteriological examination of Rajah's urine specimen?" he asked.

Meg hesitated. "No."

"Other procedures, perhaps. Microscopic, immunological RTX for viral, parasitic, bacterial disease? X ray?"

"His behavior until now hasn't warranted such an examination."

Foster looked at Meg, and she knew she should pay attention. *Listen.* Because the little man in dark suit and tie, heavy black shoes, looked agitated. In fact, his eyes appeared dilated.

"Then how can you be sure his erratic behavior doesn't, in fact, reflect feline tuberculosis?" he asked. "Here you have a tiger in close proximity of goats, deer, horses, all considered to be long-term carriers."

"Because," Meg snapped, "airborne microbacteria couldn't survive the hundreds of yards between our bovine population and our cat exhibits. They are two completely separate areas of the zoo!"

At first Meg had taken the man seriously. Now she wasn't so sure. He seemed to be grasping at straws, looking for any excuse to push the panic button.

"Nevertheless," Foster said, "it is my responsibility to consider all possibilities. Anthrax, for instance. Hydrophobia . . ."

"*Rabies?*" Despite the grimness of the situation, Meg almost laughed. "Surely you don't think—"

"It is not my job to speculate. Communicable Disease Center is concerned that Rajah may be capable of spreading a deadly disease. The California Department of Health is also worried. We all are."

"And you believe your fears are justified?"

"Why not?" Foster straightened in his chair. "You yourself were concerned enough to order an all-night vigil."

"A fairly common procedure."

"Yes, well," he said sternly, "try explaining that to Virus and Rickettsia Laboratory. No, Doctor, we have a genuine problem on our hands, and the sooner we clean it up, the better."

"Clean it up? You mean, destroy Rajah on sight, don't you?"

Foster got to his feet. "That's precisely what I mean. After which, the Bureau of Animal Industry will perform an autopsy to provide information to protect the living. My division will handle all the arrangements. In the meantime, I have been instructed to have you hand over all records pertaining to Rajah. Also any blood samples, and other data concerning his health."

Meg stiffened. How easily, how cleverly he had slipped in the fact that he wanted all of Rajah's records. As though it were common practice. No, Meg decided, this evil little man wasn't concerned for public safety. He was here for the sole purpose of confiscating her records. Without them, Meg would be vulnerable to any charges Roueche or Ellroy wished to make against her.

Or did it go deeper than that?

Meg knew that the Department of Natural Resources was a powerful governmental body that controlled almost every aspect of L.A. life. But she had never known them to send a deputy out at two in the morning. And an assistant chief at that.

Meg moved slowly behind her desk now, wondering who had sent him here. The mayor? The governor, perhaps? Yes, Meg knew she needed to protect the public, but from whom?

She said, "And if I refuse?"

Foster considered her for a second. Then he reached for his attaché case. "Any person in possession of data pertaining to an injured or diseased animal on the loose must oblige the Department of Natural Resources by handing over such documents. Otherwise, they are in violation of the law and will be prosecuted. It's the law, Doctor. I suggest you obey it."

Meg hesitated, thinking things over. They were not only going after Rajah, but her as well. She could almost feel the trap being set. The question was, when would they spring it?

"All right," Meg said. "But my office is in a mess. The lab's worse, I'm afraid. It will take me most of the night to collect all of my research."

Foster glanced at his watch. "Very well," he said grudgingly. "I'm staying at the Sportsman's Lodge. I'll expect a call first thing in the morning. Arrangements will be made to have the samples picked up. *All* the samples, mind you. They will be safe with me."

"*Quid custodiet ipsos custodes?*" Meg murmured, and then wished she hadn't.

"Beg your pardon?"

"Nothing," Meg said.

Foster nodded. "I believe you said: 'Who shall guard the guardians.' " He drew closer. "I understand your apprehension, Doctor. I am a vet myself. At least, I was. I understand how attached you can become. But think of it this way. We wouldn't want an epidemic on our hands, now would we?"

Meg hesitated. "No, Mr. Foster, we certainly wouldn't want that."

AN HOUR LATER, Meg sat hunched over Rajah's daily log reports, barely able to keep her eyes open. But Foster's visit had only stiffened her resolve to discover the *real* cause of Rajah's sudden aggressive behavior.

If Dr. Hampton's assertion was right, that Rajah was

acting out some sort of Freudian "death instinct," which, when turned against the outside world, showed itself as aggression and destructiveness, then it was Rajah's mental state that Meg had to consider, including consciousness, self-awareness, memory, thought, and emotion.

His mind! Meg thought. Am I really sitting here doing this, trying to comprehend the mind of a tiger turned suddenly violent? But if it was, indeed, the mystical meanderings of Rajah's mind she was dealing with, and not a feline sickness, then she wanted to know. Had to know.

The experts and their publications which Meg had so carefully studied offered little in the way of real guidance in this area. Each had a convincing argument, yet each seemed to contradict the other.

Meg glanced irritably at the stack of reference books piled on her desk. Mentally she reviewed the few conclusions common to all these scientists.

Cats clearly have uncluttered minds, on that they agreed. Cats exist moment to moment. They live only in the present, using working memory—or *short term* memory as it is often called. Because of this, environment, more than anything else, controls what is happening in a cat's mind.

Meg sat back now and considered this, picturing how dark the compound must have been the night Rajah pulled Carol from the ledge. That particular area was thick with trees and shrubs; not a normal place for Carol to be. Clearly, he could have perceived her as prey. But how to explain the aggressive posture he had assumed at the compound earlier in the day. Surely he must have known humans were peering down at him from the railing, not animals. Yet he refused to withdraw, despite all the human commotion. Instead, he presented a challenge, grew more aggressive. As if . . . Meg hesitated. As if memory was causing in him some sense of deep rage.

CLAW

Once again, Dr. Hampton's story of the dog who had waited to seek revenge on its owner crept into Meg's mind. Revenge? Was that possible?

Was Rajah's memory somehow *longer* than most cats', sharper, cluttered with unresolved images? Could he possibly be operating on a desire for revenge of some sort? Just as Dr. Hampton had suggested. Or had something simply gone wrong with his brain? A tumor perhaps? A rare neurological disease? Or perhaps epileptic activity? Meg wondered.

Shaking away this last, repugnant thought, she got to her feet. She knew she couldn't go any further. Her exhaustion was complete. Before lying down on the couch, she reached out and turned off the lights. The coldness of the room suddenly surrounded her, and she let the warmth of her heavy parka comfort her as she stretched out and draped it over her body.

Eventually she slept, her dreams a disjointed mixture of images, some reflecting the guilt and frustration she felt at Carol's death; others stemming from fears of what might lie ahead.

At one point she awoke with a start, aware that she was dreaming of a saber-toothed cat that had roamed North America until its extinction 11,000 years ago. It had been a particularly grisly dream as she followed the cat, hunting alone, then chasing its prey across a grassy plain. Suddenly she was there and it directed its vicious gaze at her, just about to plunge its daggerlike fangs into her neck when she awoke.

In the distance an animal shrieked.

17

THE SMALL TOWN of San Rafael Hills sat quiet and still, nestled ten miles outside of Los Angeles flush against the San Gabriel mountain range. It was a lonesome area that L.A. residents called "out there."

There wasn't much activity at four in the morning. A small gathering of people at the all-night restaurant. Two highway workers shooting the breeze in their parked truck, having coffee and doughnuts.

A burgundy Rolls-Royce was parked at the edge of town, the young woman in the backseat straining to check her makeup in a gold compact. A few truckers were pulled off to the side of the road, asleep in their cabs. Now and then a car or two would drift through town, driven mostly by locals.

The woman in the Rolls finally let down her window and watched her fiancé, a successful studio executive, shoot bottles off a farmer's fence. Friends of the executive stood off to the side, cheering him on.

Baker, the man with the gun, struck a haughty pose as he carefully loaded his weapon, then shot another rack of bottles. When he finished, having hit every one, his friends gathered around him, applauding.

"Great shooting," one of them said, and everyone joined in with words of agreement. Baker was clearly the leader of this group.

"Oh, for chrissakes!" the woman in the car shouted. "Will you *please* stop acting like little boys and get back into this car. I've got a plane to catch."

Baker turned to face her. "In a minute, hon. Stan here has bet me a hundred dollars I can't shoot seven in a row."

A bird suddenly broke from the trees and sailed down toward the Rolls. Baker, his hand steady, fired again and the shot created an explosion of feathers. The two men standing beside him murmured their appreciation.

"Damn you!" the woman shrieked and let up the window.

The men outside laughed. They considered themselves the best of sports. And, in fact, they weren't bad people. They just had too little to do, made too much money, drank too much, did drugs occasionally. They were simply bored.

Another bird hovered on the wind, its wings extended. Baker fired, and the bird fell.

"Next time wait until the bird dives and see if you can hit it in full flight!" one of the friends suggested.

Baker nodded and started to reload.

No one would remember later which came first after that, the sudden roar that erupted from the storm drain or Baker's scream. He had turned, lifting his gun, and caught just a blurred glimpse of a cat—an incredibly big cat— launching itself into the air at him. The cat struck him chest high, driving him against the Rolls door. His gun went flying. It whirled over the top of the car, to land in the roadway.

People came out of the restaurant to look, staring in stunned silence as Baker wheeled, rose, dipped, trying to break free of the cat's claws. His fiancée screamed when his face smashed against the window, leaving a trail of blood as it slid from view. The tiger turned suddenly to face the crowd. People dashed for cover.

Some were lucky, some not. A man made it to his pickup, and sat in terror behind closed windows as the cat rammed its tremendous weight against the truck door. A passing motorist swerved when the cat leapt into his headlights and the car careened into a telephone pole.

Then the cat concentrated on the restaurant. People ran inside and the owner, Lester Cook, locked the door. Perhaps those inside the restaurant would have been all right. But Lester Cook, pigheaded as he was, stood in open defiance by the plate-glass window, waving his arms and fists at the cat, threatening to kill the son of a bitch if he didn't leave them alone.

Stepping closer to the window, Lester cursed, snarled . . . and that was when the tiger crouched, roared, and then came crashing through the window. Glass showered down, and as people scattered, Lester saw the first flowers of his own blood splattered across the counter. He glanced down, saw blood spewing from his gut. Saw a thick rope of intestine hanging out of his torn shirt.

As he rolled behind the counter to protect himself, screaming as he went, the short-order cook came rushing from the kitchen and flung a skillet of grease at the cat, starting a fire.

Flames and smoke filled the restaurant. It was like a sudden, noisy ambush sprung by a silent signal. In a flash the fire jumped up, a living red weed running across the wooden floor to the walls.

"Get the hell out of here!" Lester hollered to the cook. "Get—"

The rest of the sentence was drowned in a sudden outburst of flaming timber and people smashing into pots and pans as they scrambled through the kitchen, trying to get to the back door. Some people made it, others were too scared to move.

The cat's jaws were only inches away from the waitress's leg. She held him off as best she could, only faintly aware that she was screaming. The cat's eyes were locked on her. Then he lunged forward, clawing and biting into her stomach just below the pink cups of her bra.

The waitress fell back, rolled over and collapsed onto the floor, face up. Her breath came in ragged gasps as a sharp pain ripped through her belly. She knew the cat had torn her open, and when she heard the heavy creak of the floorboards she knew the cat wasn't finished with her yet.

The cat looked at her, cocking its head to stare with one enormous green eye. Blood dripped freely from its jaws. Then it snapped its head in one swift motion and began dragging her across the floor. The horror of what was to come caused her to gag, then vomit.

The world tilted crazily as the cat lifted her by the leg, letting her dangle upside down. Then came the sickening fall, and her stomach heaved again.

But suddenly the cat had had enough.

He drew back, turned and dashed through the flames out the back door heading for the mountains where snow-covered peaks awaited him.

Thirty minutes later, an unearthly quiet hung over San Rafael Hills. A row of body bags lined one side of the street. The sheriff stopped his car by two of his deputies and rolled down the window. "Any sign of him?"

The youngest deputy said, "Gone for good, I reckon." He gestured toward the mountains. His face was ashen.

"How many dead?" the sheriff asked.

"Five, and two hanging on."

The sheriff watched the EMS team as it loaded the last victim into the ambulance. Then he drove on.

18

HANK MARLEY ARRIVED at Meg's office just as the mayor began his news conference. Hank had flown his Cessna model 402 from San Diego to the Burbank Airport, then had taken a cab to the Los Angeles Zoo.

Now he and Meg focused on the TV, heard the mayor say a few words to the press corps, then watched him stare straight into the camera. Meg had been asleep on the couch when Ray called from Loma Linda at seven and told her to turn on the TV. She had found every local station plus CNN covering the story of Rajah and the attack in San Rafael Hills. Footage shot earlier, when men from the Sheriff's Department were lining up the bodies, was shown over and over, interrupted by commentary and up to the minute reactions from politicians and city officials.

The governor, the only state official who could call up the National Guard, had refused to take that step. Instead, he tossed the ball to the Office of Emergency Services, who quickly stated that Los Angeles County Animal Control was responsible for capturing or destroying all animals—wild or domestic—that posed a threat to humans outside the jurisdiction of the Department of Fish and Game.

County Animal Control, without consulting the mayor,

quickly asked the Sheriff's Department to lend a helping hand. The mayor became outraged when a spokesman for the Sheriff's Department came on TV and insinuated that the mayor was handing them a dirty job that nobody else could handle.

The usual and inevitable angry words and heated rhetoric flew back and forth.

For over an hour Meg sat glued to the TV. She heard no mention of the Department of Natural Resources and couldn't help wondering why. Foster had clearly stated that his department would be handling things from here on out, yet nowhere was it suggested that DNR was in any way involved.

Addressing his unseen audience, the mayor said, "As you know, Los Angeles County has suffered a terrible tragedy, and our hearts go out to the relatives and friends of the five people who died in the attack in San Rafael Hills. Assistance is already being provided by state and local agencies, although I know that nothing can undo the suffering that has been caused.

"Many of you have become alarmed, and that is understandable. There have been rumors of tiger sightings in almost every locality in Los Angeles County. Most of these rumors are false—I repeat, false—the product of excited imaginations. Latest information released by the California Highway Patrol places the tiger in the San Rafael foothills, from which he will not escape. Some of the finest authorities in animal search techniques are now at work on the best ways and means of containing the animal's movements.

"This they will do, I assure you. Therefore, I urge calm. I request all Los Angeles County residents not living in the San Rafael area to go about their daily lives without fear. I will expect to be telling you soon that Rajah is safely back in the Los Angeles Zoo.

"Thank you and good morning."

As the anchorwoman came back onto the screen, Hank Marley got to his feet. He was a tall man with thick, sandy brown hair and blue eyes, heavily crinkled at the corners. He was forty-seven, but in perfect physical condition. "Hell, I don't know," he said. "Rajah's behavior certainly isn't normal."

"What I don't understand," Meg said, "is why he left Griffith Park. Usually a mature male tiger claims about ten square miles for his territory. He had that, and plenty of water and wildlife to feed on. What would make him leave?"

"Panic, I guess." Hank lit a cigarette and filled his mouth with the taste of it, then said, exhaling, "I'll tell you one thing—he's not going to be easy to catch now."

Meg clicked off the TV and glanced at her watch. It was nine o'clock; she'd had no breakfast yet, only two cups of strong coffee. Outside, the day was dreary and cold. Thick dark clouds scudded southward, so low they seemed to skim the tops of buildings.

"It's strange," Meg said. "With all that I've told you, why do I keep coming back to Rajah's memory?"

Hank shrugged. "I don't know. With cats, I thought it was out of sight, out of mind."

"I'm not so sure." Meg moved closer to the window and gazed out. "After Rajah broke loose from the compound, he headed straight for the back gate, as if he knew exactly where he was going. Now here's the strange part. The day he was delivered to the zoo, that's the same gate he came through. I remember we stopped there for a long time, waiting while the other tigers were caged. That was over two years ago."

"Could be coincidence."

"Could be. But then we came through San Rafael Hills on the way to the zoo that day too. Is that also coincidence?"

Hank sighed. "Long-term memory in a cat? I've never seen any evidence of it."

Meg turned from the window and gave him a long, hard stare. "What if we make an assumption—some would call it a huge, ridiculous assumption—but for the sake of argument, let's say Rajah does have long-term memory. Then he just might be heading somewhere, right? I mean, he might have a particular destination in mind. If so, where?"

"Are you seriously asking me where a tiger on the loose is heading? Heck, that's like asking me where this country is heading." Hank smiled, then looked at Meg curiously when he saw the serious look on her face.

"Well, hell," Hank said. "That shouldn't be so hard to figure out. Of course, that's assuming Rajah does have a particular destination in mind."

"You think?" Meg felt her spirits lift. In Hank she had the perfect partner for brainstorming, and suddenly the situation seemed more hopeful. "Wait a minute, I'll get the map."

The closet was cluttered, but Meg quickly found the material she'd ordered from the U.S. Department of the Interior, grabbed the poster-thick scroll, and spread the map out on her desk. Hank pulled a chair over and sat next to her, a coffee mug in his hand.

"This is the best the U.S. Geological Survey ever made," Meg said. "It was taken from satellite imaging systems and reproduced by electronic printers. The accuracy is within inches; depending, of course, on how much the earth's crust has shifted since the last printing."

Hank ran his finger from Griffith Park in the lower left-hand corner. Northeast about ten miles from the zoo he found San Rafael Hills. Then his finger inched over to the foothills of La Canada Flintridge.

"Well, this is only a guess," Hank said, "but so far he is

heading due east. Not in a straight line, mind you. Nevertheless, he is heading in an easterly direction."

"La Canada Flintridge?" Meg drew closer.

Hank nodded. "The gateway to the San Gabriel mountain range in Angeles National Forest. There's a lot of snow up there, plenty of food and water, and not many humans this time of year. The San Gabriel Mountains, that's my guess as to where he's headed."

Meg's eyes widened with excitement. "Fantastic! Now why hadn't I thought of that?"

Hank chuckled. "Oh, I don't know. It's not like you've been distracted or anything."

Meg studied the elevation markings. The recent lowest altitude for measurable snowfall had to be about five thousand feet above sea level. By the time the new storm moved into the mountains, the snow ridge would drop to four thousand, maybe lower.

Rajah could easily find shelter during the day, and have plenty of game to hunt at night. It was, to Meg's way of thinking, the first ray of hope she'd seen in days.

She turned to Hank. "If they find him, Hank, they're going to kill him on sight. The mayor was lying when he said they wanted to capture him safely. They're not going to show him one bit of mercy."

Meg had barely gotten the words out when someone knocked on her door. "Come in."

She didn't recognize the man who opened the door, and despite his professional, even friendly, appearance, she sensed this visit was not good news.

"Dr. Brewster?" the man said.

Meg cleared her throat. "Yes?"

"My name is Donald Newhouse. I'm deputy warden with the Department of Natural Resources. May I come in?"

Meg drew a deep breath. She looked around as if for some means of escape, then resignedly faced the warden. "Of course, please come in."

As he opened the door wider, Meg saw two state troopers standing behind him in the hallway. Strapped to their legs, which were huge, thighs and all, were holstered handguns. The trio entered the room together.

"I've come for your records, Dr. Brewster. Mr. Foster has instructed me—"

"But I specifically told him I'd call him this morning," Meg interrupted.

"It is well into the morning," the warden said bluntly, "and you hadn't called. Therefore, Mr. Foster has sent me here personally to secure your records."

"Secure?" Meg wondered aloud.

"Court order," one of the troopers said in a hoarse, deep voice. Meg knew the tone was meant to signal authority, and failing that, virility. He advanced and handed her the written order.

"All my files?" Meg asked.

"Everything," the warden said. "We are instructed to seal them. Someone will be by shortly to remove them from the premises."

Hank Marley said, "Meg, I'll, uh—I'll take a look at the mandrill now. If you need me, just holler."

"All right," Meg said, staring at the court order. She felt herself abandoned. Betrayed. Not by Hank, of course. She knew he had left the room because it hurt him to see her suffer such an indignity. It was obvious they were going to show her no mercy—that they planned to disarm and discredit her in any way possible.

As the door closed, Meg glanced at the warden, who seemed unperturbed by her predicament. The two troopers stood like statues, unseeing, intimidating.

"You are treating me like a criminal, you know that," Meg said, pumped up with outrage. "I am responsible for two thousand animals, Mr. Newhouse. Not just one tiger."

"Exactly," replied the warden. "That's why it should be a relief to rid yourself of this nuisance."

Meg moved behind her desk and sat down. Her leather chair swiveled from side to side, an outward indication of the anger Meg felt inside. "All right," she said, rolling up the map. "There are my files. Be my guest."

Meg watched them as they silently marched over to the filing cabinets. They were just affixing the first seal when the phone rang. She picked it up before it could ring a second time. "Hello?"

It was David. He sounded agitated, and in a great hurry. "Meg, we have to talk. It's important. Stan—"

"Not now, David." Meg swirled her chair around, away from the three men.

"Christ, Meg, will you listen to me?"

"*Not now,*" Meg said, emphasizing both words. "Are you at home?"

"No, I'm not at the apartment—"

"Give me your number. I'll call you back."

Meg quickly jotted the number on a pad and hung up. When she turned she saw the warden staring at her curiously. "My broker," she said. Then she said, "Well, Mr. Newhouse, if you'll excuse me, I have a zoo to care for."

Outside, the air felt crisp and cold, a relief after almost eight hours of being cooped up in a stuffy office. Halfway up the walkway, Meg plunked loose change into a pay phone and dialed.

"Hello, Meg?" David said in a rush. "Listen, I've got to see you right away."

Meg paused. "David, you're incredible. I can't stop my life every time you call. Rajah has broken free of Griffith

Park. Did you know that? And right now I've got two state troopers and the deputy warden of the Department of Natural Resources padlocking my damn files!"

"Oh Jesus," David groaned. "Meg, listen, we *really* need to talk. Not over the phone. And I can't come there, it's too dangerous. I'll be at the La Brea Tar Pits at one o'clock. If you know what's good for you, you'll be there."

"David, I—"

The line went dead.

"David?"

Meg slowly hung up the phone. As she headed down the path, a pair of gibbons, who normally would be asleep, shrieked from the edge of their compound, baring their fangs.

Meg jumped in fear. It had been a long time since any animal had startled her like that. Not a good sign. If she was going to get through this, she thought, she would have to stay calm.

19

B Y ELEVEN O'CLOCK that morning, dark gray clouds had once again descended on Los Angeles. Across the street from the Shindlers' house, a few neighbors stood and gaped at the gutted ruins. The front lawn was cluttered with debris, and a tangle of wiring hung limply from a nearby telephone pole.

A large unmarked sedan was parked near the driveway. Light vibrated off the windshield. As Dragleman approached, the passenger door swung open and Tim Howland, chief investigator for the LAPD Arson Squad, got out.

"Neat," Dragleman said.

"What's neat?" Howland's face was set in hard, no-nonsense lines.

"You, Tim. You look like you just stepped out of a bandbox or something." Dragleman gestured at Howland's dark brown suit and conservative necktie.

"Out of church, Dan. It's Sunday, remember?"

Tim Howland was a big-boned man, age fifty, gray-eyed, with black hair and a pale face. An impatient pale face. "What kept you? You said ten-thirty."

"Traffic was a mess."

"Hell, people are acting crazy with that cat on the loose. You're handling the first mauling, aren't you? I hear Carol Lewis was a pretty thing."

"She wasn't when I last looked."

"I'll bet." Howland turned to his driver. "Call my wife. Tell her I should be there within the hour."

The driver nodded, and Dragleman and Howland ducked under the yellow police tape that sealed off the area and approached the house. They didn't have to open the garage door, it was a heap of splinters in the driveway.

Howland stared at Shindler's charred BMW. "The way I heard it, the flames shot up from the car's open window," he said to Dragleman. "The side door of the garage was left open, causing a draft. The flames hit the ceiling and headed for the open door. That's why this side of the house went up so fast, and the car's gas tank didn't blow. The flames were immediately sucked up and out. Still, it would make one hell of a commercial for BMW. 'We burn but we don't blow.' "

Dragleman looked into the burnt-out car, visualizing Shindler sitting behind the wheel. He noticed that the key was still in the ignition. He was working now, stirred by the sense of a mystery waiting to be solved.

He looked around the garage's blackened interior, then at the light overhead, looking for some clue, some detail that would provide some hint as to what had happened here.

"And nothing's been touched so far, is that right, Tim?" he asked.

Howland nodded. "Right. Thorp and Fliegel are handling things. They've already done a preliminary check, but a special team is scheduled for tomorrow morning, first thing. What's this all about, anyway, Dan? Why are you so interested?"

"The Carol Lewis case," Dragleman said.

Howland didn't get it.

"I got a call last night. Somebody telling me I should come take a look. That maybe the two cases are one."

Howland still didn't get it. He said, "A dame gets careless and is eaten by a tiger. The doctor gets careless and burns himself up. What kind of connection is that?"

"Don't know until I look around," Dragleman said. He moved over to the side door, which was nothing more than a charred hole in the wall. He stepped through it and glanced around. There was a path running alongside the house, a few scorched bushes, and little else. When he returned to the garage he saw Howland glancing down forlornly at his dusty shoes, shaking his head.

"Hope I didn't take you away from anything important, Tim," he said.

"You did," Howland answered. "My mother-in-law's coming to Sunday dinner. Come to think of it, take your time."

Dragleman nodded, then went around to check out Mrs. Shindler's Buick. It was still in fairly good condition considering the intensity of the blaze. Probably because it was an old-timer, he thought. They had paint jobs hard as cement back in those days. Steel bodies, too. He walked around the car slowly. Lying on the ground by the rear tire was a piece of cloth. He crouched. Using the tip of his pen he gently lifted it into the air and brought it up to his nose and sniffed.

"What have you got?" Howland asked, picking his way through the soot and debris.

"Don't know, but I'd definitely check it out if I were you."

Howland's face tensed. "No doubt about that. First thing."

"Tomorrow morning, I know." Dragleman dropped the rag where he'd found it, then straightened. "In the meantime, Tim, there's a whole lot here doesn't make sense."

"Like what?" Howland sneezed once, and again, and then again.

"Well, for starters, why is Shindler's key still in the ignition? A guy pulls into his garage, shuts off the engine, and usually removes his key."

"Hey, he's listening to the radio maybe. Ever think of that? He lights a cigarette and sits there enjoying the music. Or maybe a news program. He relaxes. And while he relaxes he falls asleep." Howland shrugged. "Hell, Dan, it's happened to me. I just didn't get burned up."

"It was pretty cold out Friday night," Dragleman continued, still following his initial train of thought. "Raining, too."

Howland looked at him strangely. "What does that have to do with anything?"

Dragleman pointed to the BMW. "I notice that the window on the driver's side is down. Kind of strange, don't you think? Cold, rainy night. The garage must have been damp. So why sit around with the window down?"

"Maybe he wanted to let the smoke out." Howland glanced at his shoes again. "Jesus! Why'd you drag me over here, Dan? To talk keys and open windows? Somebody puts a bug in your ear and my day off gets ruined?" He shook his head, then stepped gingerly away from a puddle of black, slimy water. "Why'd you pick me to call, anyhow?"

"Because I know *who* to call. This is real crap, and you're the only one I can count on to launch a full-scale investigation."

"Ah, give me a break." Howland waved a hand in the air as if shooing away a pesky insect. "There's nothing here to investigate. The guy simply got careless, that's all. It happens all the time. Like I told you, Thorp and Fliegel were here nosing around. They didn't see any signs of arson, or they would have filed a report."

"Maybe they didn't look close enough," Dragleman suggested.

Howland wheeled around. "Hey, you listen. They're both damn good cops. Been with the force—"

"Why are you getting so upset?"

Tim Howland's eyes narrowed ever so briefly. For a split second, his anger threatened to get out of control, flashing briefly in his eyes. "You want to know why I'm pissed off? You really want to know? Because suddenly I get the feeling you're telling my department how to do its job!"

Dragleman waited a second until Howland cooled down. Then he said, "What about the side door to the garage being left open? You figure Shindler opened it before or after he decided to listen to the radio?" Dragleman quickly went over to the BMW and peered in. "By the way, anyone check the radio?"

"Check it?"

"Yes, if Shindler was listening to the radio when he fell asleep, it would still be switched on."

Dragleman looked to Howland, who was getting angrier by the second.

"No," Howland said, and sneezed. "Until you showed up, nobody suspected anything. At least not that I'm aware of."

"Sorry to ruin your day off, Tim."

Howland paused for some moments, staring at the side door. He was a stubborn man, but he was also a damned good cop. The fact that he had personally come to the scene instead of sending a flunky meant that, day off or not, he cared. He also knew Dragleman was in need of his services. Bel Air was out of Dragleman's district, and without Howland's help he would get little or no cooperation. This was the sheriff's territory, and the sheriff wasn't known for sharing information with the LAPD.

Howland turned suddenly, startling Dragleman. "And you really think somebody torched this guy? That's what you're telling me?"

Dragleman shrugged. "All I'm saying is that I got a call—maybe a crackpot, maybe not—telling me to check this scene out, that there could be something odd going on. And from what I see here, I think there are enough unanswered questions to justify a full and thorough investigation of possible arson and possible murder. But I'm not the inspector, you are."

Dragleman's eyes drifted again to the ceiling. The overhead light bulb had blown from the heat, but that wasn't what caught his eye. He could see the grooved threads of the bulb stem sticking out from the metal socket.

He climbed onto the bumper of the BMW and looked closer. The bulb had been screwed halfway out of the socket.

"What are you looking at now?" Howland stood below him, looking up.

"The way this bulb is unscrewed. You figure the fire could have caused this to happen?"

Howland sighed. His eyes, which were animated a minute before, went dull. "Not really," he said.

"Right," Dragleman said, and climbed down. "Anyway, I appreciate you letting me nose around, Tim. If you turn up anything, let me know."

Howland gave him a look of resignation.

Outside, Dragleman stopped to stare down at the blood-soaked spot in the driveway, visualizing Mrs. Shindler lying there, and imagining, with a shudder, the panic she must have felt just before she jumped. As always, the thought of the fear, and then the death, made him feel sick, and he moved on.

20

THE EDGE OF THE STREET blurred and fell away. To the east, black thunderheads loomed on the horizon. Despite the approaching storm, or perhaps because of it, traffic was snarled. The crosswalks were even worse.

Meg's Jeep caused pedestrians to scatter as she drove past the Museum of Art, then past the George C. Page Museum, which housed artifacts ranging in age from nine thousand to forty thousand years old. Breaking free of traffic, she looped around the building and parked in the Rancho La Brea parking lot on Curson Street.

As she strolled up the walkway to the museum, she glanced down at the perfect reproductions of woolly mammoths, mother and child, struggling up from the sticky goo of the La Brea Tar Pits. As any schoolkid knew, no mammoth had ever escaped the tar pits alive.

Miserable, shaking off the January chill, Meg came to an abrupt stop behind a large crowd of people. The entrance to the museum was mobbed: impatient kids in green jackets with dinosaurs on them, shapeless women in billowing coats, grumbling men—hunched, swaying, all trying to get through the door first. Over their bobbing shoulders Meg caught sight of David.

He was standing just inside the double glass doors, studying a list of scheduled lectures and temporary exhibits that would soon be on display. His back was to her, but there was no mistaking David for another man. Not ever, then or now. His broadly framed shoulders hung in the air like the center beam of a tall building. Strong arms curved back, hands tucked in the back pockets of his jeans. A fisherman's sweater, leather jacket, and cowboy boots.

No question about it, Meg thought, the man was decidedly handsome.

After checking his watch, David turned and spotted Meg on the first pass. She waved, and he flashed his biggest smile.

"Right on time," he said as she came through the doors.

Meg tried to return the smile. Please, God, make this as easy as possible, she thought. She couldn't bear another fight with him.

In silence they walked to the glass-covered table in the center of the main room. Beneath the glass, bones and teeth lay neatly arranged on black velvet.

" 'Dire wolf,' " David read, feigning interest. "Long teeth for a dog. Wouldn't you say?" He glanced sideways at the double glass doors.

"Did you ever wonder why the extinct creatures are the ones with the sharpest teeth and biggest bodies?" Meg murmured. "While we humans, puny, sickly animals, continue to exist. Could it be that we are just too devious to be killed off?"

The uneasy chuckle that had risen between them died, and David cleared his throat. "I know this isn't easy for you," he said.

"No, it isn't, but I'm here," Meg replied.

David glanced at the doors again, then took her arm and guided her to a bench in the corner.

His smile disappeared as they sat. Meg knew the look.

She could read his mind like a road map, as he could read hers. They had always been able to understand each other too easily and too well. A little deception was, perhaps, good for a marriage.

Getting right to the point, he said, "Someone threatened Stan's life last night, Meg. Hell, Stan laughed it off. But this morning I found his apartment torn up. His car was still in the driveway, but I couldn't find him anywhere."

"Threatened his life?" Meg repeated slowly. "Does it have anything to do with HAATE?"

"Anything is possible. Stan knows a lot. Too much, actually. You remember what he told you about Rajah?"

Meg nodded. "About Midway, the experimentation . . ."

"He knows a hell of a lot more than that, let me tell you."

Meg scrutinized David now, seeing, perhaps for the first time, a genuine fear in his eyes. There was also uncertainty, because whenever he was unsure of himself, his hands would creep into his pockets and stay there. "So what are you saying? That you actually believe somebody made good on his threat?"

David laughed nervously. "Hell, Meg, there's no thinking about it. The sheets on Stan's bed were blood-soaked. Someone worked him over bad. Either that, or they killed him, and then removed the body from the apartment."

"Did you call the police?"

"Not yet, but that's not the point. You have to walk away from all this, Meg. While you still have the chance. Take a vacation. By the time you get back, all of this will have blown over."

Meg took a deep breath, felt an odd current course through her body, and said, "Are you walking away, David?"

"I can stay in the background, you can't. They're watching you. I know these people. They are powerful and they are ruthless. They're not going to stop until the situation is contained. If you get in their way, Meg, you're going to get hurt."

Meg hesitated. The air seemed dry, dusty, filled with too many people crowded together. Stifling. "You mean . . . you actually know who *they* are, David?"

David took a deep breath but did not respond.

"Friday night," Meg pressed. "You told me Roueche and Ellroy *might* be involved. Are they? Or does it go higher? Is the Department of Natural Resources involved?"

He looked at her for a moment, then sighed. "Ah hell," he said, standing, then crossing back to the display case. He was obviously frustrated, Meg could sense that. He seemed to be trying to control a situation that had gotten out of hand.

Instinctively, she got up and went to him, slipping her arm into his. "David, listen, I know you're worried about Stan, but—"

"I don't give a damn about him," David stated bluntly. "It's you I'm worried about."

"Then why won't you tell me who is causing all the trouble?"

David turned suddenly, breaking off their embrace. From the glass doors, shrieks of youthful laughter reached into the room. People of all ages, their inhibitions dulled by forty thousand years of artifacts, were standing in the middle of the marble floor. How strange it all seemed! Four men stood laughing and pointing at a large mural. A teacher stood seven or eight feet away, her pupils gathered around her, as if they were her little flock. Meg's heart was suddenly beating at a good clip.

"Christ," David said, "you're not going to listen to me, you're not going to let go of this, are you?"

Meg said, "Not until I find out what is going on. Ellroy could hardly speak last night. Today, he and Roueche were nowhere to be found. Why, David?"

Without answering, he slipped an arm around her shoulder and bent to put his cheek against hers. "I'll make a deal with you," he said. "You go away. I'll go with you. We'll call it a postmarriage reunion. Separate rooms, if you like. Separate dining arrangements, if you insist." A grin played around his lips, then he became serious, his face darkening. "But don't ask me to put you in danger. I can't tell you any more."

"Why? Because you don't know, or because you won't tell me?"

David's hands slid into his pockets again, and he leaned away. His face was expressionless.

"Fine," Meg said. "But I'm staying right here in L.A. By now Rajah is holed up somewhere, exhausted. They'll never be able to find him in this weather. In the meantime . . ."

"Don't tell me you're actually thinking of looking for him yourself!"

"It's crossed my mind."

He looked at her sharply. "Why are you being so pig-headed?"

"Because my entire career is on the line. They've impounded my records. They're trying to dismiss Rajah's actions as 'just another cat who hates being in a cage.' For God's sake, David, we're talking about a girl's death. Rajah stalked her and killed her, and to do it, he jumped a wall he shouldn't have been able to mount. What he did should be impossible! That's how deep his aggressive drive goes, but they make a point of saying I'm the only one who believes this so-called aggression is actually a factor. Either I'm nuts or they're setting me up. You yourself warned me of that Friday night."

"Listen to me, Meg, leave it alone and you'll be okay. Once they have Rajah, they'll fade into the sunset. Publicity is the last thing they want."

Meg made an effort to remain calm. "I don't believe that, David. And I'm sure you don't believe that either. Besides, Harry Shindler was a friend of mine. A friend of *ours,* and if they were responsible for his death, I have a right to know."

David looked at her in surprise. "I never mentioned Shindler."

"You didn't have to. It's obvious, isn't it? First Shindler dies; now suddenly Stan is missing. Apparently, anyone connected with Rajah seems to be in danger. Isn't that why you're so worried about me?"

When David did not respond, Meg said, "Names, David. Are you going to give them to me or not?"

This time David looked away. Meg could see the muscles in his jaw tightening, could sense the tension throughout his body. Without looking at her, he answered, his voice hollow: "No."

"Well, then . . . that's that."

Once again they had reached an impasse. It seemed that neither time nor distance had brought them any closer to a true understanding of each other, and Meg felt sorrow rise in her, felt the last of their relationship crumble.

Commitment was something David had always lacked. Perhaps it was because of some old childhood battle he was still waging. Or perhaps it was simple fear of a new adversary, Meg wasn't sure.

As she started to walk away, he grabbed her arm. "You're acting insane, do you know that? What are you trying to do, get yourself killed?"

Meg remained silent, unflinching.

"Meg—how can I protect you unless you let me?"

"You can't, David," she said slowly. "I'll just have to protect myself."

As Meg moved away, David said, "Please, Meg. Call me! I really do want to help."

Meg nodded, and kept on walking. She still didn't know who *they* were, or what they were up to. Or whether or not Roueche was involved.

She decided to find out.

21

THE WIND ROSE, approached silently, and as it reached the tiger, he sniffed. It was a cold wind, the kind that kills. The kind that drives most beasts to shelter. But shelter was the last thing on his mind.

The cat, driven by hunger, urged his massive body forward. Behind him, in the west, lay the town where he had had to abandon his kill because of fire. The loose food that he had found, the dead food he had eaten had given him little sustenance, and the desire for a fresh kill pulsated through him as one beat, one purpose, one thought.

Suddenly he pressed his nose to the ground, searching for any telltale sign or scent that an animal suitable for killing and eating was close by.

There was still some daylight left, but already the temperature had dropped below freezing. The cold made his legs stiff, his muscles less limber. Because of his long period of captivity in the zoo, he had become unaccustomed to the biting cold.

Now he moved carefully along the riverbank, keeping beneath the trees and the snow-covered bushes. The ice-scape of the riverbank was a fractured expanse of jagged peaks and sloping crevices drifted with snow, and footing grew steadily more treacherous. The snow mounds were steep, the troughs between them less stable.

He stumbled, sank into the frozen whiteness, then hauled himself up onto an ice-covered ledge and was still. A small movement, far ahead and to his left, had caught his attention. The cat slowly swiveled his head.

A deer was there, at the edge of a grove of hemlock. With wide rack, bull neck, and heavy shoulders, it stared at the tiger. The tiger remained still, a fixed part of the landscape.

The deer pawed at the snow and tossed its head up and down. Then it came forward, down the slight incline, heading to the river for a drink of water.

Suddenly the cat sprang. His teeth sank into the deer's throat. Blood splattered the snow as the cat tore open the deer's neck, slammed its body to the ground. Limbs convulsed, quivered. Claws tore into flesh.

The deer's eyes remained open even in death. An image of horror and surprise shone there as the cat dug deep into the body to get to the vital organs. He ate liver, kidneys, entrails, and still he was hungry. He chewed on flanks, shredding and gutting the deer. And still he was hungry.

And then he heard them. The humans. They were high above him on the ridge. He rose up, sniffed.

Then he started upward toward them.

"YOU BASTARD!" the woman cried and slammed the car door closed, the sound echoing in the canyon. For a moment she kicked at the snow with her boot, a pretty woman of twenty-four with sandy hair and enormous blue eyes that, for the moment, were ablaze with anger.

Her boss, sitting behind the wheel of his new Honda, rolled down his window. So far his plans had been running along smoothly, so goddamned smoothly, and now *she* was going to spoil everything. Nervous energy erupted and flooded through him, gripping his face with jaw-aching pressure.

"Joan, get back in the car," he said, feeling the sudden chill rush through the window.

"No," the woman pouted. "How could you do such a stupid thing? Tell him something like that?"

The man sighed and glanced through the windshield. A light snow had begun to fall, and this made him nervous as well. Why was she acting so innocent? he thought. After all, it was the sort of thing they had done before, only in better weather.

Earlier that day, he had strolled into his office and grinned at the young woman who had taken over his desk these past three weeks. "I feel in one of *those* moods," he had said, using his charm.

"What sort of mood, Mr. Keyes?"

Mr. Keyes, he repeated silently, cursing the respectful tone in her voice that reminded him he was twenty years older than the woman whose gorgeously manicured fingernails were poised over the computer keyboard. She was a dedicated employee, conscientious, and he cursed that, too.

"Why, to get the hell out of here," he said. "It's Sunday. I know we're facing a deadline—"

"Well," she interrupted, "go right ahead. If Mr. Wallace calls back, I'll say you're in a meeting. And I certainly can finish this report by myself."

But that wasn't what he had in mind. He had started to talk very fast, very buddy-buddy, and as a result, two and a half hours later they were in the mountains. He was claiming that somehow he had gotten lost.

"I don't know what my boyfriend is going to think,"

Joan had said, looking at her gold-chain wristwatch for the fifth time in five minutes.

"Chuck will understand," Bob Keyes said matter-of-factly. "Before we left, I called him. Told him you'd be working most of the night."

"Why?" she asked, failing to recognize his empty prattle for what it was.

So he felt compelled to tell her the whole truth. How he had rented a cabin for the evening; nice place, fully stocked, liquor, food—fireplace and plenty of wood. How he knew she was attracted to him, had been all along. Each little outing they had taken together had, in some way, confirmed the fact that she was secretly in love with him. He knew it, she knew it, and now her boyfriend knew it too, because he had made sure that the lad had gotten the message.

Bob Keyes's face relaxed now. He removed the key from the ignition and got out and stood beside her. He put his arm around her and stroked her side. It was warm, or rather his hand was cold; all of him was cold, he discovered, now that he realized she was crying.

He stood still for a moment, waiting for the tears to subside. "Christ, Joan, why are you crying?" he asked her gently.

She caught her breath in a long choking gasp. "Because . . . you had no right to call Chuck like that. He's going to think this was my idea. That all those nights we worked late together . . ." She broke off and wiped tears from her eyes. "What made you do such a thing?"

Bob Keyes shrugged. "It's just . . . the way you always seemed to want to be with me. The things you said. The way you acted. I just thought . . ." He glanced up when a snowflake struck his forehead. "Look, let's talk in the car. It's cold as hell out here."

He felt her body stiffen against his, briefly, before she pulled away. "I hate you for doing this," she whispered. "Dammit, I really hate you."

He didn't move as she climbed back into the car.

How long he stood there, Joan Collier wasn't sure. All she knew for certain was that she *did* hate him, and that the sooner they got back to town the sooner she could call Chuck and straighten things out.

But Bob Keyes wasn't moving. He stood shivering, his hair and the shoulders of his blue suit covered with a fine layer of snow. It would be the way she would remember him. The image of him standing alone, an ice statue in the wilderness, just before she heard the roar.

Her heart leapt into her throat as something large and inhuman sprang from a boulder onto his back. Her first panicky thought, like a child having a nightmare, was *monster,* and she looked around wildly. There was nothing to see but snow flying everywhere.

When she heard Bob Keyes scream, she instinctively lurched toward the window and rolled it up. Outside everything wavered, started to break up. She tried to hold on to the image of Keyes still standing there, tried not to see the other images: blood splattering off trees, Bob kicking and waving his arms and fists and howling like a dog and then screaming in terror. The maddened green eyes, fangs—and the blood.

All over the snow now.

Unable to watch any longer, she ducked down in the seat and clapped her hands to her face, harrowing her cheeks with her fingernails, listening to the snorts and snaps of teeth on air, the uncanny sound as it separated itself from the wind in the trees, breath chuffing across a huge hanging tongue, roars of murderous excitement.

Bob was still screaming.

CLAW

He would not stop.

And she imagined him still standing there, the shock not allowing her to comprehend as the sound of flesh being fanged and the smell of death drifted into the car.

Yes, Bob Keyes was still standing there, she thought. And then she lost consciousness.

22

A MONKEY HOWLED in the distance, its cry shattering the silence.

Meg looked up. Above a crow flew in a short arc over the zoo, wings curved against the dark sky. She drew back in her place of concealment, and glanced again at the administration building. The hulking structure was dark. The cleanup crew had turned the last of the lights off around nine o'clock.

Ten minutes had passed, and still Meg hadn't moved. She'd been tempted to forget the whole idea, and then shook her head. No, dammit! She had to know if Roueche was involved.

She waited a second longer, then moved to the front door of the building. Slipping the key into the lock, she stepped inside and quickly closed the door.

She stood still for a moment, staring at the deserted office, trying to be calm. There were no sounds to be heard, no movement to be seen. And there was no light. She mustn't turn on her flashlight, she reminded herself. At least not yet. She would have to let memory guide her.

Refusing to succumb to panic, she moved down the hallway and, after a brief struggle with the keys, opened Roueche's door. She moved quickly through the outer office to the larger one beyond. She knew when and where security made its rounds. But security had been tightened—Roueche's orders—and new guards had been posted throughout the grounds, so she had to remain alert.

After drawing the drapes over the window, she turned on her flashlight and looked around.

Roueche was a fastidious man, a tendency reflected in the way his office was kept. The top of his polished mahogany desk was empty of the usual papers an executive normally left behind. No crammed In and Out baskets. Nothing but a sleek, oversized black blotter with gold trim and an expensive gold pen in an equally expensive gold holder. Even the filing cabinets were recessed into the wall, their oak drawers matching the oak paneling around them.

Meg's flashlight beam crisscrossed the room and found the bookcase recessed into the north wall in which she knew the books were carefully arranged by subject, and then further arranged alphabetically by author.

Meg hardly knew where to begin, hardly even knew what she was looking for. Something, anything, that could shed some light on what was going on.

She started with Roueche's desk. None of the drawers were locked. None contained anything of importance. Recent animal-purchase orders. Contact sheets with other curators around the country. Progress reports, and little else.

Now, as Meg gazed into the lower left-hand drawer, the last one to be opened, the only thought that made her the slightest bit suspicious was the fact that the desk contained not one scrap of anything personal. It was as if it were merely there as show, not tell. There wasn't even the customary Rolodex.

Meg pushed the drawer closed and glanced at the filing cabinets. She knew from past experience that the cabinets weren't locked either. Susan Blake, Roueche's secretary, was too lackadaisical for that.

Meg had barely gotten the first drawer open when she turned with a start. A resonant thumping issued from the vent above the window, heralding the coming of heat. A loud gush of air hissed through the vent. Shivering, she glanced at her watch. She still had forty-five minutes before security made its next rounds.

She quickened her pace, flipping through files, and then whole drawers, which contained case histories of all the animals Roueche had procured: tigers, eland, howling monkeys—hundreds of exotic animals from lands most people never heard of, much less visited. The metal vent began to vibrate as heat rushed through it. Outside, Meg could hear that the wind had picked up. Tree branches tapped against the window. Or was it tree branches? She shined the light around the dark room, wishing she could see what was going on outside. But she knew she couldn't risk opening the drapes.

When she got to the last file cabinet, she pulled at the top drawer, but it wouldn't open. She tried the next drawer, and the next.

Nothing. They were all locked.

She glanced at her watch. She had perhaps fifteen minutes left, no more. Suddenly Meg was suffering an acute anxiety attack. That one cabinet alone was locked was enough to arouse her suspicions. Looking closer, she realized that all the other cabinets were clearly labeled. The face plates on this one were blank.

Without further hesitation, she took a letter opener from the desk, shoved it between the top drawer and the wood frame, and pushed. The drawer popped open with a tiny click. Dust that had settled between the cracks rose, and a single screw fell to the floor.

Looking in, Meg was astonished to see that the drawer

contained a wild assortment of medications: Demerol, suc-
cinylcholine, Innovar—some containers half empty, others
yet to be opened. Among the many varieties was a carton of
unopened morphine bottles, tape, plastic tubing, and sy-
ringes.

Meg quickly closed the drawer and opened the next. It
was empty, except for two odd-looking files tucked away
in the back. Opening the first accordion-type packet, she
saw a dozen handwritten memos and several letters ad-
dressed to Roueche. She laid the entire contents on the desk,
pointed the flashlight down, and began to read.

Most of the memos were from Midway Quarantine in
San Francisco, confirming Rajah's release date. Others were
from a variety of sources, explaining the delay of that release. Meg had barely begun reading the last one, dated
1989, when she stopped suddenly. Before her eyes was the
name Shindler.

But Meg clearly recalled Roueche saying to Ellroy the
night of Carol's death: "I don't know Dr. Shindler personally."

Yet here was a memo that stated Roueche should *again* go
through Dr. Shindler for all pertinent data, that they had
worked well together in the past and that all problems could
and would be resolved. A memo written five years earlier!

Next was a letter from Howard Boss at INR in Washington, D.C., inviting Roueche to spend Thanksgiving
week with him in West Virginia. "It is most important you
accept my invitation," the letter stated. "All is going according to schedule. There are, however, a few details that
need ironing out." The letter was dated November 3, 1991,
one month prior to Rajah's release date from Midway.

Meg knew INR stood for the Bureau of Intelligence and
Research, and that INR was an agency within the State
Department. They were also linked to the Defense Depart-

ment, which, as far back as she could remember, had been involved in animal experimentation. According to a U.S. Department of Agriculture report, the Defense Department had used over 200,000 animals in experiments in less than five years; 30,000 were classified as "wild animals," species not given.

Hands trembling, Meg opened the last envelope and found a small, handwritten note. It was from a Dr. Auston, Head of the Albert Richter Institute, thanking Roueche for his services. The writing was a woman's; the stationery was blue and appeared expensive.

Meg glanced at her watch. She had run out of time, but still needed to check the second file. Opening it, she saw a smaller file—a thick wad of paper bound in brown cardboard. On the cover of the file was stenciled MANTIG, and underneath, an ominous note.

THIS FILE IS CLASSIFIED TOP SECRET
Examination by unauthorized persons is a criminal offense punishable by fines and imprisonment up to 20 years and $50,000.

Meg knew if the wrong person read the file, she or he would be in deep trouble. She hesitated, then opened it.

PROJECT: Mantig
AUTHORITY: State Department
CLASSIFICATION: TOP SECRET
SUBJECT: _____

Someone had taken a thick black marker and inked out the subject. Someone had also removed the first seven pages. Meg began to skim, hoping to make sense of the material. The print was small and the subject complex. Apparently project Mantig had something to do with neurons.

Somewhere in the middle of the file, she found a photo-graph showing six different slices of a rat's brain. She read below slice one: "Autoradiographic imaging of 3H-CDP-DAG accumulation of rat hippocampal slices."

Meg glanced at her watch again. Aware that she had exceeded her time limit, she quickly removed the autorad-iographic page, along with several others, and then moved back to the filing cabinet.

She would not recall later what had made her look up. Nor would she recall slipping the files back into the cabinet and opening the window. All she would remember was seeing the dark silhouette of a man standing outside Roueche's office, peering in through the glass frame.

Maybe she had heard his breathing, or a gun being cocked, she wasn't sure. Not that she had had time for contemplation.

By the time Meg heard the door crash open, she had hit the ground running. When she glanced back she saw the bushes still swaying below the window from which she had jumped. As the man came to the window, she darted to her left and pressed herself against the building.

A pale moon had inched its way into the sky, allowing Meg some sense of her surroundings. She looked over at the security station. It contained a lone man. He was leaning back in his chair with his feet up, reading a newspaper. Two security guards were strolling up the walkway; they were talking loudly, but they didn't seem to realize anything was wrong. With a loud bark of laughter, they disappeared over the rise, leaving the walkway deserted.

Meg waited a moment longer, sensing now that whoever was after her *wasn't* one of them. The thought rooted her to the spot. She pressed against the wall, eyes darting again to the security station. The worst thing, the absolute worst thing was to be immobilized by fear. Anything was better than that.

She bolted from her hiding place, forcing herself into action, running forty yards at top speed, then diving behind a tree. Short wait, heart beating wildly like a bird's. Another short burst as she retreated to the closest compound. She did not move fast enough, however. As she stepped over the low chain-link fence, she saw behind her a blur of sudden movement.

Coming at Meg with surprising speed appeared to be a man in a dark raincoat, his face gaunt in the moonlight, his lips frozen in a horrid half smile. Off to the side, another man quickly appeared. Two men now, not one. Both lunging.

Stifling a scream, Meg turned and dropped into the crocodile pit. She landed hard on the rocks below, but quickly got her bearings and began to run, thrashing through the murky shallow water. She heard a muffled groan behind her, followed by a loud thud as one of the men pursued her into the pit. Or had both men jumped in? She wasn't sure.

An instant later a crocodile's head rose out of the water, its horny skin glistening in the dim light from above. As Meg drew back, her legs buckled and she fell to one knee before pulling herself to safety on the other side of the stream. Terrified, she turned and saw the crocodile a few feet away from her. As it lunged, jaws snapping, she scrambled upward. Oh, dear God, I'm not going to make it, she thought, this momentary flash of fear giving her a jolt of energy that enabled her to break free.

Behind her she heard a man gasp, the sound of water being savagely thrashed. When she looked back she saw the crocodile dragging one of the men down, its jaws locked around his leg. The other man quickly placed a pistol with a silencer to the croc's head and pulled the trigger.

The crocodile released the man's leg, but before either man could recover, Meg had climbed the embankment and was running again. Animals shrieked as she ducked off the main path into a clump of bushes, plunging ahead through thick shrubs. Branches stabbed at her through her jacket, but the pain did not stop her; it drove her on.

Near the top of the rise she turned and glanced back. Behind her was only darkness. The lunatic cry of frightened baboons echoed in the distance. Overhead she heard a creak of wings and below water cascading over rocks on its way to the pond.

Meg quickly veered to her left and started toward the service road where she had parked the Jeep. The cold moon had risen high in the sky. It loomed through the pall and peered at her, then vanished.

In that brief moment of light, Meg stopped. Up ahead she had seen movement; swift, quivering. Then just as quickly she couldn't see it again. No, it could not have been them, she thought. The men who had chased her had seemed clumsy and slow. And one of them had been badly hurt. Surely they couldn't have gotten ahead of her.

Slowly she began circling the compound again, avoiding puddles of water on the distant side, and then turned toward the gate. The wind came in blasts from behind her now, chilling her spine.

When she saw the Jeep parked outside the gate, she nearly collapsed from relief. Perversely, the consolation didn't last. Whatever comfort she drew from the specific moment, there was a general misgiving. It occurred to her that the gate, which she had closed behind her, stood slightly ajar. As if someone had entered the grounds after she did.

She listened now, heard the sound of twigs snapping, someone coming closer, approaching. She turned, trying to get a fix on the sound; it might not be footsteps at all.

Standing beside the tallest pine on the crest of the hill, Meg listened and looked until her ears and eyes ached. Nothing. Silence.

She started to move again toward the fence, hearing her own footfall, listening for others.

Still she heard nothing.

Relief. She had imagined it all.

And then she heard one of the men coming, fast. As the bushes behind her broke open, she started to run. Suddenly a hand with an iron grip grabbed her right arm and yanked her back.

Meg's heart nearly stopped altogether. Frantically, she struck out at the man, flailing with her one free arm and both legs.

After the first wild fit of terror, Meg fought instinctually and brutally. Her fingers groped for eyeballs, for kidneys, for all the weak spots—but in the darkness she got only elbows and muscular shoulders. When she kneed him savagely in the crotch, he groaned and doubled over. The moment of freedom was all that she needed.

With a last burst of adrenaline, she raced toward the fence. She heard the metal latch of the gate catch behind her as she slammed it closed.

By the time it was opened again, Meg was safely in the Jeep, gravel shooting up from beneath the tires as she sped away.

23

TWENTY MINUTES LATER, Meg Brewster hurriedly ordered a hamburger and coffee at a North Hollywood diner. She was still wired with tension and tried not to show it. While the burger sizzled on the griddle, she ducked into the rest room and tidied herself up. She cleaned mud off her jacket and boots, combed her hair, and put on a light touch of lipstick. Then she went to the pay phone and called Ray. After seven or eight rings, she hung up. Apparently he still hadn't returned from Loma Linda.

Meg hesitated, considering whether or not to call Lieutenant Dragleman at LAPD's Northeast Division. On the one hand, she felt a need to get in touch with him, to tell him exactly what had happened. On the other hand, she knew that she'd just broken the law. No easy matter explaining that away, she thought.

Instead she dropped loose change into the slot and dialed her office. Hank Marley answered, sounding sleepy. Meg asked him how it was going.

"Fine, fine," he replied.

"Have there been any disturbances?" she asked, holding her breath.

"Not really, everything is quiet. The mandrill is doing fine, so is the baby tapir."

Meg sighed with relief. So whoever had attacked her was certainly *not* part of the zoo's security, or they would have identified her and the whole zoo would be alerted to it by now.

"Listen, Hank, I'm afraid I'm going to be tied up for a while. . . ."

"Take your time," Hank said.

"How long can I count on you helping me?"

"Well . . ." He hesitated. "I've already cleared tomorrow with my front office. And I'm sure another day on top of that won't ruffle their feathers."

"Hank, that's great. Listen, I'll keep checking in with you, okay? I really appreciate it. Oh, and that couch you're probably sitting on, it turns into a comfy bed."

"I figured that out already!" he said laughing.

He was still chuckling as Meg hung up the phone and quickly dialed the Research Department at UCLA.

"Dr. Shindler's records?" the security guard said.

"Yes," Meg said. "He was working on blood samples for me when—"

"That office has been sealed off," the guard interrupted. "A warden from the Department of Natural Resources left here about an hour ago. Nobody's allowed in, miss . . . uh, I'm sorry, I didn't catch your name."

"Banister. Ellen Banister," Meg said. "Well, thanks anyway." Before the guard could respond, she hung up.

Meg went back to her table. Her mind was racing fast, but, she knew, not half as fast as theirs; they were ten steps ahead of her now, and this lapse on her part angered her.

* * *

CLAW

Forty-five minutes later Meg brought the Jeep to a screeching halt in front of Gordon Ellroy's house, situated on two acres of prime Beverly Hills real estate along Benedict Canyon Drive. It was a two-level structure, in the California mission style. The ground-level walls, set forward, were whitewashed masonry draped with vines. The facade was relieved by pools of light emanating from fixtures hidden in the shrubbery below.

Meg climbed out of the Jeep and started up the stone walkway toward the main entrance. Sculpted rosebushes flanked the path to the iron gate.

She rang the doorbell and waited. The night was damp and cold, and she zipped up her jacket. Her hands and feet felt like blocks of ice.

After a moment, Joan Ellroy opened the elaborately hand-carved door. Yellow light poured out of the archway, framing her figure in half silhouette. Her short blond hair was brushed back, exposing her smooth, pale brow. She was wearing a long robe and bedroom slippers.

"Hello, Meg," she said. "Is something wrong?"

Meg drew a deep breath. "I'm sorry, Joan. I know it's a bit late, but I have to speak to Gordon."

"It's all right, come in." Joan pressed a button, releasing the gate, and together they went into the foyer. As Joan passed from darkness to light, Meg could see the stress in her face, the pallor, the dark crescents below her eyes, the anxiety behind the fixed gaze.

"I suppose we all know how crazy it's been," she said. "Gordon said he had no idea the viewing rail needed to be replaced. All those poor people. And now, more deaths." She ended in a long sigh, her elegant face as forlorn as a sad child's.

"I promise I won't stay long," Meg said.

"No, please. Stay as long as you like," Joan said. "It may

help Gordon to see you. He's so . . . well, it can't be helped, can it. I'm sure we'll get over this tragedy and go on . . . in time. But right now . . ."

The woman appeared ready to cry. Instead, her chin came up and her shoulders rose.

"Make yourself comfortable, won't you?" she said. "Gordon will be down shortly." She gathered the folds of her robe and turned to go. "In the meantime, I'll have Denise make a fresh pot of coffee."

As Joan disappeared toward the back of the house, Meg's anger was suddenly overwhelmed by compassion. Joan was a fragile woman, despite her family's millions. In New York, the name Percy was practically synonymous with money. It symbolized the dynasty of bankers which, along with the Rockefellers and the Morgans, at one time had held financial America in the palms of their hands. And when her mother had divorced her father, fifteen years before, it had been to marry into an equally eminent family, the Woodwards, holders of the last great gold-rush fortune. Joan was a proud society girl whose life had never been touched by scandal. Until now.

Her friends had most likely gone into hiding, Meg thought sadly as she entered a vast living room with rough-hewed beams spanning a forty-foot ceiling. Joan and Gordon Ellroy had always mixed with a fickle crowd, people who confused friendship with social alliance. A few had probably rushed to her side after Carol Lewis's death, offering their cautious support. But with the body count rising, those most certainly had gone into seclusion as well.

Meg glanced around. Two white-cushioned sofas held the center of the room. Ocher, rose, and faded orange dominated the hand-woven rugs, pillows, and large Aztec tapestry on the opposite wall. The rest of the furniture was an eclectic mix of the ornate and the primitive. Hung in ram-

bling clusters were Joan's own watercolors. They were re-
markably good, Meg thought, considering she'd only
started to paint a few years earlier.

"Beautiful, isn't it?"

Meg turned. Ellroy stood beneath the archway in rumpled shorts and an old Hawaiian shirt, a glass of bourbon in
his hand. He lumbered slowly into the room as he spoke,
bare feet shuffling, ice cubes tinkling in the amber liquor.

"All this beautiful crap, and my lawyers tell me I'm
screwed. First the victims go after the county. Class-action
suit worth maybe eighty . . . ninety million?" he said with
a droll smile. "Then they come after me. Some loophole in
the civil-service code. All bullshit—*reckless endangerment* or
gross neglect for the public safety or some other bullshit legal
crap, you know?"

Meg said nothing.

Ellroy's disposition turned suddenly mean. He planted
his heavy legs and slapped his chest hard. "*Me!* They're
going to sue *my* ass for everything I've got!"

"You'll get by," Meg said coldly. If Ellroy wanted to
wallow in drunken self-pity, he would certainly get no sympathy from her.

Now he laughed. His body swayed and jerked; a splash
of bourbon slapped to the floor.

"You don't get it, do you?" he tittered. "The lawyers,
Meg. Those bloodsucking whores are going to squeeze me
dry, see? Don't you think that's funny?"

"I didn't come here to talk lawsuits, Gordon."

"You're right. Forgive me," he said with mock courtesy.
"Dr. Brewster thinks she's off the hook. That she's as clean
as a whistle! So why the hell should you care if your boss
gets flushed down the toilet, right?"

"You're drunk, Gordon," Meg said. "Please be quiet and
sit down. That is, if you're capable of it."

Ellroy stood still, his eyes wide with surprise. He stared at her for a long moment, then said, "All right, Meg. Give me your best shot."

As he staggered over to the couch, Meg followed. He tried setting the glass on the table but couldn't quite make it. As he sat, bourbon splashed into his lap. "Oh, my," he sighed.

"I found the files, Gordon."

He stopped wiping himself and glanced up. His face, flushed a moment before, tightened to attention. "What files?" he asked, his voice suddenly sober.

"In Philip's office. He said he didn't know Harry Shindler, but his files show they worked together at Midway Quarantine. You knew that, but you didn't tell me."

"So?"

"Rajah was at Midway, and you know it," Meg said. "Now tell me what happened up there."

Ellroy finally managed to set his glass down. He rubbed his stubbled face, and as he did so, a peculiar expression rippled over it. "The first cat," he said, "the original cat, a gift from the Chinese government . . . he died. Intestinal infection. It happens. Only this time, some jerk from the State Department gets a hair up his ass. He says to Philip, 'Don't you know those Chinks still believe their tigers are sacred?' Like these cats are pagan gods, you see? Real touchy about it. And then he says, 'Don't you know important government officials have millions tied up in Beijing hotels?' As if this dead cat is going to start World War III or something."

Meg asked, "And Philip told you about this conversation?"

"I was there. I mean, he was on the phone to Washington in my office."

"Go on."

"Well, Philip tells the guy he'll take care of it. No one has to know, he says."

"Know what?"

"It took some doing, but he located a healthy male Siberian through a private foundation. Very close in appearance to the original cat. I said okay, and I signed the transfer documents. End of story."

He reached for his drink and swallowed it in one gulp. Then he looked straight ahead, his face as clean of blame as that of a bronze Buddha.

"No, Gordon," Meg said, "that is not the end of the story. What was the name of this *private* foundation?"

"Hell, I don't know," he muttered. "Some blueblood . . . animal outfit. Filthy rich. They keep exotic animals in a small compound in the San Bernardino Mountains. Summit Valley, I think."

Meg's heart started to race. "You're talking about the Albert Richter Institute. The same one that's here in L.A. They're funded by the government, Gordon."

"So what?" he snapped back. "What the hell is the difference? The zoo got a new tiger, and everyone was happy."

"You bastard," Meg said, "the Richter Institute is involved with the Bureau of Intelligence and Research. They are both heavily involved in animal experimentation. There's no telling what they did to Rajah, or even where he came from. Didn't you think to check his background?"

"Please, Meg, calm down. I had no idea."

"Oh no," Meg said. "You knew, but you covered your eyes. You never checked on Rajah's background because you were afraid of what you might find. So you signed the papers and hoped for the best. And now people are dead."

Ellroy's body slumped in his seat, but his head remained erect. Meg was surprised and oddly embarrassed to see tears in his eyes. They overflowed and ran down his cheeks. His face, however, did not change expression. Suddenly he sobbed, still without moving a muscle beyond the involuntary jerkings. He sounded hoarse and pitiful. Meg felt inexplicably frightened.

"Gordon?" The voice came softly into the room.

Meg turned and started to speak. But Joan held up her hand as she advanced, her eyes never leaving her husband.

"Is it true, Gordon?" she said. "Is it true you signed papers, knowing that there might be something wrong with that cat? That you've dealt with people who torture animals?"

He waved his arm in a helpless gesture, opened his mouth, but no words were spoken. He seemed to want to speak, but could not. Tears began to flow once more. In a few seconds, he was sobbing like a child.

"I'm sorry," Meg said, looking into Joan's eyes. "I really am." Then she turned to go.

At the front door Joan took hold of her arm. "Meg, wait. It might be hard for you to understand this, but I'm glad you spoke to him that way. It may be even harder to understand when I tell you that I love Gordon very much. You see, for a man like Gordon, self-deception can become a destructive habit. He might have gone out of his mind over this, or driven us both crazy by drinking himself to death. Perhaps now . . . well, we shall see. Good night, Meg."

"Good night," Meg said, and quietly left the Ellroy house.

A FEW MINUTES LATER, Meg pulled the Jeep into an all-night gas station. At a public phone, she deposited a quarter and called a number that she had committed to memory.

David answered at once, sounding as wide awake and

agitated as she was. Behind Meg, two teenage boys whooped and made wolf whistles as they jumped into their car.

"Where are you?"

"A gas station. Anyway, I've decided to go after Rajah," Meg said, and heard him groan. "Now before you say anything, let me tell you that I believe I know *exactly* where he is heading. I'm going home now to pack. I'm leaving tonight."

David said, "You really are crazy, you know that?"

Meg hesitated, watching the two boys eye her as they cruised by. She pressed closer to the phone. "Listen, David, I'm going to need all the help I can get. You said that I should call you, remember? Well, are you coming with me or not?"

A brief pause. "Okay. I'll meet you at your place in an hour."

"Right," Meg said.

When she hung up, the gas station was deserted. The two boys were gone.

24

"**H**EY, LIEUTENANT, the body is down here!"

The voice echoed up from the old trap drain that Los Angeles County had installed nearly fifty years earlier, but was now mostly plugged with leaves and sediment and, as Dragleman had been told, a newly discovered body.

He groaned and glanced down into the drain and saw Detective Richardson looking up at him, his face lit from below by a small generator light. The effect was eerie and unsettling. It reminded Dragleman in a flash of Halloween, of a small child terrified by someone in a death's-head mask, hollow eyes and all.

"How do I get down?" Dragleman hollered, shaking off the unpleasant memory. He saw only a small rope ladder dangling over the side.

The face below smiled up at him. "The ladder, for chrissakes. What's the matter, didn't they teach you anything in the service?"

Dragleman nodded and glanced over his shoulder at Cusack, who sat with his arm resting on the open window ledge of the patrol car. There were three other cars on the scene, lights flashing, as well as the van from the city morgue. A light rain had begun to fall; water pelted the windshield in dull splashes.

"Hand me the flashlight," Dragleman said, and Cusack snapped the light from under the dash and handed it to him.

"Watch your step, Lieutenant," he said. "Wouldn't want you busting a leg."

"Nice of you to care," returned Dragleman, "even if you don't mean it."

"Now, now, that's not fair," Cusack said, feigning a wounded look. "I always mean what I say."

Dragleman shook his head and then went over and shined his light down, inspecting the shaft. It was about fifteen feet to the bottom. He started downward. The closer he got to the bottom, the more he became aware of a terrible odor. At first it smelled like sewage; then it changed to the heavy aroma of decay.

"Over here," Richardson said when the Lieutenant reached the bottom.

What Dragleman saw was a man's body jackknifed in half and wedged between the brick walls and the flow pipe that pierced deeper into the spongy earth.

The body was upside down, the head resting in a half inch of water. Candy wrappers and soggy tissue were caught in the hair. Dragleman bent and shone the light on the corpse's face. "Jesus," he said involuntarily.

"He hasn't been down here too long," Richardson said. "Somebody broke his neck, at least that's my guess. Tried to make it look like an accident, you know? Like he fell. Probably figured with all the rain we wouldn't find him for weeks. By that time . . ."

"Why'd you call me?" Dragleman asked.

Richardson started to laugh, then broke off when he saw the serious look on the lieutenant's face. "Hell, Dan, he didn't have any ID on him. No wallet, nothing. He only had this."

CLAW

Detective Richardson's round eyes glinted in the beam of Dragleman's light as he handed him a piece of partially soaked paper. On it was written Dragleman's own name and phone number.

"So do you know the guy or not?" Richardson asked.

Dragleman rose, dismal in his wet shoes, sidestepping a splash from the waterfall above. "Yes, I know him," he said. "His name is Farris. Stan Farris. An animal rights activist working for a group called HAATE. I almost busted him a few years back for negligent homicide. It happened during a demonstration on a college campus."

Dragleman glanced again at the small piece of paper in his hand. So he had discovered who his mystery caller was last night. So had somebody else, apparently.

"You got any leads for me?" Richardson said, sniffing and stepping away from the corpse. The stench seemed to be getting stronger.

"Not really," Dragleman said cautiously. Richardson was from another division, and to get him involved in the Carol Lewis case would mean a ton more paperwork for the lieutenant. "Can't tell why he had my number in his pocket, but I'll sure give it some thought. I'll call you if I think of anything."

Richardson looked at him keenly. "Yeah, Dan, you do that, okay?"

Dragleman nodded and started back up the ladder. First Carol Lewis, he thought. Then Shindler. Now this. A picture was starting to form in his mind, but the image was still blurry. Vague. There was something odd about all this. Everything seemed disconnected, yet when pieced together there was some logic to the whole.

He nodded as he reached the top. One thing was for sure: it was time to call Meg Brewster.

25

I<small>F BEFORE</small> it had been bad, now it was bedlam.

Heavy rain pelted the Jeep's windshield, turning everything beyond it into a wavering hallucination. As Meg turned onto Mulholland Drive, the rain fell so hard that the wipers were useless. The area around her house was covered in mud; a river of water careened across the road, rushing downhill, taking earth and uprooted brush with it. A brilliant flash of lightning pierced the sky.

Meg drew her head back; for a moment her dazzled eyes could make out nothing. She slowed the Jeep to a crawl. Not just the weather, but everything seemed out of whack now. Roueche; Project Mantig; the INR; . . . insane, surreal. She could not have imagined a blacker nightmare.

Meg spotted her driveway and at the last second turned the wheel hard, skidding into the drive. She straightened the Jeep out and pulled into the carport. She killed the lights, cut the engine, then glanced nervously at the .38-caliber Special lying on the seat beside her.

A few months after David and she were divorced, Meg had gone into Richard & Sons Sporting Goods on Vanowen Boulevard and purchased the gun. She hadn't given it much

thought after that, nor had she felt there would ever be a
need for her to use it. Now, as she slipped it into her jacket
pocket, she wasn't so sure. She had no illusions about her
situation. She was in danger and had to be on guard. Whoever had come after her earlier would undoubtedly do so
again.

As she got out of the Jeep, her eyes scanned the street.
Everything seemed unnaturally dark. The intensity of the
downpour blocked most of the city's usual reflected glow,
and most of the streetlights were out, probably as a result of
the storm. Even the front door made an odd squeak as she
closed it behind her.

She turned and stood for a second, staring out. Cold.
Numb. Exhausted. Then, as if she were in a spy movie, she
crossed to the front window, pulling back the drape and
peering out to see if she were under surveillance. She saw
no one. She pulled the curtains closed and locked the door.
Only then did she turn on the lights. She looked around
cautiously. Everything seemed to be in order. The red call
signal of the answering machine was blinking. She pressed
the playback call button, and listened. Outside, a loud clap
of thunder shook the house.

"Meg, it's Ray . . . Bingo! I've got the answer we've
been looking for, understand? Listen, it's nine o'clock.
When you get this message, stay put. I'll be there as soon as
I can. See you."

Meg glanced at her watch; it was twelve-thirty. Three
and a half hours since Ray called, so why wasn't he here?
Probably, she thought, he had come and gone. But why no
note?

Beep. "Uh, Dr. Brewster, this is Lieutenant Dragleman,
LAPD. I believe it's time we talked. Something's come up
that I think you should know about. My number is 213-
485-2563. Call me."

The machine clicked off.

Meg stood still, biting her lower lip. Her mind raced over the events of the last few days, wondering whether or not Dragleman could be of any help to her now. If she did call him, then she would be compelled to tell him all she knew. She felt reasonably confident that he would, at the very least, detain her, restricting her movements until he launched an investigation into her allegations.

In the meantime . . . in the meantime what?

They had already confiscated her records and, no doubt, destroyed Dr. Shindler's records as well. Ray, of course, still clung to a shred of proof, but Meg knew that in order to vindicate herself, she was going to need more than that. She was going to need Rajah. And Rajah certainly needed her!

Ignoring Dragleman's call, Meg marched into the bedroom, put on her warmest winter clothes, and then began loading the Jeep with supplies needed for a prolonged hunt in the deep snow. Between trips, she tried calling Ray again, but there was still no answer.

Now she paused under the carport and looked out at the storm. The rain was relentless. Palm trees bowed in the wind, and though the latest weather report predicted clear skies by morning, Meg doubted it.

She heaved the last of the blankets and the two sleeping bags into the back of the Jeep and was just reaching for the carton of army surplus canned goods, when she saw a sparkling light suspended in the dark. One light became two, shimmering through the slant of rain.

The car slowed and stopped at the edge of her driveway. Meg did not recognize the car, and she quickly drew back behind the Jeep, slipping her hand into her jacket pocket and firmly gripping the handle of the .38.

Let it be David, she thought. *Please, God, let it be him.*

She watched as a man jumped from the car and came racing down the driveway toward her. His head was bent, his face concealed by the hood of his rain slicker. His boots sloshed through the deep water as he neared the edge of the carport.

He stepped through the curtain of rain and pulled back his hood.

A gasp of relief rushed from Meg's lungs when she saw the face. David stood still for a moment, looking at her, seeing the gun. Then his eyes went to the supplies piled up beside the open Jeep hatch.

"So you're really going through with this," he said, advancing toward her. He had an odd look on his face, as though he were annoyed, as though Meg had become as bothersome to him now as she had been during their marriage.

Meg slipped the gun into her pocket. "Yes, David, I'm going through with it. Did you think I was joking?"

For a moment David said nothing. Then he came to her and placed his palm against her face so that his fingers could lightly massage her temple. "Christ, Meg, haven't you had enough yet?" he breathed. "You look exhausted."

Meg sighed. What she felt, and did not understand, was an odd attachment for this man, a feeling that would not go away. Only now her vision of him was filtered through distance.

Meg's throat tightened and she cursed the bind she was in. Again and again, she had tried to put him out of her life. She had a genuine desire to be free of the past, yet somehow she could not completely free herself of David.

He was there and not there, like a ghost who continued to confuse her, throwing her off track. But not this time, she thought.

She lifted her eyes slowly. "My only chance of helping

myself is to find Rajah before they do, David. And I am also his only chance. It's who I am, David. I tried telling you that three years ago."

Meg began to move away, but David pulled her back. "I love you. Don't you understand that? I don't want to see anything happen to you. But what you're doing is absolute suicide. They're watching you. They know every move you make."

"They?" Meg almost laughed. "You mean Roueche, don't you? And the Bureau of Intelligence and Research? Oh yes, and let us not forget the State Department, or is it the Defense Department, David? Or both?"

Meg bent, picked up the carton of canned goods, and flung it into the Jeep. "Don't look so surprised, David. I snooped. Tonight, I broke into Roueche's office. Classified files, top secret—Project Mantig. I peeked, David!"

Before Meg could say more, David pushed her against the Jeep. "Will you listen to me! This is not a game. After what I told you about Stan, whatever possessed you to do such a dumb thing? Especially after what happened to Shindler?"

"I'm really sorry if I'm causing you difficulties, David, really I am. But those are the breaks. Now please let go of me."

"No, not until you say you'll give up this self-destructive crusade. I still love you. Do I always have to spell it out? We deserve another chance together, Meg. But you're not giving it to us."

Meg waited until his grip loosened, and then slowly slipped from his grasp. "It's too late, David," she said quietly. "I think we both know that."

She saw him stiffen almost imperceptibly. It was too late to take back her words, and there was nothing to do but go on. "We should try instead to be good friends."

David continued to look at her until he sensed her attention was being drawn away. He turned his head, following her gaze. Car lights approached, seemingly appearing out of nowhere. As Ray's station wagon pulled into the drive, the headlights washed over trees, played across their faces. Several seconds passed after he shut off the engine, before he got out and walked slowly toward the carport, his dark blue jacket blending into the blackness of the night.

"What is he doing here?" Ray asked, ducking in out of the rain, his eyes never leaving Meg.

David chuckled. "She used to be my wife, remember?" He raised his dark eyebrows. "Besides, she called me for help. Did she call you?"

Meg anxiously watched the two men stare at each other. She didn't know what to say but knew she had to say something. They had never hidden their dislike for one another, and both hated false courtesies. She said, "Listen, before you get to tearing at each other, don't." She looked at Ray. "I got your message and was worried about you. It's after twelve. Are you all right?"

Ray was still staring at David, who leaned casually against the Jeep, seeming to enjoy the encounter.

Meg went on. "What he says is true, Ray. David is only here because I asked for his help. I didn't know where you were. I tried calling you. In the meantime, I'd decided to look for Rajah myself, and I knew I couldn't do it alone."

Ray relaxed a bit, apparently deciding not to force a confrontation. "I figured as much," he said. "That's why I'm late getting here. I stopped by the zoo and cleaned out a few lockers. Then I went to the lab and picked up enough tranquilizers to put a rhino to sleep for a month. I saw Hank Marley while I was there. He said he'll take care of everything and wished us luck."

"That's great!" Meg said, and in the same breath began to tell him about her conversation with Ellroy and her notion as to where Rajah was now heading: the Albert Richter Institute compound in the San Bernardino Mountains.

"The Richter Institute? Are you sure?" Ray asked.

"Absolutely." Meg looked keenly at the two men, barely able to contain herself. "Don't you get it? Rajah is going home!"

Ray said, "The Richter Institute—it all makes sense now."

"What does?"

"The mutated neurons. Jesus, I almost forgot. Rajah's blood test! Here, see for yourself." Ray took a small piece of paper from his pocket and handed it to Meg.

She moved closer to the porch light and began to read. Almost at once a chilling picture began to form. "Oh my God."

"What is it?" David took the paper from her hand.

"I know it sounds crazy," Ray said, "but it's true. Eddie and I discovered millions of mutated neurons living in Rajah's blood. Eddie said it was the craziest thing he'd ever seen. Millions of feline neurons, only they were sprouting human axons and dendrites."

"*Human?*" David said. "That's impossible."

"Is it? Well, Eddie may live in Loma Linda, but he's a genius when it comes to genetics. It took him a while, but once he zeroed in . . ." He turned suddenly to face Meg. "I'll be right back. I've got something in the car I want to show you."

A FEW MINUTES LATER, they were sitting in Meg's kitchen with Eddie Crowell's notebook full of wrinkled pages and covered with blue ink scrawls, open on the table. So many thoughts were clamoring in Meg's head that she could hardly focus on what Ray was saying. Outside, the heavy rain continued to beat down, drenching the garden just beyond the patio doors.

". . . In '86, Eddie was working as a lab control supervisor for Comtrex, a pharmaceutical company on the East Coast. That's around the time they began tests that would reveal trace levels of stress hormones accumulated in the brain tissue of deceased infants. It's all there in the notebook."

"But what's this got to do with Rajah?" David asked.

"I'm getting to that." Ray put down his coffee cup and leaned forward in his chair. "While they were running tests, someone forgot to clean up the lab the night before. The next morning Eddie couldn't believe his eyes. One of the infant specimens, which should have been dead, had reproduced overnight. Before that day, there were only two legitimate accounts of neuron replication in the lab. But in each of those cases, the specimens stopped dividing and died within fifty-two hours.

"But then Eddie started thinking, 'What if I stirred up a solution rich in nutrients specifically vital to the health of developing neurons within the brain environment? And why not mix in a strong growth hormone, too? Say, forty percent.' So . . ."

As Ray continued to talk, Meg glanced at Eddie Crowell's notes, then looked at one of the pages she had removed from the file in Roueche's office. It was headed Experiment Objectives.

She glanced quickly down the page, which read:

1. *To enhance natural abilities*
    a. Heighten sensory abilities.
    b. Increase physical capability.
    c. Intensify instinct compulsion.

2. *To control and direct all action of test subject*
   a. Intensive training methods, such as conditioned reflexes.
   b. Drugs, designed to affect the behavior of the infused neurons.
   c. Introduction of designed genetic material to induce, or block, specific behavior.

"And?" David said, clearly annoyed that Meg wasn't paying attention.

Ray was on his feet now, heading to the stove for a fresh cup of coffee. He seemed hyper, hardly able to keep still. "Hell, Eddie said that not only had replication not slowed down, as he thought it would, but instead it was speeding up. It started dividing once every half hour!"

"In a petri dish?" Meg asked.

"You got it. Living human neurons growing in a dish! Ten days went by, and Eddie said it was like he was living in a separate universe. By this time the neurons were multiplying at an astounding rate—one thousand times per hour. By day fifteen, eight hundred divisions per minute.

"Naturally, Eddie was excited and started sending reports to the home office here in Los Angeles. But he never heard from them, until one night five guys in lab coats showed up, with State Department credentials. Right away, Eddie knew something serious was going on. He could tell by their questions that they had gotten hold of the reports he'd sent to the home office. The next thing Eddie knew, they were removing everything from the lab. All specimens, dead or living. Storage units. They even ripped the damned computers right out of the walls, and removed all the backup files."

"That sounds familiar," Meg said.

"When Eddie gets home that night, he picks up his phone but there's no dial tone. Then he realizes someone is waiting on the line. 'Good evening, Mr. Crowell,' the man says. 'If it's not too inconvenient, we'd like to talk to you.' And he tells Eddie to forget about his research. Put it out of his mind. It's over. Finished. Six months later, Eddie hears that Congress released two point seven billion dollars in funding PANRE: The Project for Advanced Neurobiological Research and Experimentation."

"And the Richter Institute received the largest portion of that funding," Meg said, closing the notebook in disgust. "It was in all of the newspapers. Something to do with neurological disorders."

"That's when Dr. Shindler probably climbed aboard," Ray said. "They went after all the top names in the field. I'm sure he thought he was joining a team to fight childhood diseases. Of course, the whole operation was a sham."

"But what are they up to?" David asked, still confused.

"Don't you get it?" Ray said. "They're growing brains! In lab dishes. Reconstructing neurons. Crossing *man* with *animal*."

"For what purpose?" David asked.

Meg got to her feet. "Only the State Department knows that for sure. But my guess is, attack animals, genetically engineered for cunning and viciousness. By combining human intelligence with innate animal aggression you would have the perfect beast, ruthless and incorruptible."

Meg picked up the sheet of paper taken from Roueche's file that she had been looking at only moments ago. "Look, under Experiment Objectives it lists: '(b) Increase physical capability.' Rajah scaled a twenty-foot wall, didn't he? '(c) Intensify instinct compulsion.' That would explain his sudden aggression."

"But why a man-tiger cross?" David asked. "Why not man-ape, or man-dog?"

"Because tigers are innate hunters. Their stalking ability

is relentless and incredible. And"—Meg hesitated—"they can adapt to almost any terrain. Asia comes to mind, naturally. South Africa. South America."

"Meg's right," Ray said, too nervous to stop pacing. "They are looking to create an animal elite. Up till now it's all been done with sophisticated animal training, but with the latest advances in genetics, they could very well remove the nucleus from a feline neuron and replace it with the nucleus of a human neuron. They could very well breed animals with human brains!"

"Wait a minute," David said. "Do you actually believe that Rajah is . . . thinking with a human brain?"

Meg remained silent for a moment, her mental computer actually considering the possibility of such an impossible scenario. She knew the science, the history of experimentation, some of it going back centuries, efforts to "humanize" animals. "No," she answered finally. "Apparently, he is a mutant of some sort. Not perfected, as they say. But it doesn't really matter, does it?"

"To me, it does," David said. "There's something we're missing here."

"Like what?" Ray asked.

"If there had been any doubt, any chance Rajah would exhibit abnormal behavior, wouldn't they have killed him rather than letting him go to a zoo?"

Ray said, "My guess is that when they decided to release Rajah, it was because they thought all of the transplanted neurons were dead. But apparently there were still a few survivors, hidden away, undergoing subtle mutation, slowly evolving out of their original composition."

"And eventually they found a more suitable environment in Rajah's blood," Meg said, getting to her feet. "Remember, we're dealing with *human axons,* which are capable of growing to extraordinary lengths. That would account for his increased memory capacity. And his furious hunger." She felt a chill and thought, *Rajah is hunting right now.*

She knew his metabolism was constantly racing to keep up with the energy demands of an immune system at war with the very strange, always multiplying, neurons.

The more Rajah ate to feed his immune system, the more nutrients the neurons received. "With more nutrients," Meg went on, "hybrid neurons multiply. When the neurons multiply, the immune system responds to the threat of a foreign invader. The alarmed immune system signals Rajah to eat more, and he kills again. And the cycle grows more horrific with each feeding."

"*Holy shit,*" David said.

"My thought exactly," Ray responded, shaking his head.

Meg quickly shoved all of the data into her satchel. She would take it with her, because there was no doubt in her mind that they would soon be tearing apart her house, just as they had torn apart Eddie's lab. Then she glanced sharply at David. "Well, David," she said, "are you coming with us or not?"

When David did not respond, Ray said, "Forget him, Meg. We'll take the Jeep and the station wagon and drive all night. We don't need him."

David sat back and sipped his coffee, ignoring the remark.

"No," Meg said, "we all need sleep. We'll have to spell each other. I'm also going to call Jack Riner. He lives in Scotland, which is directly in Rajah's path. Jack knows the mountains, and I'm sure he'll be willing to help us, too."

"Must you always do this sort of thing, Meg?" David asked. He looked at her with a bemused expression on his face. "Must you always run around trying to do the impossible?"

"If I'm forced to, yes."

"But for chrissakes, why?"

Meg shrugged. "Let's just say it's because of something my father said to me a long time ago, David. That unless you make commitments, you're not truly alive. You may be dreaming of life, but nothing will ever be real."

Meg kept her eyes on David, wondering if he was getting the message. Wondering if he would finally commit himself, not for her sake but for his own.

"I know what you're thinking, David," she said finally. "You're thinking, what's in it for me? Am I right?"

"Sort of," he answered without hesitation.

Meg said, "Maybe nothing. Then again, maybe everything. But I'll tell you this, if we don't find Rajah before they do, prove what they've been up to, they'll continue. They're not going to stop these grotesque experiments until someone comes up with hard proof. Something that will finally convince the public that what's going on is dangerous, unnatural, and immoral. Now you'll have to excuse me, David, but I've got work to do."

"Right," Ray said. "I'll help you finish packing the Jeep." He took hold of Meg's hand.

David looked at them for a second, then said, "All right, count me in."

26

"KILL THE SON OF A BITCH!" the hunter yelled. His
partner took aim and fired. And then the woods grew quiet.
Both men were crouched behind a tree, their breath steaming in the night air, boots buried in snow. Only a few hours
earlier Dale Long had stood in a warm bar, wondering
aloud which man in his small group had the most courage.
"I do!" John Palfrey had said, slapping a hundred-dollar
wager down on the bar as a measure of his bravery. Now,
away from the warmth, the strengthening liquor long since
evaporated, leaving only a bad taste and more than the usual
mental fuzziness, he wondered where that courage had
come from.

"Oh God," he moaned, fumbling to reload his rifle.
"Martin's dead, Dale. Did you see what that cat did to him?
Oh Jesus—Martin's dead!"

"Quiet," Dale Long said, listening for sounds. The whole
of Big Horn Ridge was quiet, as though every animal and
human within a five-mile radius knew there was an awesome predator on the loose.

John Palfrey listened, too, then let his body drop like
dead weight behind a tree stump. He tried to roll forward to

his knees, but it was as if every joint were locked, every muscle frozen. He groaned with the effort, but he could not move. There was no question about the wager. He was going to lose.

"He's gonna get us, Dale." His voice was as dead as his muscles. "We're trapped down here. He's—"

"I said, shut up!" Dale Long scowled at him for a second, then glanced up the narrow trail, past rows of rocks and tall pine. The moon appeared, then vanished, as heavy clouds crossed the sky. It had snowed on and off all day, and now large, moist flakes fell without sound, covering the hills and the rolling, exhaust-stained mounds of snow alongside the highway.

Dale could see his pickup truck parked on the road only two hundred yards above them. A wind suddenly rose and swung to the east, whipping his face. Then for a moment, it died, leaving them with an unearthly quiet.

"You stay here and cover me," Dale whispered. "Then I'll stop halfway up the trail and cover you as you come behind me."

Palfrey looked at him. "He's somewhere between here and the truck, Dale," he said in the same low voice. "I know it. I can feel it."

Dale stepped out onto the trail. "Cover me, dammit!"

THE TIGER TENSED, all senses focused on the human coming toward him. Slowly he dropped to a half-crouch and inched closer to the trail. The human was no more than twenty feet away from him now.

Suddenly the cat froze, its taut muscles standing out in ridges under his thick coat. Then tautness and tension exploded, and the cat rose in one gigantic leap until the bulk of its frame seemed to hang in midair, suspended there, until it came crashing down.

CLAW

DALE LONG'S SCREAM ripped through the night, a strange, terrifying scream that rose naked and final into the air.

Palfrey turned in terror, staring at the nearby copse of trees. The scream, one long, horrible, unbroken cry, kept rising and filling the cold night air, broken only by a violent cracking of tree limbs and the hasty trampling of snow.

Palfrey's heart raced and hammered in his chest. His brain filled with a rush of blood that throbbed within his skull, blurring his vision. He drew back, fired two shots into the dark, then turned and ran deeper into the woods, away from the highway.

He ran through the same forest that he had run through as a boy, everything familiar yet totally foreign, a world at odds with his shocked senses. Dale's scream had stopped; the only sounds now were his own thrashing movements. And the steady pad of footsteps behind him, growing louder.

Below, a small stream came into view, glittering in the pale moonlight. Palfrey stopped to catch his breath. Something was moving, making a straight line of agitation along the shoreline. A bird darted from the water, large enough to be seen from a distance but only against the phosphorescent glow of water. When it rose as high as the land it was gone from sight.

The rest of Palfrey's survey was made in the dark, aided only by the blanket of white around him. Making a sudden decision, he veered left, off the main path. Too late he realized his mistake, as he missed his footing and crashed down the embankment, grabbing frantically for a hold, losing his rifle in the process. He fell heavily into a drift, covering his face and hair with snow.

Struggling to overcome his shock and disorientation, Palfrey pulled himself out of the drift and staggered down the steep incline, holding his chest. Trees and snow sucked him quickly downhill until he began to run again, glancing back every few seconds to see if the cat was following him. He knew the ranger station was less than a mile away, and he began running in long strides, alternately skidding on ice and regaining his balance. A copse of trees suddenly leapt forward. He put his arms out, breaking through branches.

A low roar to his left made him veer again, down to the small stream. He ran through the water for a few moments, then pushed his way up through the undergrowth beyond. Soon the foliage around him became altered by his imagination. Nothing was familiar; every tree held a threat, every creak of a limb meant danger.

He ran on. Each time he glanced back he saw nothing; yet he sensed the cat's presence. *Oh God, oh God . . .* His rasping breath came in gasps, the words of prayer more thought than sound. He ran faster, came to a slight ridge, crossed it, and turned sharply, glancing back over his shoulder one last time. His trousers were soaked from the snow, and from the stream, and from the urine that ran down his thigh into his boot.

Abruptly a shapeless mass heaved up, momentary, swift, quivering. Palfrey stopped his frantic running, grabbing a tree for support.

Just as suddenly it was gone.

It had happened so fast that he wasn't sure that he'd seen anything. He stared at the uncertain darkness. Shadows seemed to grow into others.

He waited. Around him there was only silence.

He started to move again, listening intently. There were no echoes behind him.

Then he froze. A twig snapped, followed by a faint rustle. He turned to face the boulders. Suddenly there were more sounds, louder, pounding, shaking the ground.

CLAW

The cat exploded from the darkness, catching Palfrey from behind, bringing him down by the neck, teeth piercing his vertebrae. He sensed more than felt the claws as they tore into his flesh, and he was covered with blood and screaming into the night again and again. Thrashing, heaving, twisting—and then he stopped, mercifully unconscious, spared the final pain, no longer aware of his death.

When the body lay still in the sparkling crimson-stained snow, the cat flung its head back and released a roar, a horrifying sound—low-pitched yet shrill; powerful yet tremulous. Then he circled the body, sniffing at the wounds.

When the kill had been thoroughly examined, the cat stood still and carefully looked around. Before he could eat, instinct demanded he scan the dark for rival carnivores that might be lurking about.

Satisfied that he was alone, the cat shredded the man's clothes and cut through the meaty flesh of his buttocks with shearing teeth, then pulled out intestines with incisors.

After cleaning away bone with its tongue, the cat rose, and then stumbled forward. He coughed weakly and angrily. A scavenger bird appeared and flicked across his vision, but he did not raise his head. Instead, he licked away blood spewing from the fresh bullet hole in his shoulder.

His head lolled forward for a moment, then he glanced back. Already a light, powdery snow covered the hunter's body. If the snow kept up this way, by morning he would be buried.

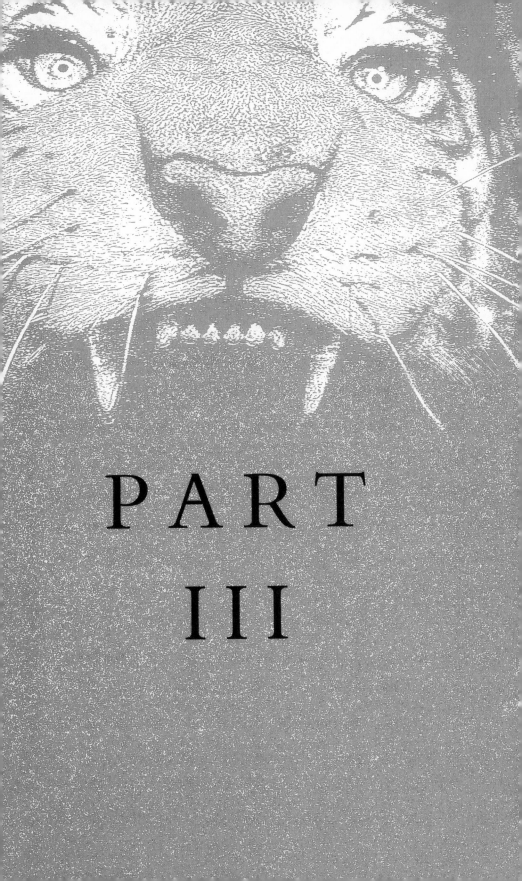

PART

III

27

MONDAY AT DAWN the snow stopped, leaving in its wake a steamy confusion: snowplows before a parade of car headlights, police waving Day-Glo batons. Traffic had slowed to a painstaking crunch of tires; those few pedestrians who were out walked hunchbacked with their heads down. Inside the Jeep the windows fogged; there was the closeness of sweaty bodies beneath heavy coats.

Meg sat with her right shoulder jammed against the passenger door, peering out. She had gotten barely an hour's sleep when gravel flew up from the road, hitting the windshield and waking her. It startled her at first. Groggily she looked around, remembering why she was there.

Still a little shaky, she stretched, then stamped her feet to get the circulation going. "Where are we now?" she asked David, who inched the Jeep forward behind a long line of cars.

"Ten miles outside of Scotland," he said. "About three thousand feet up. Did that spray of gravel frighten you?"

"Sort of." Meg looked at her watch. It was a little after six: at least another hour before they reached Jack Riner's cabin. Maybe two, if the traffic didn't let up.

Below, a crooked stream was steadily shrinking from view. The road under the snow seemed to be turning to ice. For a moment the Jeep faltered, and as they inched forward, the incline grew steeper. The only good thing was that the higher they climbed, the more the wind lessened.

"Cigarette?" David pulled a crimson-and-white box from his coat pocket and offered it to Meg.

"I thought you gave up smoking."

"Hell, I've got to have one vice." He held out the box of thin oval cigarettes.

"No, thanks." Meg turned and peered out the rear window. Ray's station wagon was still following close behind. She had spelled him earlier while he slept in the seat beside her. Then David had taken his turn sleeping. She waved now behind the frosted glass, and though she doubted Ray could see it, she smiled.

"He's okay, you know," David said. He took a deep drag on his cigarette.

"You mean Ray?"

David laughed shortly. "Of course I mean Ray. A few months after our divorce, I became jealous of him, you know? 'My assistant,' you had said, and I thought, 'Yeah . . . right.' "

Meg swung around to face him directly, her back resting against the door. "Why not say what's on your mind, David?"

A sudden enigmatic smile appeared on his lips, something of an attempt at intimacy, mingled with the remoteness Meg realized would always be a part of this man she had once married. "Just how frank should I be, Meg?" he said finally.

"What do you mean?" she said, but already with an idea of where he was heading.

"You and Ray, of course. Is an ex-husband entitled to ask if you're sleeping with the guy?"

Meg looked at him in silence, unsmiling. Ahead the traffic crawled forward. Suddenly they stopped. Ahead was a solid line of motionless cars and trucks.

"Well?" His voice with its usual abruptness broke through her revery.

"Is an ex-wife entitled to tell you to go to hell?" she retorted evenly.

"Does that mean you are or you aren't?"

"Look, David—"

"You aren't, are you?" He laughed.

"There's more to love than sex, David. But I'm sure you wouldn't understand that."

"Now," he said, "you've hurt me." And curiously, he really did sound a little flat. Almost to himself, he added, "It's funny. Here I was wondering about the sex part . . . and I never thought about you being in love with the guy. Jesus, what a concept. Not a very pleasant one at that."

Meg was no longer listening. Had she said *love*? Until now she really hadn't been sure, though she greatly admired Ray. She enjoyed the way he moved; the way he tucked his shirt into his trousers and the pure masculine act of lacing up his boots. She liked his looks, even the scent of him. But she had always felt an emptiness inside her since divorcing David, an emptiness she couldn't quite figure out.

Perhaps it was fear of being hurt again, or a wholesome sense of caution. Whatever it was had always held her back from making a final, real commitment to Ray. It had certainly put a lock on such words as *love*.

"Look," she said, a little unsteadily. "I'm not sure that I . . . maybe you just pushed the wrong buttons and . . ."

Almost eagerly David said, "You're right, forget it. It's none of my business. God, leave it to me and I'll have you married to the guy before either of us knows what's going on. Let's talk traffic. This road is a mess. Snow is hell. That casual enough?" With a heavy sigh, he began inching the Jeep again through the narrow pass.

Rounding the next curve, Meg noticed a steady stream of cars heading toward them from the opposite direction. Closer to the intersection, she saw that the road had been blocked off. Soldiers in camouflage fatigues were hurriedly jumping from the backs of army vehicles. Two men not in uniform started barking orders.

The surrounding area was crowded with police cars, but it also had an odd, deserted look, as if the officers who belonged to all those vehicles had suddenly been told to vanish. Besides the soldiers, Meg could only see a couple of state troopers pacing at the road edge.

Suddenly headlights appeared from a small service road near the intersection. A brown, unmarked sedan pulled up and stopped. A broad-shouldered man in plainclothes got out, and the trooper hurried toward him.

"Road's closed," a policeman shouted as David gained the lead in the long line of traffic. "You'll have to turn around."

Meg rolled down the window. "What's the problem, Officer?"

The trooper came to her side of the Jeep. "Wildlife trouble," he said, his face reddened from the weather.

"Oh?" Meg tensed.

"The tiger that got loose from the L.A. Zoo is believed to be in the Cucamonga area. Road is closed until further notice."

Meg said, "But we've got to get to Scotland. It's an emergency."

The air outside was so cold that the officer paused to turn up his collar. "All emergency vehicles are being routed to Lytle Creek. You can circle around and come into Scotland from the north."

"But that could take hours."

"Sorry," the officer said.

Before Meg could speak again, the broad-shouldered man from the sedan approached. "Can I help you, miss?" The officer stepped aside, bowing to a higher authority.

The man wore no hat, and his hands were buried deep in the pockets of a long cashmere coat. The lapels of the coat were flipped up, revealing a neatly folded silk scarf.

David leaned over and said, "We've got business in Scotland. Any chance of us driving through?"

The man studied David, then glanced at Meg. "I notice you've got an L.A. Zoo emblem on your plate. Do you folks work for them?"

"No," Meg said quickly. "We're just supporters."

The man nodded. "Considering the circumstances, they can sure use you."

Meg glanced over the man's shoulder. Beyond she saw another unmarked sedan shooting up the road at high speed, heading toward the cluster of soldiers. Behind it came a line of small army vehicles. They zigzagged and swerved in every direction. It gave Meg a sense of action without purpose, a kind of panicky, helter-skelter movement. She was suddenly sure that they had lost control of the situation—if they'd ever had control in the first place.

"Has the cat been sighted?" Meg asked.

The man stared at her, his round cheeks reddening from the chill. "No," he said, "but they just found the bodies of some hunters near Big Horn Ridge. Torn up pretty bad. It was that damned cat, all right."

He dropped his gaze to the road map bunched up tightly in Meg's fist. "And you're heading to . . . Scotland?"

Meg glanced at David. The jerk of his chin signaled a message: *Time to go—now.*

"Yes," Meg said. "Family illness. But we'll head back to Mount Baldy and send a telegram. No problem."

The man said, "Well, the Mount Baldy cutoff is at the bottom of the canyon. That's rough traveling, though. Plenty of ice."

"I think the Jeep can handle it." Meg motioned for David to turn around. "And thanks again for your help."

"My pleasure," the man said.

As David swung the Jeep around, Meg saw the man say something to the officer, and then stroll toward the National Guard unit.

"Jesus!" David exclaimed, signaling for Ray to follow him. "You are still a lousy liar!"

"What difference does it make?" Meg said. "It's obvious he knew I was lying. The point is, he let us go."

"That's what worries me," David said.

FACING EAST, the second unmarked sedan sat motionless on an overhang three thousand feet above the canyon. The man in the cashmere coat—agent Howard Boss of the Bureau of Intelligence and Research—approached the sedan slowly, thinking the Richter Institute fiasco had done a lot of damage.

In fact, it was threatening to blow INR out of the water. He knew that the whispering around Washington had begun. The whispering, the memos, the secret reports, and all because Meg Brewster wouldn't stop digging into matters that really didn't concern her. He sighed deeply; no one stepped from the car to greet him when the rear door swung open.

Boss climbed in and closed the door. The man beside him in the backseat barely stirred. "It's her, all right," Boss said. "Both men came with her, just as you predicted. Two cars: the Jeep and the station wagon. She pretended they were heading back to Mount Baldy."

Philip Roueche did not look up. A new intelligence profile had arrived from Washington and he found the contents fascinating. "She's lying, of course," he said. "She won't stop until she reaches Scotland. That's where Riner lives."

Boss nodded. "Should we continue air surveillance?"

"A pass or two will suffice," Roueche replied. "But not too close."

His eyes remained on the confidential profile in his lap. Jack Riner was a real piece of work: fifty-one years old. Single. Four years in Vietnam. Decorated for valor. Six years with the World Wildlife Fund. Two years Operation Tiger: protection of Bengal subspecies, Bhakra, India. Tracking expert. Weapons expert. Reclusive.

A talented man, Roueche thought. Tough. Experienced. Such a terrible waste.

Boss shifted uncomfortably beside Roueche. "I just spoke with Washington," he said sullenly. "They're saying we've lost control of the situation."

"Temporarily," Roueche said. "The cat will be dead within hours. We have complete authority over disposal of the remains. Without a thorough postmortem examination, there will be no proof. And I believe we needn't fear Dr. Brewster's allegations."

Boss said, "Correct me if I'm wrong, Philip, but I distinctly recall you giving us assurances that the Richter Institute could be trusted. Top-notch, you said. So how do you explain the crisis we now face? Someone—"

"Misread a code," Roueche interrupted. "It's as simple as that. The incubation period had long since expired. No one, including myself, expected this, Howard. 'Top Secret,' 'Highly Classified,' these are terms, not guarantees. Besides, I've taken every precaution to see that INR's position isn't compromised."

"Encouraging, but doubtful," Boss said. "No, my friend, INR is not safe. Not anymore."

Roueche stared at him. "What was your shop expecting, Howard? We were dealing with the fundamental reconstruction of life! Interspecies nuclear transplantation. Where neurons are concerned, nothing is absolute. It is still a gray area. A new poetry, if you will. And we were so close. . . ."

Roueche broke off, sighing. He knew that trying to explain all the scientific nuances to Boss was useless. He knew more about military hardware than he did about a human body. And now he was behaving much as Roueche might have expected—a disgruntled buffoon on the verge of panic.

"Why is it all crises have a disturbing sameness," Boss said irritably. "A certain inevitability. Especially those brought about by stupidity."

Roueche shrugged. "I assure you, it's nothing that can't be handled."

"Handled? That cat is out of control, Philip. You know that."

"Not necessarily," Roueche said, his gaze drifting to the outdoors. "Animal brains can only react. The ape hand may exist, but not the human brain to guide it. Isn't that what INR was looking for? The perfect beast. Animal fierceness controlled by human cunning."

Boss looked at him inquiringly. "I'm not sure I know what you're driving at. Are you suggesting the earlier experiments were a success?"

"It's quite simple, Howard. You can't make choices based on abstract thoughts. Only humans are capable of assessing the circumstances of conflict before hostilities begin. We can ask ourselves, 'Are the conditions of battle favorable to us?' Or, we could ask, 'Does our analysis of the situation reveal obstacles that lessen our chances of victory? Are these obstacles insurmountable?' In short, humans are the only animal capable of formulating a plan. Isn't that what the cat has been doing all along? Hasn't he displayed an uncanny amount of forethought?" Roueche smiled. "If anything, Howard, I'd say our experiments were too successful."

In the brief silence that followed, Boss's lips tightened in angry confusion. From the front seat, a voice said, "What happens next?"

Roueche slowly lifted his gaze, fixed his full attention on Paul Gaddis, who sat hunched over the steering wheel. Roueche felt annoyance at having to deal with such a man. Gaddis had a personality that was fundamentally ungovernable. He was merely a hit man, and hit men always self-destructed sooner or later.

So be it, Roueche thought with a certain grim comfort. He had always welcomed challenge. "For the moment, we'll split up," he said, closing the Jack Riner file. "You take this car. I want you to hook up with Meg Brewster in Scotland."

Paul Gaddis turned and flashed a smile that became suddenly, horribly, predatory. He said, "You should have let me snuff the bitch days ago. So, naturally, it will be my pleasure."

28

SOMETHING WAS HAPPENING. He was sure of that. But what was it?

Lieutenant Dragleman had hardly slept all night—maybe three or four hours. His mind kept coming back to the recent series of events.

He had tried calling Meg Brewster again, right at dawn, but had gotten the answering machine again. Around 8:00 A.M. he had breakfast—a small glass of tomato juice, a toasted bagel with cream cheese, a cup of black coffee. The eight o'clock news reported the tiger was still on the prowl somewhere in the San Gabriel Mountains. Three more deaths, unconfirmed, were being investigated.

Dragleman put his dirty dishes in the dishwasher, tried one last call to Meg Brewster, then went to work.

The morning dragged. After sending Detective Reese to try to establish personal contact with Brewster, Dragleman called Chief Inspector Howland at the Fire Department and was told Howland was out sick. The Albert Richter Institute wasn't answering its phone either. A HAATE spokesperson said Stan Farris's funeral was set for Wednesday, 9:00 A.M. at Our Lady of Grace Church in

Hollywood, and that no one from the organization was allowed to comment on his death until after the services were concluded.

Chief Medical Examiner Kirkwood was busy performing the Shindler autopsy, which Dragleman had ordered despite criticism from his superiors.

The investigation so far showed nothing—no angle, no handle.

Disgusted, Dragleman dropped into his desk chair, drummed his fingers on the desk. Then he picked up the phone. He dialed Detective Richardson, left his phone number, hung up, waited patiently. Richardson was back to him within ten minutes.

"Anything yet on the Farris case?" Dragleman asked.

"In less than fourteen hours, are you kidding?" Richardson complained. "How about you? You figure out yet why Farris had your name and number in his pocket?"

"Not a clue. But I'll keep at it."

Dragleman had barely hung up when Detective Reese walked into his office.

"So?" Dragleman asked.

"She's disappeared, Lieutenant."

Dragleman stared at the young detective. "What do you mean by *she's disappeared?* You mean you couldn't locate her?"

Reese drew closer to the desk. "Well, I don't know. That, too, I guess. She's not at the zoo, where she's supposed to be. Some guy from the San Diego Zoo, Marley, is filling in for her. Then I go to her house like you said and find a state trooper stalking the place. I tell him I'm from LAPD Homicide, but he isn't impressed. Wouldn't say anything, just gives me a number to call. I call it, and I'm given another number, on and on. I'm calling until I get some guy from the Department of Natural Resources. He tells me his department got a court order and confiscated all of her records."

"The Department of Natural Resources. Are you sure?"

"Absolutely." Reese flipped open his small notepad. "I've got it right here. Uh—now where the hell is it?—Mr. Foster, that's it! Department of—"

"Did you ask him why they confiscated her records?"

"Sure. He told me it was none of my business and hung up. I figured, hell, maybe you'd like to call him."

Dragleman took a cigar from the inside pocket of his jacket and bit off the end. Reese knew this routine and rummaged his pocket for a book of matches, then leaned over to hold the flame to Dragleman's cigar. The latter exhaled a cloud of smoke. He took the cigar from his mouth and looked ruminatively at its bitten end. "Where was that cat last sighted?" he asked.

"Uh, the Cucamonga area, I think."

"Then that's where Meg Brewster is, dammit!"

"How do you figure that?"

Dragleman got to his feet. "Because, my friend, that's the kind of woman she is. That's her character! Listen, send out an APB on her and that damn Jeep. Get the plate number from MV. But I don't want her apprehended, understand? I just want to know her whereabouts."

The phone rang and Dragleman picked it up. It was Kirkwood from the morgue.

"Dan, you were right. Shindler was torched," Kirkwood said. "There's no doubt about it. I found traces of chemicals throughout his remains—highly flammable. Also, the way parts of his body burned indicates a sudden eruption of flames, rather than slow burning caused by, say, a fire started by a cigarette or a match."

"How was his blood?" Dragleman asked.

"Clean. But there's a connection with Farris all right. I

just ran into Webster from Latent Prints. He said there's no doubt about it. The footprints taken from the drain where Farris was dumped match the ones found at Shindler's house."

"I knew it!" Dragleman boomed. "Same fucking killer, I knew it!

"But you better go slow, Dan. Honest. There's a lot more here than meets the eye. I had a little surprise waiting for me when I got in this morning."

"What kind of surprise?"

"The Lewis girl's blood samples are missing. Not a trace of them anywhere. My notes are also gone. And someone accessed my computer and erased the data. Jesus, Dan, whoever you're dealing with has access into our department. That scares me. It seems dangerous." He paused. "Do you agree?"

Dragleman drew a short breath. "Yeah, Larry. Dangerous."

29

COMING DOWN the gravel road from the north, they finally saw a sign indicating "Scotland—one mile." At the sign they turned onto a dirt road, covered by snow so it was difficult to follow, and without the benefit of gravel underneath. Under the best of circumstances the road was in terrible shape. They had had to beware of every kind of pitfall, swerving sharply to avoid tree stumps and boulders, deciding which was the least impossible course, with one wheel crunching through snow while the other rode the crest of a rut. From time to time Meg would glance back to make sure Ray was still behind them. Both she and David were tense, constantly on alert; except for a few grunted exchanges, they rode in silence.

A few minutes before noon, they pulled up outside an open gate that was broken and leaning crazily. There were no signs marking the private forty acres known as Jack's Blue Meadow.

"This it?" David asked, glancing back over his shoulder. Ray brought the station wagon to a halt behind them.

"Yes," Meg said. "That small road over there."

David took the road parallel to the foothills. The sky had finally cleared, and the sun shone brightly, reflected by the blanket of white all around them. To the left of the road was a low, flat sweeping grassland buried in snow. To the right were steep thickly wooded slopes of aspen and poplar that rose up tier after tier to the evergreens and the craggy mountains beyond. The road suddenly grew more narrow, and deep parallel scars—recently made by the wheels of a wide-traction vehicle—appeared in the lane.

Jack's Land-Rover, Meg thought.

She knew they were close.

When she saw the smoke rising above the treetops, she pointed at an opening in the dense forest and said, "Go that way."

David gunned the Jeep down the wooded alley, and the lane abruptly widened into a snow-covered glade.

At first glance, Jack Riner's cabin appeared to be floating above the snow. It was on a level, back from the edge of the slope, hidden from the road, two stories of well-mortared logs above a foundation of thick stones. A wide deck, with planked railing, stretched across the front of the cabin. A big man clad in a brown canvas windbreaker with a sheepskin collar was leaning against the railing, watching them as they stopped. There was a six-pack of beer at his feet; the man sipped slowly from an open can.

"That Riner?" David asked, killing the engine.

"That's him," Meg said, waving and climbing out of the Jeep.

Jack came toward her, a smile on his lean face, his skin stretched tight over high cheekbones. He was a giant of a man, nearly seven feet tall, with immense shoulders. He crushed the beer can in his fist and sent it sailing, then put both arms around Meg in a bear hug.

"Well, well—if it isn't Miss City Gal!" he boomed. The voice was deep and Scottish-sounding. "I expected you long before this. I was starting to get worried."

Meg sighed. "I know. We almost didn't make it."

"Never knew you to change plans because of bad weather," he said. "But then this last storm was a real pisser."

Meg said, "The weather is the least of my problems, Jack."

"I guess." He took Meg's fingers in his enormous fist and squeezed gently. David and Ray appeared over Meg's shoulder. Jack studied and sniffed at the two strangers like a bloodhound as Meg introduced them.

"Well, best go in and talk," Jack said, leading them into the cabin.

The ground floor was divided by a large, see-through fireplace and cluttered with old farmhouse furniture, odd-looking plants, boxes, magazines, and a dozen guns, some of which lay casually around the room, while others were stacked neatly in a gun rack near the north window. A pinball machine and a fifties jukebox hugged the south wall. The yellow and orange lights from the jukebox cast a dim haze over the roughly planked floor.

"Sit down, make yourselves comfortable," Jack said, putting the six-pack on the captain's table. "Have a beer?"

"No, thanks," Meg said.

"How about you two? If beer isn't to your taste, I've got brandy or rum. I'd join you, but the old gut is starting to spread. Fat is what I'm getting," Jack said casually, winking at Meg.

David and Ray both asked for brandy. Jack poured them fair-sized glasses. Then he filled a small glass with gin for himself and downed it in one long, unhurried swallow.

"I thought you were watching the waistline," David said.

"I am. One beer a day is all. Gin is a different matter. It helps clean out the system. Keeps the blood flowing. That's a fact." He shrugged out of his coat, revealing a leather belt that supported the biggest dogleg holster Meg had ever seen, with the flap buttoned. "You folks look hungry. Let me get you started on something."

CLAW

Twenty minutes later Jack's venison stew had been eaten. A fire blazed and crackled in the hearth, filling the room with the scent of scorched pine.

". . . So you think you're being followed?" Jack asked, methodically pressing a pinch of fresh tobacco into the bowl of a short-stemmed pipe.

"Yes, I think so," Meg said. The four of them were sitting around the table, finishing their coffee.

"There's one thing in our favor," Ray said. "I dropped back a few times on our way up here. And I didn't see anyone following us. I think we lost them."

"I'm afraid you thought wrong," Jack said.

"You mean somebody came up here asking about us?" David asked.

"Not exactly," Jack said. He lifted his freshly packed pipe to his lips and bit hard on the stem; a quick scrape of the blue-tipped match across the table and the small plume of flame was cradled in the palm of his hand. "Spotter plane . . . National Guard, I think. Passed over the northern ridge around ten this morning. Flew over again at eleven, then again right before you got here. Not too close, mind you, but close enough to have a look around." The flame dipped into the pipe bowl as he sucked a few times, until a swirl of white smoke floated around his head.

David said, "How can you be sure they were checking you out?"

"Well, they sure as hell weren't looking for forest fires."

"But if they were looking for the tiger . . ."

"It isn't that hard to figure out what they're up to." Jack leaned back in his chair and puffed slowly on his pipe. "We're surrounded by two hundred thousand acres of forest." His hand made a lazy circle above his head. "Goes on and on as far as the eye can see. Now this last storm just took a short breather, it isn't over by a long shot. They haven't had a chance to do any serious tracking, no searching of any kind until, say, well, this afternoon. So if they don't know where to look yet—and believe me, *they don't*—then with all these miles of woods, they don't need to be flying over my property three times in two hours. No, they're snooping around. You can bet on that."

"You think they're waiting for us to track Rajah down?"

"Looks that way."

Meg's throat felt dry as she looked carefully at David. "The man at the roadblock?"

David shrugged. "Could be."

"In any case," Jack said, "they might know where you are, but they don't know where you're heading. I know back roads and trails that aren't even on the map."

Meg suddenly heard a growl behind her. She turned, not knowing what to expect. A dog was standing in the kitchen doorway, a shepherd of some kind, huge, its snout blotched. It snarled again, directing its stare at David.

Jack said, "Go on, Bruno, you dumb mutt."

The dog's eyes remained fixed on David. He growled once more.

"I said get!" Jack picked up a magazine and flung it at the dog. "Go on, he's not a federal agent."

The dog bounded forward, jumped playfully up at Jack's outstretched hand, took a few comforting pats on its head, then ran back into the kitchen, disappearing out the flap set in the back door.

"Does he really bite?" David relaxed a bit and sipped his coffee.

"Only people he doesn't like," Jack said, relighting his pipe. Then he glanced curiously at David. "Anyway, where were we?"

"The tiger," Meg said. "Jack, I know you're going to think I'm crazy, but I'm sure I know exactly where he's heading. Honest, I've mapped his course and so far it's been dead-on accurate."

"Let's have a look."

Ray unrolled the map onto the table, and Meg pinned two corners down with coffee mugs. Jack pinned the other two corners down with a kerosene lamp and a loaded Glock 9mm automatic pistol.

Meg said nothing. She simply stared at the gun, then looked at Ray, who seemed more curious than alarmed.

"If you don't mind my asking," Ray said, "do you plan on using that thing any time soon?"

"Just a precaution," Jack said.

David said, "Against what?"

"Varmint, mostly," Jack replied. "A bear came snooping around my window just the other night. Or maybe it was a man, I'm not sure." He bit down hard on the stem of the pipe and grinned at David, who was not amused.

Dammit, Meg thought. Bringing David along might have been a mistake after all.

The two men had never met, but each knew about the other. Meg and Jack had become friends during Operation Tiger, in India, and after the divorce she had told him about her frustrations over David, never suspecting that Jack might harbor such deep resentment against the man who had hurt her.

"What about the cannon you've got holstered on your hip?" David asked. "That for varmints, too?"

"Uh-huh." Jack nodded. "Colt forty-four, nine-inch barrel. Put a hole in a man the size of a baseball. A clean shot to the head takes the brains right along with it."

David got to his feet. "Look, I didn't come here to take part in an old-fashioned shoot-out. Capturing a tiger is one thing—killing a man is another!"

Jack looked at him steadily a long moment. "Son," he

said softly, "I don't know what your beef is with me, and I don't want to know. But this isn't L.A. There are all sorts of dangers in these woods, including crazy humans." He picked up the 9mm automatic; it looked like a toy in his huge, scarred hand. "Packing a gun is second nature to me, I guess, living alone up here. But if it makes you nervous, well . . ." He released the bullet clip and tossed the gun into the stuffed chair in front of the TV.

David eyed the gun for a second. Meg saw him relax, and she said, "Good. Now, can we get down to business?"

"Suits me," Jack said.

Meg moved behind Jack's shoulder and stared down at the map. "Rajah was last reported to be in the Cucamonga area," she said. "My guess is, he's heading north by northeast to Summit Valley. That he'll make his way down the San Andreas Rift Zone and cross into the San Bernardino Forest here." She pointed to the map.

Jack squinted, put on a pair of silver-rimmed glasses, and then studied the map. "Well, he'll have to cross Highway 15 to do that."

"Not necessarily. There are plenty of storm drains that run under the highway. That's how he got out of L.A. County. Look here." She placed her finger on the map. "The Cleghorn Ridge. He follows it to Cajon Canyon, travels the ridge and then drops into Horsethief Canyon. Summit Valley is dead ahead. He was raised in a private compound there."

"That Richter Institute hellhole?" Jack asked.

Meg nodded.

"Near the Mojave River. Damn. Some of us tried shutting that place down. Would have, too, if it hadn't been for them bringing a whole army of silk-tie lawyers up from L.A." He spun around to face Meg. "Count me in. And don't you worry none about that cat of yours. From what

I've heard, he's a shrewd one. He won't be poking his head up until well after dark. That's when we get him." He paused, then stood up and nodded to Ray. "You see that rug?"

Ray glanced at the floor behind him. "Yes?"

"Roll it up," he said, and then turned to Meg. "There's something I want to show you."

Meg and David followed Jack's lead to the center of the room and watched Ray as he rolled up the heavy Navajo carpet. The tongue-and-groove slats of oak flooring were pegged at both ends, each row looking the same in every direction.

"Nice floor," David said. "But what are we supposed to be looking at?"

Jack turned around from the storage closet holding a flashlight. "Keep your pants on," he said with a grin. "There's more to this floor than meets the eye."

He knelt on one knee and pushed his thumb into one of the hundreds of pegs in the floor. Meg heard a soft click, and up popped a second peg in front of her toe. "Step back," Jack said. He squeezed the protruding peg and a small metal handle sprang out to the side. He hooked it with his finger and pulled.

"Down there is where I keep all my goodies," Jack said, shining his flashlight down a set of old wooden steps. He went down first, the others followed.

At the bottom, Meg glanced around. To her amazement, the cellar was filled with high-powered night-vision sur-veillance equipment. It included electromagnetic field de-tectors, ionization monitors, scanning devices, and scopes that had barely been introduced into the military, let alone the private sector.

"We'll set up shop at Horsethief Canyon," Jack said. "A friend of mine has a fishing cabin close by. I've got a solid holding cage, too. Used it myself while nursing a bear cub back to health. And chain-link fence for setting up our blind." He smiled. "And that's just for starters."

He moved further into the room and pulled open a large door. Steamy, frosted air spilled out and swirled around his feet. He groped for a light inside the door and switched it on.

Before them was a freezer at least ten feet wide and twenty feet deep. Inside were a dozen animal carcasses strung up on steel hooks, their bodies frozen stiff, bloodied and stripped of skin. Meg felt suddenly sick, but Jack didn't seem to notice. His face showed no emotion, although Meg did detect something different about his eyes, a gleam she could not diagnose—excitement, perhaps, or challenge. Or both.

He turned slowly to face David, smiling. "Hell, a tiger's got to eat, right?"

30

THE BELL JETRANGER helicopter flashed over Telegraph Peak, its shadow running ahead of it because the sun was to the east.

Below, the tiger remained in a rigid crouch, his paws gathered beneath him as the helicopter swooped by. He sniffed the air and scanned the surrounding area, his tawny striped coat blending with the rocks and the shadows and the tall reeds of dry grass.

As suddenly as the helicopter had appeared, it vanished over the next ridge. The cat waited a moment, then loosened his cramped muscles and joints, and let his massive body relax on the ground. Over the past few hours, he had doubled his efforts to find something to eat, searching in vain for the meal he needed. Now he was too exhausted to go on.

Listlessly, he swung his head around and licked at his wound. An errant wind crossed the canyon, wafting toward the knoll, and the cat flared his nostrils without moving anything else. His nose quivered for a second or two, telegraphing to his brain the identity of the scent. But it was an odd scent, like nothing he had ever encountered.

Then came the faint barking of dogs, an angry sound that came and went on the wind.

A low growl started to rumble in the cat's belly. When the sound of the dogs grew louder, he bounded to his feet. He was too late to elude them, however, as the pack of wild dogs was suddenly there, surrounding him. They circled, heads slung low, fangs wet and dripping saliva. They could smell the tiger's wounds and the blood, could sense but not gauge his vulnerability.

The black mongrel lunged first, going for the tiger's throat. The cream-colored bitch came next, snapping at his shoulder. The cat growled as he dropped into a defensive crouch, and both dogs quickly retreated to the edge of the circle, eyes glaring.

From the rear, three more dogs darted beneath the tiger's flank and snapped at his limbs, the mongrel and the bitch barking furiously to confuse him.

As the tiger turned, the mongrel sprang onto his back and tore into his flesh. He rolled away, but the pack was on him now, biting, tearing, slashing at his legs until he reared up with his claws fastened on the mongrel, and slammed it against the rocks. He bounded full speed for cover, but within six strides the pain returned as dogs snapped at his flanks. He stumbled, groaning, then knifed his way into the tall brush that lined the riverbed.

The cream-colored bitch and a boxer continued the chase as closely as they could. The tiger lunged, brought the bitch down by the throat, then his legs pushed forward, propelling him into the water; but the boxer held on, riding his back into the river.

When the dog bit into his ear, the cat flung his head back and started to sink into the water. Still the boxer wouldn't let go—its teeth held, and the cat couldn't get a breath, the shock overwhelming, until he sank beneath the surface.

CLAW

When he came up again he had the boxer's body held firmly in his jaws, which opened once and then slammed shut.

Silence enveloped the tiger as the boxer stopped thrashing. Already he could taste the animal's hot blood as it mixed with water and rushed into his mouth. Holding the dead carcass between his teeth, the cat drifted a ways, until he could get his footing and hurl himself ashore on the other side.

The pack, suddenly quiet, sensing defeat, had gathered on the far bank and watched as the tiger roared triumphantly over the kill, then bent and ripped away the skin, exposing the pink under layer of flesh. Slashing, ripping with his teeth, he tore open the dog's stomach and quickly gorged himself.

After gulping down the last of the entrails, the cat stared up at the face of the cliff. Hawks, crisscrossing above the pale surface of the water, swooped down to have a closer look.

The cat growled and rose up to his full height, scattering the birds. Then he glanced across the river.

The pack was gone.

31

CAJON JUNCTION at 3:00 P.M. was at least ten degrees colder than it had been at Riner's cabin. The ground was carpeted with ice, and the wind hissed through the trees. Behind her, Meg heard the noise of a small animal crashing through the underbrush and suddenly realized that if she left the Texaco station they had stopped at, a walk of no more than a few hundred yards would bring her into a natural fortress of towering peaks and harsh, forbidding canyons that would give even the hardiest mountain traveler second thoughts.

Nonetheless, she was determined, and the longer she stood watching Ray pump gas into Jack's old, two-ton jalopy, the more impatient she became. David was off making a phone call. Jack had gone straight into the small diner across the street. "Tiffany's—Open Twenty-four Hours," read the sign above its battered exterior.

"What could Jack be doing in there?" Meg asked.

Ray looked up from the pump and shrugged. "Getting something to eat, I guess." His eyes went to the meter, where flashing green digits blurred rapidly together.

Meg looked at her watch. They had already lost time at

a remote ranch outside of Blue Cut. The owner was a Mexican Jack had known for years, an old ranchero from a whiskey-making family before whiskey-making was illegal.

When Jack had asked him for the keys to his fishing cabin in Horsethief Canyon, he'd looked at him strangely. Then he had grinned, showing tobacco-stained teeth. "Ah, *el tigre*," he had said, but he knew better than to ask any questions. He and Jack merely swallowed a shot of tequila in silence, then had one more for the road.

Meg glanced now at the pale winter sun barely visible through thin clouds. If they hurried, they could still get to Horsethief Canyon in time to set up the tiger blind and lay down bait before nightfall.

"Just how much gas does this piece of junk hold?" Meg grumbled, moving to Ray's side.

"Relax," Ray said. "Rajah's probably holed up somewhere and won't be out until well after dark."

"I hope so," Meg said. She was growing increasingly nervous. She went to the back of the truck, undid the canvas flap, and peered in. The holding cage was a pretty good size, and it was solid, just as Jack had promised. Six buckets of horsemeat and two sides of beef were putrefying in the corner. Jack had used acid to thaw the meat. Then he had wrapped it in plastic, and wrapped it again in an electric blanket to draw out the blood.

The stench stung Meg's nostrils, and she drew back. As she let go of the flap she heard Ray's whistle. She came around his side of the truck. He was still leaning over the nozzle, nodding toward the street where a patrol car was moving slowly through the intersection. It crept past the gas station and then came to a stop.

The officer behind the wheel seemed to hesitate. Meg saw him check his rearview mirror and knew he was seeing only a deserted street. The yellow light flashed caution. Then he swung the car around and pulled into the station. The official markings on the side of the door shone clearly in the slanting sunlight: San Bernardino County Sheriff— Dedicated to Your Safety.

"Looks like trouble," Ray said, pretending to study the pump meter.

"I knew it," Meg said. "We stayed here too long." She took a quick step, glanced to where David was chatting, and leaning casually into the public phone. "David, time to go!" Meg yelled. He nodded and waved back.

When Meg turned she saw the patrol car inch closer to her Jeep and stop. Ray hurriedly hung up the nozzle and screwed the cap closed on the gas tank.

"Let me talk to him," Meg said.

"Okay," Ray said, "and I'll just wander over and get Jack."

As Ray started across the street, a gust of wind kicked up. Meg heard a lazy flapping sound and realized she'd forgotten to tie the canvas down. She hurried to the back of the truck, flipped the rope through the steel loop and cinched it. From the corner of her eye she could barely make out the officer's face. He appeared to be looking at his dashboard, as if checking something out, then he rolled down his window before opening the car door.

Meg could hear the crackling of a dispatch voice on his police band, but couldn't make out what was being said. She took a small step toward the officer, knowing that something was wrong. Maybe Jack had been right. Maybe they had been following them all along.

The sun emerged suddenly from behind the clouds, glinting off the Jeep window. The officer's shadow fell across the drive.

"It's turning out to be a nice day," Meg said crisply, staring into the officer's green aviator glasses.

"Don't let a little sun fool you," the officer said. "There's another front moving in." He put both hands in the small of his back and stretched. "Funny, isn't it? We can go for years with only a few inches of snow, then *woosh!* In it comes . . . big fuss. Vehicle fatalities, bodies found frozen in the foothills." He straightened and looked directly into Meg's eyes. "Then the second it's over, everybody goes straight back into the mountains. You coming or going?"

"What?"

"The mountains," he repeated slowly. "Are you leaving, or did you just get here?"

"Uh . . . both."

"Beg your pardon?"

"I mean, we *were* up there. Cucamonga. But the snow, the cold, you know?"

"Hummm."

"But now the sun, and . . ." Meg smiled and nodded up at the sky, though she was certain he wasn't buying a word of it. "So we've decided to go back up and stick it out."

"Then you'd better be careful, ma'am." He slipped his hands into his jacket pockets and began circling the Jeep slowly, peering in. As fast as the sun had appeared, it vanished.

"The roads, you mean? The ice?"

He turned his face up to the sky, appearing to consider it for snow. Then he looked down at Meg and gave her a large, kindly smile that was far too much like a grin for her. "Heck, no, I'm talking about that tiger. I'm sure you've heard, a man-eater. Not like one of these local bobcats that just hisses at you and runs away." He glanced at the Jeep again. When he removed his sunglasses, Meg saw that his eyes were a deep blue. A handsome face, once fully revealed, she thought. Friendly. "This your Jeep?" he asked.

"Yes," Meg said.

The officer nodded. "An old-timer. My son is thinking

about getting one. To tell you the truth, I'm scared to let him drive a Jeep. Not the best when it comes to handling the curves, are they, Miss . . . ?"

"Brentwood. Pam Brentwood," Meg said.

He nodded. "Well, I sure wish he'd settle on a normal car. But you know how teenagers are." He sighed. "Well, Miss Brentwood, you take care now."

Meg watched dumbfounded as the officer ambled back to the patrol car and climbed in. He had most definitely picked up on every lie she had told, yet he hadn't challenged her. Not really. She watched him roll up his window, adjust his mirror. Ray and Jack were just crossing the road when he started his car, Ray hopping over puddles and Jack following, unscrewing the cap of a small pink bottle.

"What did he want?" Ray asked, coming up beside her.

"I'm not sure," Meg said.

As they watched the patrol car leave the service station, Jack pressed a bottle of Pepto Bismol to his mouth and took a huge swallow.

"What's that for?" Meg asked.

"Damn tequila," Jack grumbled, rubbing the large circle of his belly. "I think I swallowed the worm."

BACK AT L.A.'s Northeast Division, Dragleman slammed the captain's door so hard that the walls shook. Small flakes of twenty-year-old plaster fell to the floor. Voices and the incessant purring of telephones spilled out from adjacent offices as he angrily made his way down the hallway. Faces looked up; the loud and often heated conversation inside the captain's office had gone on for almost an hour.

The captain had finally laid down the law: "Orders from the top, Dan. Back off. Don't even mention this tiger bullshit or it's your ass!"

Screw you, Dragleman thought, coming to an abrupt stop near the water cooler. He scratched his jaw thoughtfully, trying to get a handhold on reality. The *top?* he wondered. Just who might that be? The chief, the mayor, the governor . . . who?

A good question. It started others ricocheting around his skull. Was the tiger somehow connected to Shindler's murder? Obviously, Stan Farris had thought so, because he had made that clear the night he called Dragleman. *My advice is not to hang up,* Farris had said. *Not if you're interested in what happened to Carol Lewis. In a way, it was murder. Same with Shindler.*

Dragleman thought about that for a second. In a way, it was murder, he reasoned. What did that mean? A tiger kills a girl and Farris claims that "in a way" it was murder. What way?

Dragleman puzzled over these questions as he gulped water from the cooler. He hated mysteries; they gave him a headache. Perhaps that was why he had become a detective. The sooner riddles were solved, the better he felt.

Head throbbing, Dragleman fished around in his pockets and dug out a fresh cigar. Cigars were as good as aspirin.

"Hey, Lieutenant, you've got a phone call!" a voice behind him shouted. He turned and saw Detective Reese heading his way.

When Dragleman entered his office a few minutes later, Cusack turned and yelled into the phone, "Wait a second, he's right here!"

Dragleman snatched up the receiver. "Hello, Joe?"

The lieutenant had called Deputy Singer earlier for help in locating Meg Brewster, but the San Bernardino deputy had said at the time it was hopeless. It was just too big an area. But now . . .

"That's her, all right." Dragleman snapped his fingers

and pointed, and Reese quickly closed the door. "Where did you say—uh, come on, Joe. Outside of Cucamonga *where?*" Cusack rolled a rumpled map out on the desk and tapped it with his finger. Dragleman looked down, saying, "Cajon Junction?" Cusack put his finger right on the spot.

Dragleman leaned back, listening. "Right, I owe you, Joe. And like I said, don't tell anyone . . . and thanks."

When Dragleman slammed the phone down, Reese jumped. "It's her, all right. She was just spotted at Cajon Junction. Let's go." He stood.

Reese frowned. "But what about Captain Peterson?"

Dragleman froze in mid-step. His face creased into a grin. "I don't think the captain wants to come," he said casually. "Of course, I don't know that for a fact."

Reese shook his head. "Captain Peterson will nail our asses to the wall if we go up there, Lieutenant. Cajon Junction is out of our jurisdiction. We don't have any authority there."

"We really don't need any, Billy," Dragleman said, his eyes focused on the younger detective's uneasy face. He thought he could see himself there: before Vietnam, before his wife's death. Before the disillusionment, and the loss. If I feel less afraid than Billy, Dragleman wondered, is that maturity . . . or have I lost interest in my own life?

Or maybe it was control. And discipline, something he had surely learned. In fact, it had become a personal conviction of Dan Dragleman's that the one absolute qualification for success lay in such self-discipline. Virtually every powerful person he had ever met possessed it.

Like Meg Brewster, he thought, his focus coming back to the young veterinarian. Her passion for animals was the force that drove her; the control over the passion was what gave her the strength to be so good at what she did. The self-control was what he admired and why he felt drawn to help Dr. Brewster.

"What do you mean, we don't need any authority?" Reese was saying uneasily.

Dragleman smiled at the young officer. "Just what I said, Billy. We're all about to go off duty, aren't we? So why should the captain care?"

"We are?" Reese said, and heard Cusack chuckle.

Dragleman suddenly crossed to the door. "You bet we are! This is a big day, Billy Boy. We're going to have an adventure. Everyone loves an adventure, and *you're* included. Now get your boots on. I'll meet you both in the motor pool in fifteen minutes."

"Should I bring a shotgun?" Cusack asked.

Fucking good question, Dragleman thought as he disappeared down the hall.

32

THE BROWN-AND-GREEN-SPLOTCHED National Guard plane circled low over Horsethief Canyon, then headed south as the last traces of sunlight eased from the sky.

When the tiger heard the odd purring sound, he opened his eyes but did not move. Though he smelled the scent of fresh blood, he knew it was his own. His right shoulder throbbed where the bullet had lodged. Blood still flowed from the wound and from the deep gashes on his hind legs. A vision of angry dogs, teeth snapping, flashed through his mind.

He glanced upward, outward, without moving. Then he sniffed. No predatory scent was carried on the wind, so once more he closed his eyes.

Agonized, he drifted back to sleep.

A FEW MILES AWAY, Meg Brewster froze for a moment, until she was sure the plane was gone. The trunks of trees shone damp and glistening around her, and the lowest branches were immersed in ragged layers of snow. The wet chill had penetrated to her body through the heavy parka she wore, stiffening her arms and legs. But despite the cold, she stood resolutely at her vigil, staring up at the sky.

Her thoughts had been almost a total swirl of images from the past three days, but as she watched the plane disappear, they focused suddenly on what she was going to do. She felt a confusion of emotions knot her stomach. The fear was there, but there was also a certain anticipation, a gnawing awareness of the need to capture Rajah safely, to whisk him away before they could destroy both him and the secret that swam in his blood.

"All clear," she called down to the others, and watched them emerge from their places of concealment into the fading light. Heavy sweat beaded Ray's brow as he picked up his shovel, drove it into the ground, and continued digging the postholes on either side of the cave. Jack and David stepped closer to the two sides of beef dangling by a rope from a tree branch, the blood dripping into a ten-gallon bucket.

As Meg scrambled down the embankment, she caught a whiff of the raw meat. Even yards away, the stink was awful.

"How can you be sure the tiger's coming through the canyon at this spot?" David asked, watching Jack cut a sliver of beef from the dangling carcass.

"I can't." Jack tossed the bloody strip of flesh into the bushes a few yards away. "All I know is he has to eat. A Siberian is the biggest cat of them all. A cat his size can eat forty pounds of flesh in one day, and still look for more. With all those exploding neurons, hell . . . ninety pounds would be more like it. Am I right, Meg?"

"Maybe more," Meg nodded, trying to catch her breath. A trail of horsemeat had been tossed from the vehicles earlier, a quarter of a mile on either side, hoping to draw Rajah to this one spot. Then the vehicles were hidden in a lone stand of trees.

"One healthy deer might satisfy him," David persisted.

Jack cut off another slice of beef, blood spotting his hands and face. "Maybe," he said. "Of course, he'd have to get his claws into it first. He's tired now, pretty near exhausted. I doubt he'll catch much. Besides, if he's in this area, the rest of the animals will clear out."

"Still, it's a long shot."

"Not quite."

"Why's that?"

Jack smiled, and pointed to a narrow dirt road running through a stand of pine. "Because that Richter Institute hellhole is in a pocket at the bottom of this canyon. That road leads to the back entrance. If you look close, you can just make out the chain-link fence running along the ridge. That's part of their property. If Meg's right"—he looked at her and winked—"he'll be through here." He sniffed. "And the wind is running good, son. Running real, real good."

He picked up the bucket and tossed blood in several directions over the snow. Then he poured water into a canteen cup. He emptied it in one gulp, spilling it on his chin and down his chest, but obviously not caring.

Then he leaned forward, his face frozen for a moment as if in a silent convulsion before a cough. When it came, it was a phlegmy sound, rattling deep from his chest. When it was over, he held his hand at his mouth for a long time.

"Are you all right?" Meg asked.

Jack Riner laughed. "Hell, I never did like cold weather. Hot weather either, for that matter. The last time I was in the tropics I nearly died. A friend of mine did. Wasn't the weather killed him though but a panther. The cat had raked the guy's face with its claws. Four vertical lines slashed over his temple and his eyes still open, like he died of fright before the cat actually clawed him.

"He was lucky in a way," Jack went on, "because the cat never did eat him. Panthers always go for the belly first. That's where the tenderest flesh is. The belly or sometimes the cheeks. Or the buttocks. I have never understood how so clean and elegant a beast as the panther can bring itself to feed off corpses—off the nastiest sort of carrion. But then, tigers are pretty much the same."

David kicked at the snow. "Was that little story meant to scare us?"

"Just thought you should know what you're in for," Jack said.

"And you think that blind will protect us?"

Jack considered. "Don't know. Never dealt with a seven-hundred-pound Siberian before."

"That cave isn't very deep. What if the fence doesn't hold?"

Jack motioned to the rifle in David's hand. "That weapon might stop him. Of course, you'd have to stay calm. It isn't easy to hit a moving target. Especially when it's charging straight at you."

Jack stared at David for a second, then looked over to Ray. "Hey, Ray! Give me a hand with the cage, will you? I want to get it in place before we lose the light altogether."

Ray nodded and put down his shovel. He and Jack ambled toward the truck.

David looked around, shaking his head. "Christ, this is insane," he said to Meg. "Even disregarding what Jack just said, we could get trapped down here. If another storm blows in—"

Meg cut him off. "That's why Jack made sure there was a cabin close by. There are enough supplies in there to last us a week."

David stared down the steep rock embankment. Ahead, halfway between them and the river was the fishing cabin, amid a stand of pines that had grown to maturity around it. Jack had made sure none of the lights were left on.

"Still, I don't like the feel of this," David said. His face was white, as if the chill had permanently iced his cheeks and forehead. Worry shone in his eyes.

"Are you suggesting we quit?" Meg asked. "That we cut and run?"

"It's crossed my mind," he confessed gruffly.

Meg hesitated a moment. Above the sky was rapidly darkening to night. The cry of a great horned owl floated down from a giant pine.

"All I know is this, David," Meg said finally. "To be human is to be in danger. We've made a commitment here. I hope it works out for the best, for *all* of us. Now I've got to get the rest of the supplies into the cave."

TWENTY MINUTES LATER, night flooded in like a tide. A breath of wind passed through the canyon, rustling the leaves as it went.

Jack Riner took his night-vision Starlite binoculars and studied the canyon one last time. The dense tangle of trees was no longer green but pitch-black, a close-knit universe that seemed private and impenetrable.

"It's like a big hand," Jack said. "Five ridges running and enclosing this canyon. Let's hope he takes the low ground."

Meg said, "Let's hope."

Jack wrapped his arm around her and gave a gentle squeeze. "He'll be through, Meg. In the meantime, we'd best be getting inside." He pulled the chain-link fence back and disappeared into the cave.

Ray was just coming from the truck with the last load of

supplies. Meg hoisted her Cap-Chur rifle and started toward him. Ray's legs disappeared into a snowdrift and he tossed the crate he was carrying to the ground and sat on it, catching his breath.

Meg sat beside him, her back resting against a mammoth white pine, its bark gnarled, which soared upward to a lofty pinnacle etched against the dark sky.

"Is it my imagination, or does everything out here seem to be constantly moving?" Meg asked, taking two tranquilizer darts from her pocket.

"I don't know," Ray said. "The light is playing tricks, I guess."

Meg nodded, uneasy with her emotions as she began loading her rifle. Then she watched Ray lean over to help, encouraging her with every gesture. Their eyes met and Meg felt herself tremble. Something like a shock wave followed. She realized new ground had somehow been broken between them and that suddenly she was as vulnerable toward him as he had always been with her. She had always known Ray looked at her differently from the way he looked at other women, and tonight, for some reason, that pleased her intensely.

He was handsome, yes. But deep down she believed it was the quality of his character that attracted her most: his great patience, his respect for all living things. And she deeply appreciated his tolerance for her point of view. No matter how narrow or impassioned her ideas might seem, he was willing to listen and not prejudge. She said quietly, "Thanks, Ray."

"For what?"

"For sticking around. Especially after all that's happened."

Ray considered her for a moment, then reached out and took her hand in his. "You know, Meg," he said, "it might sound funny, but I never asked myself if I *should* or *shouldn't* come along on this crazy trip. It was just the right thing to do . . . you needed me, so here I am."

Meg could feel the power in his body and leaned closer to him for an instant, aware of his maleness. "Maybe," she said, "that zoology degree and those four years of vet school will come in handy tonight. What do you think?" Before he could respond, she leaned in and kissed him passionately.

When it was over, he stared at her, obviously searching for words.

"We've got work to do," Meg said, and quickly got to her feet. "And let that be a lesson to you. Never become compassionate under a dark sky. It's just liable to get you in trouble."

Ray laughed; then both of them, at least for a time, were laughing.

As DRAGLEMAN and the others drew closer to the canyon, an almost palpable cloud of dread formed in the car, and conversation lagged. When Reese pulled off the main road at the large green reflectorized sign that read HORSETHIEF CANYON, Dragleman glanced nervously at the wavering darkness below.

Traveling through the mountains hadn't been easy. Deputy Singer had given them official police maps, but still the going had been rough. Some of the roads had been closed earlier because of rock slides and snowdrifts. Others hadn't been sanded properly, and were more ice slick than road.

But Deputy Singer was sure Jack Riner and the others had gone to Horsethief Canyon. The old Mexican was sure, too. "My cabin," he had said, swaying against the bar with a glass of tequila in his hand.

Dragleman looked up now, concerned. The car had

dropped suddenly and then bounced over a mound in the road. Loose snow shot up and smacked the windshield.

The wipers batted at the flakes slightly out of sync. Was the snow falling or was the car rising? Dragleman felt the stale heat on his face and the car's tires sliding beneath them, the residue of a hurriedly eaten dinner in his stomach, the sweat under his arms.

Reese slowed the car a bit. "This road's a mess," he said, straightening the wheel. His boyish face looked pale and frightened. "Christ, I can't even see where I'm going."

Cusack said, "Stay to the middle and you'll be all right."

The road was pitch-black and deserted. Halfway down the next incline they passed a small panel truck stuck in a drift. Dragleman glanced back, looking for signs of life. "Hold up," he said.

Reese jammed on the brakes and the car slid to a stop. Cusack looked inquiringly at the lieutenant.

"What do you think?" he asked.

"I don't know, the panel door was left open, so I figure we should check it out. No telling what we'll find."

Dragleman and Cusack got out, and Reese shone the spotlight on the truck. The two detectives approached slowly. Underfoot, snow mixed with gravel and ice crunched at every step. As they reached the open panel door, Dragleman shone his flashlight inside. Then he sniffed.

The smell was definable instantly, and Dragleman felt his nostrils cringe against it and try to shut it out. The smell was not as strong as it had been at the zoo, but it was just as basically offensive—a wet, putrid odor. The smell of a cat marking his territory.

"Anything interesting?" Cusack inched forward to have a look, his shotgun loaded and ready.

"Empty," Dragleman said. "But that damned cat's been

here, all right. Christ, what an odor." Peering in, he could see the muddy paw prints on the compartment floor and the warm puddle of urine in the corner.

"Any signs of trouble?" Cusack glanced around nervously.

"No. Apparently the cat just stopped to take a leak, then moved on. Or he's still close by." Dragleman's mouth had gone cotton-dry. He turned suddenly to face Cusack. "Let's go."

"Where?"

"Down there." Dragleman turned and pointed somberly to the canyon three thousand feet below.

33

THE CAVE WAS CRAMPED and cold, the kind of place better suited to animals than to humans, Meg thought. She watched as David slid off the box of canned goods he was sitting on, then stretch upward as far as he could, which wasn't much. Outside, the sky was heavy with snow. It seemed to lower itself over the treetops, pressing down on the earth and on every standing thing. Branches creaked; the wind moaned.

"It's easy to see why primitive man worshiped fire," David said finally, blowing hot breath into his cupped hands.

"And why he feared the night," Ray said. A twig snapped in his hands and he threw the broken pieces aside.

Jack stared at the two men for a moment, then pulled his jacket collar up, pressing closer to the opening and peering out. Meg felt the gesture, however, like a bead of sweat on her back.

They were all edgy, she realized. They had every reason to be. They had lived with fear and danger for many un-relieved hours now. It was bound to take its toll. Finally they were nearing the climax, the greatest danger of all.

And the chain-link fence that separated them from Rajah provided little comfort.

Meg glanced slowly around the cave. Water dripped from the ceiling; dampness seemed to impregnate everything they touched—their guns, the flashlight casing, the canvas bed-rolls. Meg hunched her shoulders and began to shiver. In the dim light she could just make out faces.

"Is there any place colder than a blind on a raw January night when the sky is bursting with snow and the wind is whistling through you?" Jack Riner wondered aloud. "I doubt it. Hell, my feet feel like blocks of ice. My nose feels like it belongs to someone else!" Jack carried a flask in each of his coat's deep pockets, one containing gin and the other rum. He removed the gin flask, uncapped it, and drank. Then he handed it to David. "Have a snort, son. It won't warm your hands, but after a while you'll forget all about them."

David took a swallow, then passed the flask to Ray, who drank slowly, a sip at a time.

"I wish I had a cigarette," David said.

"They're poison," Jack told him without looking up. "Actually, so do I. I quit about a year ago. But I'm always thinking about that carton of cigarettes I keep by my bed."

"Why keep cigarettes if you don't smoke?"

"Test of character, son. Same as a preacher keeps a dirty magazine tucked away under his underwear. Willpower."

Ray laughed out loud and handed the flask back to Jack, who held it out to Meg questioningly.

She shook her head. Her nerves could use the break, but she wanted to have all her senses about her.

By eight o'clock, the brief nervous bouts of laughter had all but died and the strain of waiting had become a throb-bing ache. Meg's feet felt completely frozen. Every few minutes she flexed her hands to keep them supple for the moment when she would aim and fire. The thermos of coffee and Jack's two flasks were nearly empty. David had grown increasingly restless and had begun asking Ray all sorts of personal questions. Both men were irritable, David because he felt Ray was being evasive, not telling him the whole truth, and Ray because he did not want to talk at all.

Only Jack remained perfectly still and relaxed. He peered intently into the dark, eyes shifting slightly to track the wind, or the faint sound made by a small woodland creature.

Meg watched him closely, although his features were difficult to read in this dim light. Still she could see his gaze dart rapidly over the shadows outside, and could feel his doubts and misgivings.

Meg whispered, "Jack, what is it?"

He did not move; his gaze was locked on the outside gloom. "The tiger is here."

"Are you sure?"

"It's him, all right."

Meg jerked her rifle up. The possibility that Rajah could be just outside made her heart pound. She wiped her hands on her Levi's and gripped the rifle.

"I can't see him," David said, and Meg wondered if Jack was wrong. The silhouettes of dangling carcasses swung slowly in front of them but that was all.

"Too damn quiet," Ray whispered, and Jack nodded. Then he looked up. They all did when they heard the sound of twigs breaking. Meg patted her pockets to make sure she was carrying extra tranquilizer darts, then raised her rifle, cocked the hammer, and sighted down the barrel.

In the darkness outside they could make out the shape of a buck as he stepped out from behind an outcropping of rocks some twenty yards away. It was moving at a brisk walk, unaware that humans were close by. Then it veered left and came up onto a small knoll.

There the buck stopped. It turned, and went rigid when

Jack flashed his light on it. The buck trembled, too stunned to move. It peered at the light, terror in its eyes.

Meg was never quite sure what came first after that.

Suddenly the buck's body crashed to the ground, the snow flying up in a violent shower around him. Out of the frenetic whiteness, Rajah's massive head emerged, his teeth sunk into the buck's neck.

"*Shoot him!*" Jack screamed. A second later an explosion of fur and claws smashed into the chain-link fence. Meg had not seen the cat move; now he was on top of them, ramming his claws through the fence.

"Watch out!" Ray shouted, and Meg stumbled back and fell, hands out, palms scraping against the walls of the cave. Mud smeared across her chin as she rolled over and groped frantically for her rifle.

Before Meg could get to her feet, Rajah lunged again. This time the fence snapped loose, pinning them to the back of the cave. Growls and shouts erupted as Ray heaved on the fence, trying to right it.

"Kill him!" David yelled to Jack, but Jack's coat sleeve was snagged on the fence and his arm was pinned between rock and steel.

The tiger's teeth tore into the chain links, quickly snapping metal until a twisted gash in the fence lay open above Jack's face. He lurched back, his free hand flailing wildly to protect his throat as the tiger's claws shot through the opening and slashed furiously.

Suddenly everything seemed to explode, to be happening at once, as Ray shouted to David, ". . . Jack's rifle. Get Jack's rifle!" then moved toward it himself, reaching out, while Jack screamed, struggling violently to elude the cat, then howling as sharp claws sank into his rib cage, while Meg's finger froze on the trigger as she tried to get a clean shot, feeling her own strength drain out of her.

CLAW

The cat lurched back on his hind legs and Jack rose screaming into the air, the fence thrashing in the dark.

The violence of Rajah's attack unhinged Meg: she rocked back on her heels and fired in panic. Screams, moans, the sound of rushing wind as Meg realized she had missed.

Grabbing Jack's rifle, David pushed her aside. The cat drew back and turned sharply, ready to attack again. He charged, rammed into the twisted steel, straining to get at David.

"Get back!" Ray cried. He yanked David aside, heard something rush past him, saw the cat reach in and snag Jack's arm, saw David fire without aiming. The two shots hit the ground. Meg fired her Cap-Chur rifle again as the cat lurched back with Jack's arm in his mouth. Jack's head slammed against rock as the cat began dragging him through the opening.

"You son of a bitch!" David screamed, firing again. Blood erupted from the cat's side as the bullet entered just below the rib cage.

Stumbling back, the cat let go of Jack's arm, swung around and dropped into the snow, rolling and growling until it staggered to its feet and in slow, painful strides disappeared into the darkness.

Things immediately got quiet. For a second Meg couldn't think, could only gasp for breath, feeling her heart pound frantically. Her scalp burned where it had hit the ground. Her whole body felt numb.

THE SOUND OF GUNFIRE had made Dragleman's heart jump.

They had stopped again to nose around, and now he wasn't sure it had been a good idea. From where he stood on the rocky ledge he saw only a blur of diffused, ash-colored light, without images. Then to his right, below the small gravel road, in the same direction they were heading, he saw two sets of headlights creeping over the lower road at the base of the mountain.

Dragleman turned with a start when Cusack came stumbling up from the lower ridge. "Did you hear those shots?" he yelled up to the lieutenant. Cusack was a big man, and his voice rumbled.

"Yeah, I heard them," Dragleman said, tossing his cigar away. The tip hissed as it landed in the snow.

"They came from over there." Cusack paused beside the lieutenant, out of breath and pointing at a long gap a thousand feet below. "That Mexican was right. Those crazy bastards are down in that canyon!"

"Singer said we could trust him."

"Yeah, but as drunk as that Mexican was . . ."

"Look over there." Dragleman lifted his gloved hand and pointed at the headlights snaking through the trees. "What do you think?"

"Two cars," Cusack said. "Not moving very fast." He shrugged his huge shoulders. "Poachers, maybe."

"In a national forest? I doubt it."

Though Dragleman's eyes followed the headlights through the darkness, his thoughts were miles away.

Deputy Singer had warned him not to go it alone. Too cold, he had said. Hell, the blustery canyon winds can play tricks on the listener, imitating the sigh of a lonely woman, or the groan of a beast in the throes of death. God help the man who follows the cries of the canyon.

Cusack nervously ran long fingers through his hair. "What do you think?" he asked.

Dragleman wasn't sure. He was definitely out of his element, and completely out of his jurisdiction. He really hadn't counted on gunplay. He turned his eyes unwillingly to the mountains and slowly raised his head. The wooded shafts poked into the sky, tapering slightly as they rose. A sudden wind rose from the gap and the trees bowed, their snowy covering shaken to the ground until the dense pine was but a single black shadow. The canyon mouth gaped wide before him, its groan fading into silence.

"The hell with it," he said. "Let's go down and have a look."

Detective Reese was waiting in the car. When he saw them coming, he opened the door and shouted, "They're looking for us, Lieutenant. On the dispatch. They sound real ticked."

Disgusted, Dragleman kicked snow from his boots. "And what did you tell them, Billy?"

Reese caught a rush of cold air and shivered. "Hell, not a damn thing. I didn't even pick up the mike," he said.

Dragleman nodded. "Good. Now get back in the car and let's go."

THE TWO SEDANS whispered along the treacherous lower road leading into the canyon. Behind the wheel of one, Howard Boss sat with his hands firmly at ten and two o'clock. Roueche sat beside him, glancing from the window. Harsh static erupted from the CB radio beneath the dash, then a low voice as the static cleared.

"TC One, this is TC Two, do you read me?" the voice asked.

Roueche picked up the radio receiver, his gaze fixed ahead on Paul Gaddis's sedan. "Yes, TC Two, I read you loud and clear."

"I heard thunder."

"I know," Roueche said. "Perhaps those below just encountered the storm. If so, we are in luck. Go slow until you reach the bottom."

"Right," Gaddis said, his voice replaced by more static.

Roueche glanced through the windshield as he put down the receiver. Outside, snow fell against the windows, driven by a strong wind. Howard Boss leaned forward and turned on the wipers. Roueche could see that the whole affair had aged him; he was not the same cocky man who had sauntered into his office five years earlier. Lines on his face that had been barely noticeable then had now deepened into fissures. He now had to wear glasses, and his hands sometimes shook. These were the outward signs of how things had gone so crazily, maddeningly wrong.

"Well, Howard," Roueche said with a slight inward sigh, "I believe things are nearing an end."

"I don't like it," Boss complained. "Even if they have the cat, they won't give him up. Not without a fight."

Roueche laughed. "Well, then, Howard, I'm afraid we'll just have to let Mr. Gaddis deal with them."

"Jesus Christ, more killings?" Boss looked at him for a brief moment. "Is that what you're saying?"

Roueche shrugged. "May I remind you, Howard, that in any crisis basic losses are assumed. There are always casualties."

"Casualties, hell," Boss hissed. "Call it what you like. We're talking murder."

Roueche was silent. What can I say? he thought. You either get it or you don't. And Boss, obviously, doesn't get it.

"Damn," Boss said, squinting through the windshield. "To think one woman could have caused all this trouble."

"Yes," Roueche said, picturing Meg Brewster as he had first seen her. So young, so deliciously lovely and naive. At least, he had thought so at the time. A mistake, of course.

Roueche stared into space, thinking of his own verbiage. The word *casualties* had made him realize that nothing was ever as simple as it first appeared.

It didn't matter, since he now found himself in charge of the situation by default. He had held back as long as he could after Carol Lewis's death, convinced INR would be able to bury the incident. When that didn't happen—and when the tiger escaped from the zoo—he saw clearly that it was every man for himself. Washington had withdrawn its support. Ellroy had crumpled. INR had quickly pulled all of its men from the field, emptied the compound, leaving only a lone guard and Roueche and Boss on their own to solve the problem. So be it, Roueche thought.

He sat perfectly still for a moment, eyes fixed straight ahead. Then he steadied himself, prepared for the fight.

34

ONCE THE MOMENTS of terror and panic had passed, Meg felt her usual steadiness return. There was no room for nerves now, no margin for error born of hysteria. Jack lay between her and Ray. The top of his head was a mess of torn flesh; one eye socket was filled with blood. His abdomen and right arm were badly shredded; his jacket was covered with blood.

Meg took charge. While Ray cut off part of a towel and made a tourniquet for Jack's arm, Meg soaked the rest of the towel and covered the gaping stomach wound. Quickly shredding a T-shirt, she made a dressing out of it and wrapped it tightly around Jack's head to apply pressure to that area. Checking the beds of his fingernails, she saw that he was profusing well, and felt relieved that he was moving his limbs spontaneously, all positive signs that he had no spinal-column damage or broken bones.

"Lift him as gently as possible," Meg said, getting to her feet. "Let's get him out to the Jeep."

David and Ray slid their arms under his groaning body, locked hands, and lifted. Jack was a big man and carrying him was not easy. Even with the dressings, there was still a lot of blood, and David had a hard time keeping Jack's head elevated, especially since both he and Ray kept stumbling in the snow.

Meg caught up, placed her hand under Jack's neck, and tried to keep pace with them. Fighting knee-high drifts, they finally reached the Jeep and got the door open. Ray climbed in first, carrying Jack with him until he had Jack lying across the backseat.

As Meg climbed in behind the wheel, Jack groaned and blew a bloody bubble through his cracked lips. It was a harsh gurgle but at least he was breathing. Ray was still clinging to Jack, strapping him down under the blanket while Meg started the engine.

"Is he secured?" Meg asked.

"Pretty much." Ray stepped from the Jeep and closed the door.

"You better go now," David said, not looking at Meg. He stood gripping his rifle, eyes scanning the surrounding woods.

"There's a little town up top, just past the high ground," Meg said. "I'll try calling Valley Community Hospital from there. Maybe I can have an ambulance meet me halfway."

Ray came around to Meg's side of the Jeep. "Be careful going up. There's got to be ice under the snow, so the roads are going to be bad."

"I will," Meg said. Then she paused. "Look, if you find Rajah, don't shoot him straightaway. He's already wounded pretty badly, and I'm sure I hit him with the last dart."

Ray said, "We'll take Jack's truck and check out the animal compound. If Rajah is there, we'll try capturing him safely. Now you go on. We'll catch up to you later at the hospital."

Ray suddenly leaned in and kissed her. When he drew back, his face was tight with concern. "Hang in there, okay? We're all behind you."

"Thanks," Meg said. She hesitated, then shoved the gearshift into first and eased the Jeep from the tree cover. The silhouettes of the two men disappeared from her rearview mirror as she bumped and crawled out onto the narrow road.

In the backseat, Jack thrashed about and groaned louder. I'm responsible for this, Meg thought. Not completely, but I'm part of it. I insisted. I'm the reason Jack Riner is hurt or dying. I'm the reason Harry Shindler is dead. Me. Determined, single-minded Meg Brewster.

"I'm sorry, Jack," Meg said, though she knew he could not hear her. "That doesn't fix it, I know, but for whatever it's worth, I'm sorry. Just please hang on. I'll get you to a hospital or a doctor . . . or something. Just hang on."

Meg followed the rutted road through a long row of trees, holding her breath as each bump produced a groan from the backseat. As she went over a bridge, she became aware of the headlights of two cars blocking the road ahead.

Meg downshifted and pumped the brakes. The Jeep slid to a stop. Squinting into the glare, she immediately recognized the cars as the two unmarked sedans from the roadblock earlier in the day.

Meg heard a car door open and someone shout, "Shut off your engine, Dr. Brewster. And turn off your lights."

As Meg flicked off her lights and killed the engine, one of the sedans came forward slowly and then shot past her, disappearing across the bridge.

The man who had stepped from the car stood peering at her, the glare of headlights casting his face in darkness.

"Is the cat dead?" he said, his voice so low that Meg could barely make out his words.

She hesitated, wondering if she should reach for the handgun she had stashed in the glove compartment. She watched as he stepped closer.

"Is the cat dead?" he repeated, his body angling oddly

toward her. There was something sinister in the way he moved, the way his hand was held frozen at his side. Even motionless, Meg could sense a tension to his body, an air of evil to his presence. *Oh Jesus!* Meg thought suddenly. She could see the gun in his hand now as he moved alongside the Jeep.

Gaddis looked at Meg a moment. He smiled. Then he raised his pistol, cocked and locked, and pointed it straight at her face.

And Meg knew in that moment he was going to kill her, that there was nothing she could do or say that would change that. She stared at him and, at the last moment, ducked and reached frantically for the glove-compartment latch.

Suddenly a voice yelled: "Police! Put your hands on top of your head and freeze!"

Meg was still groping for her gun when she heard the first shot. By the third shot she was down between the seat and the dash, armed. When she glanced out, she saw the man stagger and fall to his knees in the snow. He yelled—a scream mixed of pain and fury—and fired three shots into the dark.

Responding shots came from the woods; Meg could see men firing as they ran, fanning out right and left. Each blast shook the Jeep and sent snow flying, as the man rose to a squat and began to weave in and out of the closest trees, keeping low.

All during the gunfire there was shouting back and forth, but garbled so that Meg couldn't understand what was being said.

As the fight moved away from the Jeep, Meg instinctively turned on her own headlights. In the sudden glare of light she saw the man thirty yards away, standing beside a tree, trying to reload.

For a moment he stood still, stunned, breathing heavily; the gun gripped tight in his hand; he looked around in every direction for some egress to safety, for some defensible position.

Then, dimly, Meg heard the final shot; it sounded like a pop of a balloon. The man turned, wide-eyed, his hand going for his throat. He rocked back on his heels, and then fell face down in the snow.

Apart from Jack's gasping breath rising from the backseat, everything was suddenly silent and still. Someone knuckle-rapped her window, and she turned with a start. Dragleman's face stared back at her.

"Evening, Doc," he said. "Looks like you should have returned my calls."

35

SNOW CRUNCHED UNDERFOOT as Meg and the lieutenant approached the body.

There had been a powerful eight-cell flashlight in the carry compartment between the Jeep's front seats, and now, as Detectives Reese and Cusack transferred Jack into the police car and called the hospital, Dragleman rolled the corpse over and ran the flashlight's bright spotlight from chest to face.

"Well, do you know him?" Dragleman asked in a low, hoarse voice.

The man's eyes were still open; blood oozed from the bullet hole in his neck and from the corner of his mouth.

Meg looked closer, and then turned away, fighting off her revulsion. "I'm not sure. It could be one of the men who came after me at the zoo. But I can't be positive."

She turned to stare again. How many others? she thought. How many others would die before all this was finally over?

Dragleman raised the flashlight, aiming its beam at the two detectives. They both turned and stared into the light.

"I'm all set to go, Lieutenant," the younger man said.

"Okay, now listen up, Reese," Dragleman said. "After you get to the hospital, let headquarters know what's what. But don't let them give you any crap about jurisdiction. And if they ask for an exact fix on our location, tell them you're not sure, then get your butt back here as fast as you can. Now get going."

"Right!" The young detective hurried toward the car.

Detective Cusack held a shotgun to his chest as he watched Reese climb into the car. First the headlights went on, then the emergency lights atop the roof.

"*Turn those damned things off!*" Cusack yelled the command so loudly that his voice distorted and broke up. "And no siren. You want the whole world to know we're here?"

The lights atop the car blinked off and the tires spun for a second before the car lurched forward, jigged up the road, and then vanished over the rise.

Meg watched the car disappear, then stepped toward the Jeep. Suddenly she stopped, uncertain which way to turn. Somehow she could not think. All the feeling had gone out of her. Dragleman and Cusack watched her for a second; then both moved to stand at her side.

Dragleman said, "How many men were in the other car?"

"I couldn't tell," Meg said. "Everything happened so fast."

Dragleman looked across the black expanse of trees. The snowfall had stopped, and the night was harsh and streaked in white. He turned to Cusack. "You can bet whoever was in that car has plenty of firepower."

Cusack raised his shotgun. "So do we."

Dragleman kicked snow off his boots. He suddenly looked incalculably weary, as if he had been condemned to carry a stone on his back all his life. "It isn't that simple," he said to Cusack. "We just killed a man we can't even identify. Plus we've gone way the hell out of our jurisdiction."

"Uh-huh," Cusack nodded.

"Look here," Dragleman said, "when this is cleaned up, I've got to deal with the Sheriff's Department. Not to mention the state boys. When they find out I knew a couple of homicidal maniacs were holed up on state property and didn't let them know, they'll be mighty put out, don't you think?"

Cusack dug the toe of his boot into the snow. "I know you're right, Lieutenant," he muttered. "It's just . . . well, we've come this far, and . . ." He looked at Dragleman. "And there are still two civilians down there."

Meg came to life. "He's right, Lieutenant. There is no telling what danger Ray and David are in."

Dragleman said, "Listen, Doc, I've been in this business a long time, and I know what my responsibilities are. We shouldn't have come here in the first place!" He turned irritably away and stared down the deserted road.

Meg started to speak again, but held back. She knew that no matter what he had said, he was weighing his chances. This had to be his decision.

"All right," he said, turning to face Meg. "Cusack and I will go down and have a look. But you're staying here."

"Not on your life." Meg walked straight to the back of the Jeep and took out a twenty-gauge Remington pump, thirty-inch full choke barrel. "I know the layout down there," she said. "You don't. Where the cabin is, the cave. Besides . . . there's still a tiger on the loose."

Cusack said, "She's right, Lieutenant."

"Okay, she's right! You win," Dragleman boomed. "We'll take the Jeep. No lights, you drive!"

THE CAT LIFTED ITS HEAD SLOWLY, straining to see, its vision blurred. High gray walls grew out of the trees. Sharp light broke through the darkness and the sound of an engine grew louder and louder.

The cat dropped to a crouch and watched the fast blur of lights go by. He sniffed, caught the strong scent of his own blood. The sound of the engine suddenly quit. Voices shrilled. Human voices.

Now the cat was almost running.

36

DRAGLEMAN FLUNG open the cabin door, and Cusack darted into the room with his shotgun aimed and ready. Dragleman, close behind him, shone his light around. The room was empty. He flashed the beam of light on the bathroom door. Cusack went over and nudged it open with the tip of his shotgun.

"Police!" he hollered, and disappeared into the darkness.

Meg stood with her back to the room, glancing over her shoulder, then eyeing the woods and the riverbank close by. She could see Jack's truck still parked in the trees. But there was no sign of Ray and David.

"Empty," Cusack said, relaxing just a bit.

Dragleman let the beam of light play around the room. Sheets covered furniture. The curtains were red and dusty. An old print of a galloping white horse hung over the fireplace, which reeked of damp ash. There were a few books, an old, wood-based "cookie-cutter" phone with hand crank attached to the wall.

"Nothing's been touched," Meg said. "And from the look of things, nobody's been in here either."

Cusack eyed the phone. "I haven't seen one of those in years."

"My aunt has one just like it," Dragleman said, and headed for the door.

Outside, Meg got as far as the beech stump halfway up the drive and stopped to stare down at the deep ruts scored in the snow. A cold dampness closed down on her. No Ray. No David, she thought. Please, God, let them be all right. "The sedan took off in a hurry," she said, catching Dragleman's eye.

He nodded.

Meg pointed to the road leading farther back into the canyon. "The tracks lead that way, toward the animal compound."

"There's a compound back there?" Cusack wondered aloud, seeing merely an old disused wood road.

"It's a service road to the back of their grounds," Meg said. "They have at least fifty acres. Look, here." She started to follow the tire tracks. "There's no doubt about it. They've driven to the compound. That's where Rajah is heading."

"I see," Dragleman said. He hesitated, thinking things over. Then his eyes went reluctantly to Jack's truck. That it was still there seemed to bother him. That Ray and David were nowhere to be found seemed to bother him even more. "Okay," he said, "let's take a ride in your Jeep. But slowly."

THE CAT FELL heavily to the ground, rolling in a puddle of his own blood. He sniffed, groaned, then looked up when a giant shadow swept over him. As the shadow came abreast of the trees, it slowed.

Drawing on the last of his strength, the cat rose up, recoiled, and with a mighty push of his legs, ran toward the clearing, breaking tree limbs, until the bulk of his frame lifted in the air, came down, crushing the snow with one elongated crunch of exhaustion.

"WHAT WAS THAT?" Meg slowed the Jeep to a stop. Her eyes darted through the windshield, and then scanned the surrounding area.

"Kill the lights," Dragleman said, and when Meg did, their eyes quickly adjusted to the dark. Dragleman was sitting up front. Cusack was covering their left flank from the backseat, hunched down, eyes fixed on the dense woods.

"I heard something," Meg said, still staring. "What was it?"

"I don't know," Dragleman said. "Ease forward slowly. But keep the lights off."

Meg slipped the shift into low gear and inched forward. Around the next turn, their path grew more narrow, and the canyon walls began to close in. The cliffs rose sharply, and gray rocky gaps appeared in the rows of spruce like patches in a scraggling beard. "I can barely see where I'm going," she said.

"How much further is it?" Dragleman asked.

"I'm not sure." Meg pulled to the side of the road. "But if we drive the rest of the way, they're bound to hear us coming."

Dragleman agreed, and Meg killed the engine and together they climbed out into the snow. Dragleman started off first with light, flatfooted strides; Cusack stumbled after him. Meg was right behind them as they made their way single file down a faint path winding through the trees.

When they turned the next bend, it was Cusack who saw it first. "There!" he said, pointing, and they froze in their tracks.

The concrete structure rose out of the clearing like a monument, completely dark, its rear grounds and driveway devoid of life. Tall fencing surrounded the complex, and the unmarked sedan stood near the deserted guardhouse. Skid marks showed where the rear wheels had locked and whipped around from a hard slamming of brakes.

The gate was open.

"I don't like this," Dragleman said, inching forward, his breath steamy in the cold night air. "Gate open, no sign of your friends."

Meg moved in tandem with him, straining to see in the darkness. Cusack had moved to the other side of the path, looking for a movement in the driveway ahead of them.

"Do you think they could have taken Ray and David as hostages?" Meg asked quietly.

"I don't know. We haven't heard any shots fired. They could be using silencers, but if your friends fired back . . ."

Cusack signaled, and they moved forward until they had reached the building. Dragleman climbed the steps and tried the door. It was open. He went into the foyer and looked around.

Cusack moved ahead and checked the hallway. "Real quiet," he said.

Meg backed in last, keeping her eyes on the darkness behind them. Until Dragleman waved her on, she had not been sure that she had the strength and the courage to take the first step over the threshold. Even then, she feared for a moment that she would cry out.

Dragleman reached out and hit the light switch. Nothing happened. "They've cut the power."

At the rear security desk, the surveillance monitors were dead; the controls useless. Dragleman swept his flashlight beam across the room. "There," he said, and held the light steady on the security door. Beside the knob was a slot for identification cards and an access panel for numbered codes. A red diode light on the panel blinked faintly.

"Emergency power," Meg said. "Every security door inside will be activated."

Dragleman checked the clip on his Beretta 9mm service pistol. "Okay, we're going in to have a look. But no hero stuff, Doc. Any shooting starts, you hightail it out of here and get help. Now strip."

"*What?*"

"Coats," Dragleman said; he laid the flashlight and gun down on the security desk, unbuttoned his coat and dropped it to the floor. "I don't want anything hampering our movements."

Meg and Cusack removed their coats. Meg's arms were still constricted by the bulky sweater, but at least the heaviest weight was off her shoulders.

"Cusack?" Dragleman said.

"Ready . . ."

"Go!"

Cusack spun on his heels and delivered two blasts into the wall, obliterating the security panel. Dragleman quickly opened the door.

"Go!" he yelled, and they raced into the dark hallway with Dragleman at the lead.

Fighting off panic, Meg moved into the pitch-black void, her rifle pointed, her elbow lightly brushing the wall as she went.

Cusack said, "Aim straight down the middle."

"But—"

"Just keep it there!" he said.

Aim at *what?* Meg thought. She saw nothing, but followed orders.

The flashlight clicked on. Dragleman and Cusack were both crouched beneath her line of fire, glancing down corridors, and Meg could finally see what Cusack meant. She had a clear shot at anyone coming from the other end of the long hallway, some forty feet away.

Dragleman tapped the air with his finger. Suddenly Cusack was on his feet and running. Meg kept him covered until he reached the end of the hallway and signaled an all-clear. Dragleman and Meg ran to join him. "What do you think—nobody home?" Cusack asked, reloading his shotgun.

"They're here all right," Dragleman said. "And they certainly know we're here, so keep moving."

Meg gripped his arm. "Wait," she said, and pointed to the lettering on the door behind them:

RESEARCH LABORATORY
AUTHORIZED PERSONNEL ONLY

Dragleman nodded, and Cusack turned the handle. The door popped open with a loud click. They moved inside and immediately took cover. A faint smell of ash permeated the large space.

Meg looked up and saw the ceiling was nearly thirty feet high; the moon hovered brightly above a huge, slanting skylight. Below, strange objects showed dimly through the grayish pall. Vague. Peculiar. A sudden trepidation swept over Meg like a draft, and she looked away.

No such fear seized Dragleman. He worked his way through the chamber, his flashlight scanning the dark space between counters, computer stations and large standing equipment. "All clear," he said. "Cusack, watch the door. Doc?"

"I'm here," Meg said reluctantly.

"I think you'd better have a look," Dragleman said, and Meg forced herself out into the open.

With Dragleman at her side, she followed the beam of light across countertops covered with racks of test tubes, electronically controlled cooling units, and specialized equipment used for blending and storing blood and tissue samples. At the end of one counter stood a large, state-of-the-art incubator.

Dragleman shined his light against the wall. "What's that?" he wondered aloud, staring at a steel platform with leather restraining straps. A steel skullcap with connecting electrodes hung limply above the restraints.

"It's a torture rack," Meg said.

Dragleman eyed the contraption but said nothing. He swept the light across the floor: waste bins stuffed with burned documents and computer disks dotted the room. "You can bet they destroyed all the evidence," he said. "We're not going to find anything here."

Meg gripped his hand and shifted the light onto a strange-looking cage. They moved closer. "Treadmill," she said, a tremor shaking her voice. Two rows of parallel bars prevented the animal from escaping the rolling pad beneath. From a nearby control panel, the animal could be forced to run faster and faster, its brainwaves monitored through a skull harness connected from above.

Dragleman turned the light to his left and rocked back on his heels. "Jesus," he whispered, and Meg saw rows of glass jars containing animal brains floating in milky fluids. All were labeled with their species, date of death, and . . .

Meg looked closer. *Nicknames,* given to them by their captors, were also printed on the labels.

"Asian Panda," Meg said softly as she stared at one of the jars. ". . . Little Ling-Sing."

Dragleman called out. "Cusack?"

"Still clear, Lieutenant. Not a peep."

"We better get moving, Doc, or—"

"Wait a minute," Meg said. "What is that smell?"

Dragleman sniffed the air. His gaze narrowed, eyes searching the dark. Meg knew from the expression on his face that he recognized the peculiar scent.

But he would not answer.

As he moved to the south corner of the room, Meg followed.

When Dragleman stopped suddenly, Meg thought he had stopped to stare at a blank wall. But when the flashlight beam arced over the white surface, she realized it was a massive door, the kind usually seen at a loading dock or warehouse.

The odor grew stronger.

37

THAT WAS THE MOMENT, Meg would think later—just as Cusack and Dragleman rolled the door back and the fetid odor wafted into their faces—that she felt something horrible and cold inside her.

Dragleman inched into the room first and shined his light around. Above, a huge, vaulted ceiling with steel crossbeams revealed itself. Loading decks were mounted on every wall. Below was a long row of transport cages; a forklift stood close by.

Meg's foot brushed against something soft and powdery, and she jumped back when Dragleman shined the light on a pile of scorched carcasses: lions, tigers, and jaguars. They were clumped together, hides singed, blackened flesh exposed. Some were only kittens, barely old enough to be weaned from their mothers.

"Whoever's responsible for this panicked," Dragleman said. "No time for a mass grave in the woods."

Cusack bent down and studied the charred remains. "Looks like they used gasoline. They probably threw a match and hoped the fire would cover up the rest."

Hatred kindled in Meg. She took a quick glance to her

right and saw another mound of dead—primates. Only they were mutants of some sort. Meg looked closer, saw that one of the monkeys had had its limbs cut off. Or they had never grown in; Meg couldn't decide which. Another monkey's head was misshapen, and had electrical wires running from its eye sockets to holes on either side of its skull.

Meg saw deformity everywhere. One ape had what looked like a human hand. Another was devoid of hair and almost white in color, and looked more like a human child than an ape.

Meg drew back with a shudder, nauseated. She took a deep breath, trying to control the acid rising from her stomach.

"Jesus," Cusack said, coming to stand beside her.

Dragleman's eyes stayed on Meg. Compassion shone there, and Meg knew that he understood the horrors of animal experimentation and was grateful he did not say anything. Instead, he led her back to the laboratory.

"Are you going to be all right?" he asked.

"Yes," Meg said, regaining her composure. She knew she had come too far to get sidetracked now.

Cusack said, "We better keep moving, or—" He broke off when he heard the sound. Footsteps in the hallway. Hesitant. Halting.

Dragleman's flashlight blinked off. "Take cover," he whispered, moving to his left. Cusack grabbed Meg's arm and together they crouched down behind a counter.

As Meg adjusted her rifle, she heard the sound of footsteps settle just outside the door. There she saw a man's silhouette in the moonlight coming through the skylight. He looked in, turning slowly. Meg had all she could do to stop herself from putting a bullet through his head.

"Hold it! Police!" Dragleman yelled.

Bullets ricocheted off the concrete floor and thudded into

the walls as the man opened fire. Specimen jars exploded, and chemicals and glass came showering down.

As Dragleman dived for cover, Cusack reared up and delivered two blasts at the doorway. He glanced at Meg, signaled for her to stay put, then scrambled away into the darkness.

Meg crouched in silence for what seemed like hours, then she raised her head and peered over the shattered face of a computer monitor. Broken glass sparkled in the moonlight; metal and torn gray plastic littered every surface.

"Get down!" Dragleman yelled. More shots ripped through the room.

Meg's mind swirled as she scurried for cover. A second volley struck the floor and wall. Plaster dust whirled above Meg's head as Dragleman slid up beside her.

"Follow me, and keep your head down!" he said. Together they half-crawled along the counter toward the back of the room. The firing began again, wildly, indiscriminately. Meg could feel the vibration as the bullets spiraled into the wall above them.

"In there!" Dragleman said, following his words with a hard shove.

Meg felt his body shielding hers; gunfire sprayed over her head as, along with Dragleman, she hurled herself through a small rear door. Cusack flew into the room right behind them.

Together they rushed between storage crates and racks of medical supplies; and then, hunched down in the back of the room, they waited, watching the door.

Cusack supported himself against a crate. "How many were shooting?" he asked, fumbling to reload.

"Only one," Dragleman said. He checked the door, then turned the light on Cusack's hands. The fingers were trembling, the palms sticky with blood.

"Christ, you're hit," Dragleman said, and passed the light to Meg. He took the shotgun from Cusack. "Why didn't you say something?"

Cusack said, "Like what? Hey, Lou, that bastard just blew the back of my hand off? Forget it, I'm fine."

"You're not fine," Meg said. She could see his adrenaline reserve was almost gone. His teeth were clenched; his breathing labored. The trembling of his hands would not stop.

"Whoever he is, he's not stupid," Cusack said. "He's got us boxed in."

Dragleman said, "That's why they left the lab door open. They knew we'd be trapped back here."

"Over there." Meg pointed to a small window. It was just barely large enough for her to climb through.

"Can you crawl through there?"

"Yes, I think so."

"Okay," Dragleman said. "We'll cover you. Once you're outside, go back to the cabin and call for help. Cusack and I will make a stand here."

"But—"

"Do it! You'll have a better chance out there. No heroics. Just get to the cabin and *call*." In a low crouch, Dragleman reached the window and wrenched it open with one hand. Then he took aim at the door. "Come on, and keep low!"

Meg started forward in a belly crawl, then imagined she heard a loud click behind her, something like a gun cylinder snapping into place. She lurched to her feet and made a dash for the window. She paused for a dizzying second, catching a glimpse of snowy ground sloping downward, away from the building. Ten feet to the bottom, she thought, or twenty; the near-blackness made it difficult to tell. She dropped her rifle out to the left, swung her legs through the narrow opening and pushed herself out onto the ledge. As she kicked off from the wall, a shower of bullets shattered the glass behind her.

THE CAT LIFTED his head slowly. The harsh and confusing sounds coming from the building had caused him to retreat twice. Now he stood close by, eyes baleful. Pain, fury, the need for revenge had made him take the chance.

He inched forward. Saliva dripped from his slack jaw. He heard the sounds of other night creatures but ignored them. His nostrils flared, caught the scent of a human.

The cat's body suddenly shook with rage. He raised one paw and clawed furiously at the air. Then he swirled around, as if chasing his tail, and bolted through the trees.

38

OUTSIDE THE COMPOUND silence lay like some brooding, hibernating beast. The silence was worse than the gunfire, Meg thought. She got to her feet, grabbed her rifle, and then climbed the embankment and scrambled to an inner gate. It was open, and through it went tire tracks filled in by snow. She stopped suddenly. There were also fresh tracks made by a cat.

Oh God, Meg thought, kneeling down for a closer look. There was no mistaking the large pads of a Siberian tiger.

Meg hoisted her rifle, pulled herself up, and began moving cautiously through the darkness. Her breathing sounded terribly loud. Occasionally the wind knocked snow from a tree branch and it plonked onto the ground, startling her.

Because it stood before a background of snow, the chain-link fence seemed to spring at her. It was topped by triple strands of barbed wire. Meg had no doubt that the fence surrounded the entire compound, and that her only way out was through the rear gate. Ahead were holding cages and lean-tos. Further ahead were eight smaller cages in two rows. Meg ran to the nearest cage and dropped down.

From her vantage point she had a full view of the north side of the building. The door to the loading dock was open; a truck was backed up to the ramp. A refueling tank stood off to the side.

Meg hesitated, thinking things over. With Rajah on the prowl, Dragleman's order to leave the compound became more difficult to obey. Even if she did manage to get back to the cabin and call for help, she doubted she would reach it in time. There were too many forces working against each other now. She began to inch toward the shadows at the side of the building.

When at last she moved in behind the truck, she was holding her rifle calmly, though her hands trembled slightly. The gunfire inside the building had begun again. She could hear the harsh blasts and knew the battle was shifting to another part of the complex.

Meg peered into the shadows of the loading dock. She listened for a hint, a clue, anything that would tell her where the battle was moving.

PLAYING HIDE-AND-SEEK in the dark, following the hallways and tunnels of concrete, Dragleman came to realize there were five men in all; three of the men holding two men hostage, using their bodies as shields, threatening to kill them, as they tried scrambling for cover in the warehouse. They were all carrying machine pistols.

As they broke from the tunnel, Dragleman fired another round, cutting off their exit. Cusack's blast sent them scurrying through the closest archway, before he dropped against the wall, too exhausted to go on. "Christ, I'm fading fast. I don't think I can go much further . . ."

"Hang on," Dragleman said, sensing the men fanning out in the dark. The building had so many passageways, doorways, tunnels, that it was hard to tell where the next assault might be coming from.

Dragleman inched forward, pressing himself against the wall. He strained to hear—anything.

Silence. Yet not silence! A faint scraping sound drifted out from the passageway to his right, a passageway cluttered with wooden crates.

At first it was barely audible. Then it became slightly clearer, less hesitant. Dragleman strained to focus, found himself staring at the dark-haired, almost skeletal face of the guard as he slid behind one of the crates.

Dropping to his knee, Dragleman pointed the gun in the man's direction, but never pulled the trigger. Just as quietly, he saw the cat take three steps into the passageway and then lunge.

Dragleman jumped to his feet as the cat caught the man by surprise. The attack was so sudden that Dragleman felt his heart stop.

Oh Jesus! he thought, hearing the man scream, watching chunks of flesh leave his body. In one bite, the cat removed his arm, tossed it aside. Then, as the man screamed, rolling over in pain, the cat went for his leg. Dragleman heard more than saw the blood splatter the wall.

Then everyone inside the building was running for cover, firing as they went, hearing the man scream in terror behind them—screams that grew louder, shriller, drowned out by gunfire and a hideous, bloodcurdling roar.

MEG BOLTED for cover when the first shots rang out. Bullets slammed into the wall, ricocheted off the truck. She threw herself to the ground as another blast whirled over her head and struck the fuel tank.

Meg screamed, rocked by the explosion. Flames shot

into the sky as she rolled under the truck to the other side, trying to escape the heat. There she jumped to her feet, eyes straining to see through the smoke and glare.

"Hold your fire!" someone yelled. Four men, their backs toward Meg, started inching their way out onto the platform. There was a scampering sound, followed by a terrible, terrifying roar of fire as the wind picked up, sending flames shooting into the sky.

The noise now became muffled and more distant, then suddenly ended. Meg waited, pressed against the side of the truck, straining to hear, to see through the black swirls of smoke. She looked closer, then realized what she was looking at. The man she recognized from the roadblock had a handheld machine pistol pressed to David's spine. His cashmere coat got in his way as he yanked David closer to him. Off to the side, Philip Roueche had a pistol pressed to Ray's skull. Ray's arm was pinned behind his back, and Roueche twisted it upward as he pulled Ray to the edge of the platform.

Meg stared at the scene, unable to comprehend, to feel any emotion at all. Her heart had been numbed by all the terror and death that had gone before and the endless screaming tension of the past four days. All she felt was a sickness in the pit of her stomach.

"Give it up!" Dragleman yelled, and Meg saw the two detectives crouched behind the forklift. Both men had their weapons aimed at Roueche.

"Don't bargain with him!" Ray shouted. "He's crazy. He's—" The rest of his sentence was drowned in a sudden outburst of flames.

Now the whole area was darkened over with smoke and grime. In a few seconds it would be impossible to see anything. Roueche said, "I'm warning you, stay back. If not, I'll blow his fucking head off."

Meg raised her rifle and saw Ray turn slightly to stare at her. Then a sound cut across the snow. A sound that was not wind, not the crackling of fire or snow falling.

It was Ray's voice, thin, high-pitched, desperate.

"Meg! Take cover!"

"Ray!" Meg screamed, looking wildly around; a roar had come from somewhere just as Meg screamed. As the man in the cashmere coat turned in panic, David broke free and dashed back into the warehouse.

Suddenly gunfire rang out. The man in the cashmere coat dropped to his knees. He sat down, looking at his bloody hand. He lifted it away slowly and looked at the hole that went through his coat, chest high. Then he crumpled on his side.

Meg froze, heart pounding in her chest. Long, quickly lashing tongues of flame were licking at the side of the platform. Through the hissing and crackling of fire, she could hear Rajah growl, but very dimly, almost lost to the ear. Roueche must have heard it too, because he turned slowly and glanced over his shoulder, still with the pistol pressed tight to Ray's head.

Meg screamed, "Let him go, Philip! For God's sake, it's over!"

Roueche said nothing. Did nothing. Light from the flames flickered across his face as he peered at Meg, through her, into the darkness.

Now the platform was completely black. Meg could see nothing. "Ray . . ." she began to say to herself, but a sudden weakness stopped the words in her throat. She heard the blood thumping in her head and then a loud, whistling wind. The smoke cleared.

"You wanted to come here, Meg," Roueche said, inching closer to the platform steps. "I warned you to stop prying. To stop digging into matters that didn't concern you. But you persisted. *You* made all this happen."

"It was you, dammit. You!" Meg sighted down the barrel of her rifle, zeroing in on Roueche's back. "Let him go, Philip. Let Ray go or I'll kill you."

But Roueche kept backing toward her, as though unafraid. At the edge of the platform, his right foot found the first step and he started down, dragging Ray with him.

"It would have been all right if you hadn't interfered, Meg," he said in a monotone. "Everything would have been all right. I would have taken care of everything. Gotten rid of the whole mess."

Gotten rid of?

Meg listened, realizing he was talking about killing Shindler. Perhaps even Farris.

The man was a monster, a cold-blooded killer. All along Meg had sensed something not right with him, something strange and menacing, but she had expected nothing like this. "Why?" she said. "How could you do it?"

He turned slowly and glanced at the truck, then at the large drifts of snow off to the side, melting in the fire's heat. "Because it's what I *do*. My *thing*. A way of making incredible amounts of money, more money than you can ever imagine. But then what would you know, Meg? You're a *vet*, a desperately lonely woman whose concern for animals has turned to nauseating sentiment."

"You're a madman!"

"Perhaps," he said with a chuckle, "to someone who is incapable of seeing past primitive ethics. I used to find you interesting, Meg. I really did. But you're a coward. Clinging to that damned cat. He's nothing but a hunk of meat. A freak of science. Do you feel yourself cringe at the idea? That's your ethics, Doctor. It's incredible how many good people we've lost to ethics."

"Like Shindler?" Meg yelled, trying to get a clear sight with her rifle through the rising black puffs of smoke. She shook her head, saw David jump up and dash across the

CLAW

warehouse to join Cusack and Dragleman. Off to the side, Rajah's low growl rose above the hissing and crackling of heat against damp wood.

"Shindler," Roueche said, glancing around. "He wanted to play at being a genius without paying the price. At least the others were willing to sacrifice for larger goals. Fantastic goals, perhaps, but then they do have a certain passion for playing God. And, as I said, they pay big bucks."

"Philip, please—"

"Sorry, Meg, it's years too late to reform me. Now I'm going to open the truck door, have Ray slide in first. Then I'm going to get in and drive off." He shouted over Ray's shoulder to Dragleman and the others, "Hear that, Mr. Policeman? I'm driving the truck out of here. As soon as I'm clear, I'll let Ray go. If not, I'll kill him. Understand? I've got nothing to lose."

Coming off the bottom step, Ray stumbled and Roueche was thrown slightly off balance. For an instant, Meg had a clear target. She took aim, holding the barrel steady—her finger was on the trigger. "Let him go, Philip, or so help me God, I'll kill you!"

Roueche immediately yanked Ray upright and put the gun squarely against his temple.

"Go ahead, Meg. Shoot," Roueche challenged. He kept his back to her, eyes fixed on the detectives, gun still pointed at Ray's head.

Meg once again took aim. Sweat rolled down her face and stung her eyes. A terrible uncertainty made her finger tremble around the trigger. If I shoot him now, she thought, will he shoot Ray? Does a dying man pull the trigger on another man? Would *Philip* do something like that? She didn't know, couldn't be sure what he was capable of doing. The only thing she did know with crushing finality was that she wanted desperately to save Ray.

Roueche laughed. "What's the matter, Meg, can't you do it? You see, it's those damned ethics. Or is it sentiment?" Carefully, he reached out and opened the truck door.

Shoot him, Meg thought, feeling a surge of panic. Suddenly, the rifle felt very heavy. Her muscles ached, her eyes were stinging from the smoke. "Stop!" she yelled. Her voice was pitched higher than she had intended, and it sounded shrill and hysterical.

Roueche stared at Meg and, at the last moment, began maneuvering Ray behind the open truck door. Now, Meg thought. If she did not shoot him now she never would. As Ray came alongside Roueche, she wrapped her finger around the trigger and started to squeeze. Then everything seemed to happen at once.

Ray suddenly pulled free and kicked the truck door back, ducking for cover.

There was the rush of Dragleman and Cusack darting forward, but they stopped when they heard the tiger's roar. Roueche must have sensed the cat coming, or heard the roar, or seen a blur of ghostly movement to his right because he raised his pistol a split second before the Siberian jumped him, crushing him against the truck.

Meg heard his muted scream and saw the eyes squint shut in pain. Then fanged teeth went for his throat. The cat brought Roueche down by the jugular, its massive head swinging from side to side with the proficiency of a hunter making his kill.

Still Roueche would not quit. He rolled over, trying to slide under the truck, but sharp claws stabbed into his rib cage and dragged him back. He tried to ward off the cat with his legs but the awesome reserve of desperate strength that had animated him was gone. The cat slashed at his thighs and then went for the stomach.

Dragleman leapt from the platform and took aim at the

cat, trying to see past the flurry of snow. Cusack came off the platform from the other end, shotgun ready. Amid the confusion, the cat opened his mouth and sank his teeth into Roueche's skull.

"No! Don't shoot!" Meg cried, knowing that it was too late for Roueche. She saw Dragleman hesitate, his face a mixture of horror and fascination as Rajah stood over the curator's lifeless body, clawing at it, snapping with his jaws. And then the tiger seemed to lose his strength. He stumbled, dropped to the ground, rose again, and turned suddenly to face Dragleman, who once again raised his gun.

The cat's legs dropped out from under him. He pulled the bulk of his body away, then collapsed a few yards in front of Meg. His breath was tortured; his body seemed more dead than alive.

The cat lay there for a moment, then closed his eyes. Meg watched for a few moments, then took a step forward. Dragleman fired a warning shot. She turned toward the detective who, facing the tiger, seemed suddenly as uncertain as she had felt all that anxious time when the bullets had whizzed over her head and slammed into walls. Then he had been the calm one; now it was her turn.

"Put your gun away, Lieutenant," she said gently. "You won't be needing it anymore. I don't even know if he's alive."

Wiping tears away, Meg went to Rajah and knelt beside him. She could feel the warm plumes of his shallow breath on her hand, hear the heavy thud of his heart.

"Don't worry, Meg. He'll be all right," Ray said, coming to kneel beside her. The others drew closer.

Meg looked toward David, but even as he took a step toward her, she gripped Ray's hand and hung on. Then they were all staring at the tiger who had been almost strong enough to vanquish them all. There was awe, and a deep sense of shame, as they watched his massive body shudder.

No one moved for a moment. Behind them the fire had started to subside. Off to the side lay the body of Roueche—arms twisted, head flung back, eyes still open and staring in horror.

Soon there was just silence again.

39

A CHEER ROSE from the delegates of the Chinese welcoming committee as the C-17 transport dipped into a wide arc on its final approach over the Yichun airfield. A late spring storm had lingered that night, sweeping the black tarmac with rippling braids of snow, but just before dawn, when Flight T-105 was scheduled to arrive, the snow subsided, as if demanded by providence.

Engines roared and tires sprayed out sheets of snow as the blue-gray girth of the plane settled to the ground. It taxied toward the delegation, sunbeams glinting off its wide expanse of wings.

"Where is she?" a small voice shrilled in English, and the child's father, the American consul in Harbin, pointed to a tall woman in a red wool coat who had emerged from the plane and stood waving and smiling to the delegation.

"That's Dr. Brewster," the consul told his daughter, who clapped her hands excitedly.

"We're all set, Dr. Brewster," a crewman told Meg. Ray stood beside her in the open doorway, a fur cap in his hand. Off to the side, a truck with a crane mounted behind the cab inched closer to the C-17's cargo hatch as it was lowered to the ground. The truck that would carry Rajah back to the wilds of northern Heilongjiang Province, the mountain land of his ancestors, waited nearby.

"I don't know if I'm ready for this," Meg said, and felt Ray's hand close around her arm.

"Sure, you are," Ray whispered into her ear. "You're a hero, remember? And I'll be right here beside you."

As they started down the platform stairs, three men came forward to greet them. Two of them were bulky and forceful-looking. The third man, striding between them, was slimmer and older, and had cheery brown eyes. He introduced himself in English as Mo-Tzu, head veterinarian from the Ministry of Forest.

"We are *most* excited," he assured Meg, clasping her hand warmly. Soon the entire delegation had gathered around Meg, and with the help of the American consul, members of the Chinese Science and Technology Commission were introduced. Then the consul introduced his seven-year-old daughter, Melissa.

"Can I pet Rajah?" the little girl asked Meg.

Meg smiled down at the girl. "I wish you could, sweetheart. But I'm afraid he'll be kind of grumpy after such a long trip."

"Oh," Melissa said, disappointed.

Meg stooped down to the girl's height and said, "I'll tell you what we'll do, Melissa. You can ride with Rajah and me in the truck. We'll keep him company. How does that sound?"

The girl's eyes sparkled and she smiled. "That's a deal!" she cried, and her father gave Meg an appreciative wink.

AN HOUR LATER, the caravan of trucks and Land-Rovers started its climb into the Khingan mountain range. The

American consul sat with Mo-Tzu and Meg for most of the trip: though worlds apart, the two vets exchanged vital information on the needs and habits of Siberian tigers.

Above all else, Mo-Tzu complimented Meg on discovering the right combination of antibodies that had eventually wiped out the hybrid neurons in Rajah's system. Meg, naturally, gave credit to the dozens of consultants from around the world who had provided valuable input in the unprecedented effort.

Occasionally, Meg glanced into the back of the truck, where Ray was keeping company with Melissa. He had put the little girl in charge of tiger checking. Every twenty minutes, Melissa would dutifully peek through the tightly wrapped tarp over the cage. "It's okay," she would say in a serious tone, "he's still asleep."

Finally, they came to a clearing high in the mountains. Sunlight shone brightly against the snow-covered peaks. A vast field of evergreens covered the sloping valley ridge.

The release site had been carefully chosen. During the previous summer, local farmers had sighted two female tigers in separate, heavily wooded areas of the upper Nemor River. Subsequent observations and tracking revealed that both cats were young and healthy, and probably of a lineage from the Sikhote-Alin Mountains, three hundred miles away on the Russian Pacific coast. If the last remaining Siberians in the region could travel that far undetected by poachers, there was a good chance this new breeding group could thrive for years to come.

Meg and Ray stepped aside as the final phase of the release project got under way; they were only consultants now, unless Mo-Tzu needed a helping hand.

A wave of excitement came over Meg, something close to jubilation, as she looked over the beautiful wilderness. And yet underneath the joy was a tiny sense of regret, something so slight that surely no one could have detected the change in her. She turned and looked into Ray's steady eyes and knew that he understood what she was feeling.

Almost to Meg's regret, Mo-Tzu needed no assistance. Rajah's cage had been placed in a clearing where he was easily observed; the caravan withdrew to a high ridge about eighty yards away. Mo-Tzu reached into the cage and inserted a hypodermic into the sleeping cat. For a moment, his hand lingered on the gold fur and then withdrew.

Mo-Tzu himself raised the cage door and secured it while his assistant looked on, a tranquilizer rifle hooked over his arm. A moment later, both men came to wait with the others on the ridge. The cat was now free. It wouldn't be long until the drug worked through Rajah's blood system, reversing the effects of the sedative.

"Any time now," Meg whispered, her hand finding Ray's. She felt his fingers tighten around hers in a reassuring squeeze.

And then Rajah began to stir. His huge yawn brought a ripple of laughter through the Chinese delegation. The American consul perched his daughter on his shoulder to give her a better look as Rajah slowly pulled himself to his feet.

It took a moment for the cat to realize his cage was open. He left it somewhat cautiously, as though he feared a trick. Pausing for a last sniff at the human scent on the cage, he moved more rapidly toward the shimmering brook that meandered along the edge of the clearing.

When he lowered his massive head to drink from the clear water, there was nodding and smiling from the Chinese, an acknowledgment that the release was a success. Only Meg and Ray were silent, gazing hard at the cat who had, for them, come to be much more than just another Siberian tiger.

Then Rajah turned in their direction, his beautiful face held high in the shimmering light.

Yes, it's time, Rajah, Meg thought in silent communication. Time to be free.

Acknowledgments

IN PREPARING THIS NOVEL, we have drawn on the works of many eminent zoologists, scientists, and social psychologists, particularly those works of Adam Paul, John Mc-Crone, and Russell Arthur. Richard M. Restak's two books *The Mind* and *The Brain* were also valuable sources of information in helping us to understand the complex nature of the human brain and the new technologies, controversies, and developments surrounding this area. Other reference materials include Jonathan Winson's *Brain & Psyche,* Susan Jacoby's *Wild Justice/The Evolution of Revenge,* Steve Fishman's *A Bomb in the Brain,* and Anthony Smith's *The Mind.*

Certain ideas presented here about animal and human aggression were first articulated by Robert Ardrey, in his book *The Territorial Imperative,* and by Desmond Morris and Peter Marsh, in their book *Tribes.* Genetic information was gathered from a variety of sources, including *Scientific American, U.S. News & World Report, National Geographic, Discover, Science News,* and *Newsweek.* A special thanks to Jeffrey R. Boehm, DVM, for his valuable input and shared knowledge.

This book is entirely fiction, and the views expressed here are our own, as are whatever factual errors may exist in the text.